Okechukwu Nze[...] [...]e
was the recipien[...] [...] [...]y
Writing North. His debut novel, *The Private Joys of [...]a Maloney* (Dialogue Books), won a Betty Trask Award; it was also shortlisted for the Desmond Elliott Prize and the Polari First Book Prize, and longlisted for the Portico Prize. In 2021, it was selected for the Kingston University Big Read. He is a regular contributor to *Kinfolk* magazine, and a Lecturer in Creative Writing at Lancaster University.

'A beautiful exploration of grief and family. Through exquisite prose, Okechukwu Nzelu delves into the lives of the complicated men at the centre of this story with compassion and tenderness. A lyrical and insightful novel.' Brit Bennett

'*Here Again Now* is a novel of great tenderness and understanding. Okechukwu Nzelu's words feel both wise and fresh on the page.' Elizabeth Day

'A truly stunning love story. Heavy themes captured with grace and lightness. Tender, erotic, a total pleasure to read.' Daisy Buchanan

'A deeply intimate novel. Nzelu's incisive style probes beneath his characters' layers to expose vulnerability, joy, and love. This is a work of aching possibilities, unearthed warmth between distant bodies, the blurred limits that masculinity sometimes affords ... *Here Again Now* is a revelation.' Courttia Newland

'Nzelu has written a tender and probing book. I've not read anything like it and its impact will be far reaching. Baldwin-esque and honest, pulsing with love. I honestly believe Nzelu is the future of Black British writing.' Derek Owusu

HERE AGAIN NOW

OKECHUKWU NZELU

dialogue
books

DIALOGUE BOOKS

First published in Great Britain in 2022 by Dialogue Books
This paperback edition published in 2023 by Dialogue Books

10 9 8 7 6 5 4 3 2

Copyright © Okechukwu Nzelu 2022

The moral right of the author has been asserted.

A CIP catalogue record for this book
is available from the British Library.

ISBN 978-0-349-70109-7

Typeset in Berling by M Rules
Printed and bound in Great Britain by
Clays Ltd, Elcograf S.p.A.

Papers used by Dialogue Books are from well-managed forests
and other responsible sources.

Dialogue Books
Carmelite House
50 Victoria Embankment
London EC4Y 0DZ

www.dialoguebooks.co.uk

Dialogue Books, part of Little Brown, Book Group Limited,
an Hachette UK company.

For anyone who's ever stood at the edge of something

PART I

Thou comest, much wept for: such a breeze
Compell'd thy canvas, and my prayer
Was as the whisper of an air
To breathe thee over lonely seas.

For I in spirit saw thee move
Thro' circles of the bounding sky,
Week after week: the days go by:
Come quick, thou bringest all I love.

Henceforth, wherever thou may'st roam,
My blessing, like a line of light,
Is on the waters day and night,
And like a beacon guards thee home.

ALFRED, LORD TENNYSON, *In Memoriam A. H. H.*

Chapter 1

Ekene always heard the music first.

Achike gave him something different every time. Some days, Ekene would open the front door and there would be Samuel Coleridge-Taylor before him, in Achike's hands. There might be Elgar, or Chopin, things Achike had taught himself, heard somewhere and reined in to his own keen fingers. Reined in to himself and then played out, wild again, like the first time it was ever played. Or he might come home early from filming and Ekene would walk across the courtyard to an improvisation on something by Frank Ocean, something Achike had listened to on the way home. Something that made Ekene think of fresh air and cool evenings after long, hot days.

Something of this was for Achike himself. He worked too hard, these days, and he loved to leave hard work and bother behind. He loved to step off the tube and go, step by step, to his home, and close the front door, and hear the busy world continue, just outside. He loved this feeling of safety, and so some of the pleasure in his music was for him.

But what he did was not for him alone. His music was like offering joy; all his training and listening, and the hours of practice were like joy, plated up and pushed across a table to a smile. Achike loved to play, and think how his playing could be heard in the street. He didn't care if the neighbours had questions, or might complain in the morning. They might, and sometimes did. That was for them.

But Achike . . . he might make Ekene happy with a song. He might take music that had been two pieces and make them one. He might loop them both together and play them out, to please Ekene. Two favourite things of his, noticed and known and offered. Or he might fly into Heathrow a week late, cursing the director all the way home, and let himself into the flat at one in the morning, tiptoeing in so that Ekene woke to the sound of him humming a new piece of his own making, woke to the sound of some creation pouring into his ear, as though Achike were feeding him a dream.

And how he fed him. Ekene often dreamed about Achike when he was gone. He was gone too much. Ekene always thought to be happy for his friend in his success, and to think of him doing great things, but sometimes it was hard. When it was hard for him, he thought about the way good light might hit Achike's face in some perfect scene, or how Achike might inspire someone to write some new thing charged with beauty, or perhaps only to change a scene, knowing it could be better with Achike in it. Sometimes it was enough just to think of Achike, to think of him smiling in good light.

Ekene was rewarded for his faith. He would wait for Achike as long as he could, but the trains were late, and filming ran on, and he sometimes fell asleep before Achike arrived at the big flat with its large windows for the fresh, cold light of the day. Ekene slept, and dreamed of his great friend in the world, and of his friend coming near while the world kept its distance just outside. And sometimes, after dreaming, he woke to find Achike next to him in bed, barely awake, still singing under his breath. Had he sung all night in readiness?

*

Over the past three years, Achike had spent more and more time away on set, and less and less time at home in Peckham. His career was taking off at speed, and time with Ekene became increasingly precious. Shakespeare productions in pubs with Ekene and their friends fresh from drama school became low-budget independent films with up-and-coming directors, became walk-on roles in bigger productions. He played a boxer with bipolar disorder; a longshoreman who hadn't seen his children in weeks and who had exactly eight words to say about it. The role of a plucky juror in a historic trial won him praise from critics. Then there was silence for a couple of months, and Achike wondered if everything that would be, had already been and gone.

Then, one day, Achike received a call from Julian Trent, an agent with a client roster so famous, the first few moments on the call had silenced Achike. Achike had been at his desk in the co-op agency, chasing a potential lead for another of the actors, when Julian told him he'd seen his reel and outlined Achike's future for him in bold, ambitious terms.

First, Achike would have to quit the co-op agency and sign with Julian. Then, everything he had wanted would be his. The world, Julian said, was waking up to the possibility of young black men playing a wider range of roles than ever before, and he knew that Achike Okoro had the range for whatever was needed to build a career that nobody would forget. If he trusted Julian to make it happen, it would.

Two years later, Achike had filmed minor roles in two major Hollywood films: one, a period slave drama (for which Julian was slightly apologetic), the other a tragic family epic, whose screenwriter was nominated for three major awards.

Then, this year, more good news.

'You'll like this one,' Julian had said. When he was this excited about a project, his voice lost its weary breathiness and became somehow sharper, taking on a kind of shimmering quality that Achike could almost see through the phone.

Here Again Now was an almost-big-budget film with a small cast. Its screenwriter-director, Mercy Oruche, had a new degree in film direction and a story to tell: a young doctor named Helen Izundu is murdered by police in New York City, but after her death she reincarnates multiple times in Nigeria. There, in each new life, Helen – now Adaeze, now Grace – meets people who help her shape the country's destiny and her own, before returning to a life in America and launching a historic dissolution of police brutality. As the film ends, she is about to be reborn again to a new life, new possibilities.

'Oruche is a visionary,' said Julian. 'Her work is unparalleled. There's nobody in film who's doing what she's doing. And you know – I don't say that often.'

'No,' said Achike, 'you really don't.' Like many father figures, Julian was hard to please. He could advocate fiercely for 'his own' (he never called his clients 'clients'), but he would have only the best of things. Those best things he wanted urgently, but he was impatient, even scathing, of those whose talent he deemed less-than. Achike had heard Julian dismiss actors and directors as 'blips on the radar'. Julian had been known to write off creatives after a single trailer; more than once, Achike had wondered what Julian would say about him if his own career ever stalled.

The doubt made Achike work harder. Julian had quickly become much more than an agent to him; Julian saw greatness in him, advised him, kept him away from bad choices. And, though his career was on the rise today, Achike lived in fear of the day when the roles and the money would slow down or stop coming – a fear that was not born out of love of acting, but out of a need for something like love. He wanted to keep his work coming; he wanted to keep Julian smiling down on him. When he heard of the young director who could win Julian's approval so resoundingly, Achike knew he had to work with her.

And then there was his real father. Chibuike had always

criticised Achike for letting white Hollywood subsume him into itself, and Achike had been waiting for an opportunity to prove him wrong. When he saw his father's culture in the script – names and locations he knew his father would recognise and approve of – he knew it was the right thing. It was from traditional Igbo beliefs that the idea for a film about reincarnation had sprung.

Only in a corner of Achike's mind was there any pride in himself for being a part of a project he believed in, or for bringing his father's culture to the world; only dimly did he understand that his work on this film was a profound act of love, and that through his work he was joining a lineage of storytellers that reached back through generations, from one life to another, stretching back endlessly through time. Achike could present himself on screen as firm, bold, persistent, capable, but he was always little to himself, barely a man, only a little man. He hardly knew that he was connected to something infinite and strong.

'I think Oruche's work has a magnetism to it, you know,' Julian mused, on the phone. He had a way of speaking almost to himself, only allowing the listener to be present. Achike was completely still, listening. 'She's doing something transformative. Her work is really *in the world*. This is where cinema is, now. And where it needs to be. You know, I really believe it's the kind of film that audiences all over the world will fall in love with.'

'I want in.' Achike was almost breathless. 'I want to be a part of it.'

'You need to be part of it,' said Julian, plainly. 'This is where you go next. It has to be.'

There were some weeks of preparations. There was practice to be done, and research. There were exercises and drills. Achike sent in a tape of himself, and then his in-person audition came next. For this, he stepped into a small, plain, soundproofed room with no air conditioning. Julian had prepared him well, as had Achike's prior films: he showed an earnestness, a directness and a vulnerability, which were his own, and which became the character's.

Then there was the screen test: the director and producer wanted to see the chemistry Achike and the female lead would be able to offer. Achike would be acting opposite an American named Dacey Douglas. She was shorter than Achike, who was just over six foot two, and very slim. She was from California but, when the script called for it, her Nigerian accents were as Achike's mother's and father's. She did not seem afraid, as he was. Perhaps she was afraid.

It was upon him to be the man now. The director was watching, and she wanted to see what love could look like. Achike tried to imagine how he might love Dacey, in another life. He might be a different man, then, and tower over a woman, and not long for a man to hold him. He might watch Dacey's dark eyes shimmer under lights and feel an urge to hold her, to envelop her in himself. That was the thing, wasn't it? That was what they wanted. He tried to imagine reshaping the love he had for Ekene, and giving it to a woman to hold.

Achike stepped into the shape of a big man. He pushed his little self away, and gave the man they wanted. He did it for the film, and for his father in his mind, but how strange it was to hear his whole world carry on, only just inside. How strange, and sad.

He was cast as the male love interest for the film. And, because the film kept its cast small by doubling, Achike would play Helen's husband and her extra-marital lover – and, once, her adversary – across multiple lifetimes. He would be the one to help Helen evolve into one woman after another, evolving himself as the story was told.

They shot the film out of sequence, to save money. They had spent months in Nigeria, filming scenes in Lagos and in rural

Igboland, following Helen's story across the country. Achike had spoken in a southern English accent as the idealistic graduate returning to his parents' country, and then in Chibuike's Nigerian accent when he played Helen's Nigerian-born lover. He did other acting as well, in Nigeria: he kept his sibilants under control, or kept quiet. Growing up under his father's eye had taught him how. He knew how to walk and move 'straight', how to hold his body to account from moment to moment, how to live like a ghost.

The opening and closing scenes were set in New York, but the outdoor scenes were shot in central Manchester, in the final stretch of filming. There, in the Northern Quarter, where the architecture still resembled old New York, scaffolding was thrown up and yellow taxis were artfully placed: within hours, one city was much the same as another.

In those final weeks, Julian found Achike's big break. Achike signed the contract between takes. For this film, Achike was being paid more than for all his other jobs combined. His name would be made, and audiences everywhere would be made to learn how to say it. He moved out of his flatshare in Brixton and bought in Peckham. He was proving himself now. One day soon, auditions would become a thing of the past. Soon, he would only need to read scripts, and accept roles or politely decline.

The rest of the cast and crew of *Here Again Now* had spent time together in hotels, but now that Ekene was home from Berlin – now that Oskar was gone – Achike could only race home to see him after every day of shooting. Who knew when either one of them might disappear again? Any more distance between them would be too much. The material of their relationship was already so fragile, and it might disintegrate one day, if the two of them found themselves in different cities, countries, hemispheres. It was for this reason that, as soon as Ekene had asked to stay with Achike while he looked for work and a place of his own, Achike had told him, 'yes'.

And it was Ekene who had asked.

So what else would Achike do, but sing? What else could he do, but play out music for Ekene to hear as he ascended the stairs to their home, for as long as the home was theirs?

Achike lived in a spacious flat near Bellenden Road, where he'd never have thought even to rent before. A few streets away in one direction, people were selling plantain. A few streets away in another direction, people were selling plantain at twice the price. Achike's apartment block was exposed brick, open-plan living, tall windows, high rents, big mortgages, mostly white residents. Achike had used much of his first payment from his latest film to pay the deposit.

The building was exclusive, but Achike had told Ekene that Julian wasn't happy. Julian thought that somewhere close to the airport might be more convenient, but Heathrow and Gatwick were only an hour's drive away. Julian had frowned. One day soon, he warned, Achike would have to leave Peckham. One day soon, too many people would recognise him. An actor like him needed peace. He needed a building with a real security system, not a place in the middle of town with a part-time concierge. He should be in Notting Hill. But Ekene didn't want to move again; they'd already moved to London from Manchester for drama school. That was enough.

Achike stayed for Ekene. To Achike, London itself was nothing, Peckham only slightly more. He had never made friends easily, and years on, he barely had any more than when he'd first arrived as an undergraduate, his drama school cohort notwithstanding. There was a division in his mind: home was Manchester; work was London, LA, Lagos.

Still, Achike tried to make the flat feel warm for Ekene, adding mismatched vintage furniture and soft lighting: a deep blue velvet sofa with plump upholstering; a circular rug made of bright, patchwork patterns; an upcycled bookshelf he'd found at auction; heavy velour curtains in mustard yellow. The piano he was playing was an antique that a nearby café had thrown out when they closed down; Achike had had it varnished and tuned, and set it in the middle of the living room. It was the first thing visitors saw when they came in.

Ekene wedged the bottle of wine underneath his armpit and, with his free hand, fished out his keys from his back pocket. He tapped his fob against the reader on the door and heard the lock release with a click. He raised his shopping-bag hand and waved to Tom, the concierge behind the desk. In the first few days after Ekene moved in, Tom had looked questioningly at him, not quite understanding his role in the young actor's life. A friend? Family? Lover? But recently he seemed to have accepted Ekene for whatever his presence was, and these days he was uncurious, even friendly. On another day, Ekene might have stopped to talk to him. On another day, he might have asked how Tom's day was going, asked for gossip on the downstairs neighbour who once complained about Achike's music. He had been out all day, walking along the Thames, thinking, reading, missing Achike, until he got the text message and hurried back. Otherwise, he might have wandered home more slowly through the streets, not having anywhere to go. He might have checked the postbox, or his reflection in the window. But not today. Achike was home.

Ekene walked briskly through the tall glass doors and entered the courtyard, a huge open space with potted plants scattered around. The staircase was across the way (he made himself take the stairs, even to Achike's flat on the sixth floor, unable to bear the long wait for the slow, old lift) and as he walked towards it, he could look up and see the figure of Achike, bent over at his piano. Ekene told himself to walk calmly and push his excitement away, but he heard his footsteps speeding up regardless. He heard his shoes clacking hurriedly on the flagstones and echoing against the walls, announcing his excitement, answering Achike's steady music with his own palpitating rhythm.

Ekene did this every time. Every time, he found himself racing up the stairs, through the heavy fire door and along the corridor. Soon, he would be pushing open the unlocked door to flat 618, and Achike would be waiting for him, and Ekene would hug him tightly, so tightly his arms could not move far enough along the keyboard, and they would laugh. And Achike would hug him back, and they would share a bottle of wine while Achike told him all about his latest film, and the producer's girlfriend, twenty-eight years his junior, and the eye-watering lighting budget, and the last-minute changes to the script. Achike would tell him where he had been, and what he had learned, and the things he had failed to do, and the dreams he had for himself that were always changing. And they would go out for dinner, just the two of them, to a place where there was more music, and candles lit for them. And they would talk and talk and talk, and then come home under a soft night.

Ekene was breathless at the sixth floor, but he did not slow down. Racing through the corridors, he pushed open the door to the flat and found Achike playing something shimmering and ethereal, his fingers advancing and retreating up and down the keys, beating out something so fine it was almost impossible to recognise the tune at first. This arrangement was one of Achike's own: he did not sing the melody, giving the voice to his right hand, playing gently discordant harmonies with his left. Ekene had to stop and breathe and listen. 'Pink + White'. Frank Ocean. The song lasted only three minutes and five seconds, yet Achike played as though he had until the end of time to unfurl the slow, easy magic. Yes, Achike was home.

Ekene set down the wine and the shopping bag on the counter, took three giant steps towards Achike and wrapped his arms around him. Achike kissed his neck softly.

'Ekene.'

'I'm so glad you're home, Achike. What time did you get back?'

'Not that long ago. Did you like the music?' Achike's voice was eager and strained. He sounded a little tired.

'Of course I did,' said Ekene. 'I always do.'

'Good,' said Achike.

'What's wrong?' said Ekene. 'You look sad.'

'There's something I need to tell you,' said Achike.

Ekene withdrew and stepped back to face Achike. Ekene closed the keylid, gently leaned on it, and tried to fix patience into his face.

Achike had told Ekene he loved him before this. Many times. He would do so again. Ekene never quite believed it. Could never quite depend upon it. And yet, every time it was something for Ekene to withstand. He must always hold himself still against it, as against strong winds behind him.

'What is it?' Ekene asked, patiently. 'What do you want to tell me?'

'It's not that,' Achike smiled. 'Not right now, anyway.'

'You're being weird.'

'The thing is,' said Achike, 'we're not alone.' He took Ekene's hands in his. Ekene was standing, Achike sitting, as if he were about to propose something momentous.

As Achike opened his mouth to explain, a man emerged from the spare bedroom. He was older than both of them by about twenty-five years, but his hair had gone completely grey and was thinning, and the lines on his face recalled deep frowns. Ekene tried not to react when he saw that Achike's grey cardigan was loosely draped around the man's shoulders, over wrinkled pyjamas.

'Oh,' Ekene said. The old habit of respect for elders was still alive in him, and he forced himself to brighten his expression and stand up straight. He took his hands away from

Achike, clasped them chastely in front of his body. Whatever Achike might have proposed was, for the moment, forgotten. 'Hello, sir.'

'You okay there, Dad?' Achike called. His body became strict with itself, and stiff. His father nodded only a little.

'That's what I was going to tell you,' Achike said to Ekene, softly. 'He'll be staying with us for a bit. I thought it could be good. For all of us.' He took Ekene's hands back in his.

'Yes,' said Ekene. He seemed to struggle for air. 'Yes, of course. Nno, sir.'

The old man nodded again, and gave a distant smile. He looked at Achike and Ekene carefully, his gaze resting for long moments first on one, and then on the other. He seemed as if he wanted to say something, but then he only smiled and turned away. He padded into the kitchen with an empty glass and held it against the refrigerator's ice dispenser until two cubes tinkled out. He seemed to think for a moment before going to the tap. He filled his glass too quickly, and sipped the excess before he trudged slowly back to his room as though nobody was watching him, as though he had intruded on nothing at all.

'Is he dying?' Ekene tried to keep his voice neutral. It was twilight by now. It was winter, and the world was not as it had been. The sun was setting earlier, and fewer people were outside at this time of day. Still, it was just warm enough for them. There might be snow tomorrow, but for now it was not too late for them to walk and talk to one another in the evening air.

They had taken the tube and then walked in silence for a few minutes, to a square lined by restaurants and bars. In the middle were sunken steps built in a square where people ate food in takeaway boxes and drank their cocktails from plastic cups. Had they been elsewhere, a square like this would have been perfect for the hot weather. It would have been a place where people might sit outside and be cool. There might have been children playing in a water fountain. But it was England, and the weather was not to be played with.

It was December now, and the restaurant's space heaters gave them only just enough warmth for an evening outside with coats on, and with some stoicism. At the restaurant's door, Achike ignored the light of recognition in the hostess's eye, and would not use his name; outside, he huddled with Ekene and made do.

'No,' said Achike. 'He's not dying.'

'Achike,' said Ekene. He spoke softly and put his hand on Achike's knee. 'Do you really want to do this?'

'He drinks too much,' said Achike, simply. He would not meet Ekene's gaze.

'I know he drinks too much. He's always drunk too much.'

'Not always. There've been times.'

'Achike.'

Achike sipped his wine quietly and ignored the sympathy in Ekene's voice.

'Achike,' Ekene said again. 'Why now? He's been like this for years. This isn't new.'

'I got a call from his landlord. He'd not paid his rent for months. He'd missed so many bills. And he was living in chaos, Ekene. It was like an animal was living there. He never cleaned anything. There were cockroaches. You should have seen it.'

'But hasn't he always been quite . . . high-functioning? What happened?'

'He got fired.'

'From the hotel?'

'Yep.' Achike shrugged. 'He kept turning up late, or not turning up at all. And sooner or later he would have been visibly drunk at work, and that would have been it anyway.'

'So you went to his flat, bundled him up and took him home in your pocket?'

'I had to take him with me,' said Achike. 'He's my dad, Ekene.'

'I know that,' said Ekene. 'Jesus, Achike. You don't have to talk to me like that, you know. You don't have to – to shut me out just to let him in.' He waited for Achike to respond, but he didn't. 'And you don't need to say "he's my dad", like he's some perfect father, either.'

Achike frowned. 'What?'

'Come on, Achike, he's . . . he's let you down. He's really let you down.' He formed the words slowly so that they could say things to Achike. 'And I know you haven't forgotten it. So why should you change your whole life, for him?'

'Because sometimes you have to make sacrifices. That's what you do for people you love.'

'Is it, always?'

That was the problem. Too often, for Achike, this *was* love. Love could never be everyday for Achike; never. His love was for emergencies. It always had to be, Achike thought, essentially corrective. Love must be a red pen. It must be a bright, sharp blade, to cut deep into flesh and come out clean. Years ago, as teenagers together in Achike's bedroom, their clothes dismissed and bodies under question, Achike would make scissors of his fingers and mime the blades through Ekene's penis. *Snip! Snip!* As if he were easier without all that.

But who could blame the boy? Or the man. Ekene leaned over and kissed his friend's forehead gently. Achike smiled and made the smallest movement to turn his head away; Ekene might have missed it if he hadn't known it would come.

As long as they had known each other, Achike had done this, inching towards Ekene, his best foot first, only dipping in his big toe – and then withdrawing it, quickly, as if from a scald. That was what his uncle had done to him, years ago. Although Achike hated to discuss it, this was what he saw in himself, and what the man had put in him; a thing in his soul that was dirty and wouldn't go. Nobody wanted to touch a thing like that. Nobody could bear it. Unless they really, really loved you.

This was Achike. This was the love that he gave, and he gave. But Ekene did not recognise love this way. He would not have it so pristine, and so untouchable.

'Look, Achike,' Ekene said. 'I know your dad needs help. But what about what *you* need?'

Achike went quiet. He picked olives off his half of the pizza and put them on Ekene's side, before picking up a slice and eating it, watching the city's lights.

Ekene tried to catch Achike's eye, knowing that he would be calculating the amount of exercise he would need to do the next day, to compensate. Food could never be food. Achike's mind metabolised it into carbohydrates, proteins, calories, macros, targets, sin, guilt, penance. This pizza should have been sundried tomato and broccoli. Instead it would be a ninety-minute workout the next morning, before Ekene was out of bed.

Achike never spoke about this balancing act. It was for Ekene that Achike pretended. It was for Ekene that he tried to keep up a façade of normality. The pizza had been Achike's idea. He never wanted to be an obstacle. He couldn't let himself be the reason Ekene might leave him, might turn from him in disappointment and leave him.

But how much closer Ekene would have allowed himself to get, if Achike had only been himself? Ekene missed the way Achike used to slip into his Manc accent when they were together, sloughing off his non-regional actor self. He hated the show that Achike put on for him. He wondered what it would be, never to be Achike's audience, but to be allowed merely to *see* him.

Ekene took one of the olives and chewed it thoughtfully.

'Look,' he said. 'I think it's so good that you want to look after your dad. You're so good for doing that. And I'm not singing his praises, but I don't want anything bad to happen to him, either. In some ways, he's been like a father to me, too. You know he has. So, I do understand what you're trying to do. God knows it's more than I've done for my dad. It's just—'

'That's not the same,' Achike said, softening. 'Your dad isn't the same.'

'No, I know,' said Ekene. 'I just meant I appreciate what you're doing.'

'Are you okay?'

'It's fine. I'm not talking about that. I just mean ... you know.'

Who had a heart like Achike's? Ekene watched him wipe tomato sauce from the corners of his mouth, and wished he could be the one to do it. He wished there could be something inside him that was tender enough, and brave enough to do a thing like that for Achike. How sad, to be able to offer up only an approximation of love, to bark consternation at Achike when he only wanted to take a napkin and clean his skin.

'Okay,' said Achike.

'But, I mean ... how will this even work, really? What will be the cost for you?'

'*Cost*? Ekene, come on.' Achike frowned, as if Ekene had used foul language.

'I don't just mean money. How long do you want him to stay?'

Achike turned to look at him. 'Why does it matter?'

'Achike ... '

'What does it matter, Ekene? What are we doing?'

'I don't know,' said Ekene, simply. He wanted to take an index finger and run it through Achike's hair, and see Achike close his eyes, soothed. He didn't. 'I don't know what we're doing. I don't think I've ever known what we're doing, and it's been more than twenty years.'

'I've come back here, Ekene. To you. When I was away in LA, I came to see you. When I was in Manchester, I came to see you.'

'I know,' said Ekene.

'And then that night in Berlin—'

'I know,' said Ekene, quietly.

'When are we going to talk about what happened?'

'Don't, Achike.'

'You said you wanted to wait until we could talk about it properly. And I got that. You were in Berlin. And then I was away, filming. But it's been almost a year now, Ekene. And you're not with Oskar anymore. And we're both here.'

'I don't know what that night means, Achike. I don't know what any of this means. Do you?'

'I know what I want it to mean,' said Achike. 'Don't you know what you want by now?'

They were both quiet for a moment, and then Ekene said, 'We were talking about your dad.'

But Achike ignored him. 'If Berlin didn't mean anything . . . if we're not together, then I don't see why my dad can't stay with us. He's not intruding on anything.'

'It meant something. I never said it didn't mean anything.'

Achike looked at him. Ekene wanted to run a finger through his hair.

'I've been thinking,' said Achike, after a moment. 'Whatever it is we've been doing, we've been doing it since we were at school. How many relationships last that long? How many marriages?'

'That's not what we're talking about.'

'But think about it, Ekene,' he pleaded. 'Even if we're not together, we're together. We are. We're not nothing.'

'I'm not saying we're nothing. I've never said that.'

'And if we'd been married,' said Achike, 'he'd be your father-in-law. Think about that.'

'But we're not married, Achike. Don't be ridiculous. Why are you saying all this?'

'It's not ridiculous.'

Ekene took out a paper napkin then stood up and slowly wiped the grease off his fingers, taking far too much care over it, and then went to put the napkin in a bin nearby.

Ekene did this. He walked away. Whenever they argued, he did this, and hoped that things would change in his absence, that Achike would change his mind, or that Achike would change. Ekene's parents had been the same, though he hadn't seen them in years. They were quiet people, hated confrontation, hated conflict. They went years without fighting each other, but the anger never went away. They fought Ekene instead: the mother battled what she saw of the father in him, the father battled the mother in him. Ekene always lost.

Achike's parents were the opposite. Before his mother died, they shouted, raged, railed. Achike didn't know how to be quiet about something so important. Ekene only knew that fighting wouldn't work.

When Ekene sat down again, Achike persisted. 'When you lost your job, we said you'd move into my flat for a bit while you found your feet. Four months later, you're still here.'

Ekene flinched as though he'd been touched somewhere sore. 'I know.'

'So what do you want?' asked Achike, eagerly. 'Don't you want to just ... do this properly?'

How can you do love properly? How can you do this love properly?

'I'm not sure yet. I need more time, Achike,' Ekene said.

Achike relented; Oskar had only broken up with Ekene a few months before. 'And you keep changing the subject,' said Ekene. 'Do you even have a plan? Who's going to look after your dad when you're away? Are you hiring someone? A specialist?'

'He's not infirm, Ekene. He doesn't need round-the-clock care. He's just ... lost. He needs something to anchor him. He needs to be around family, and he needs someone to remind him of why he should give up drinking again.'

Ekene let himself glance softly at Achike, this beautiful, kind man for whom all kinds of sacrifice would be worthwhile.

'He has nowhere else to go,' said Achike. 'He has no job, no savings. He only has me. And I've finished filming, now, and then I'll be able to—'

'Okay, but what about after that? What about the next film? What happens when you have to fly to Nigeria again? Or ... I don't know, Siberia, or something? What happens when you get cast in some North Pole explorer biopic? Even if he doesn't need round-the-clock care, he needs you around. You just said. He needs family. Have you thought about that?'

Achike shrugged.

'I can't look after him, Achike. He's not my family. I haven't forgotten what he did for me when we were kids. But I'm not his son. It's not me.' His face clouded over, and Achike searched his eyes for the unnamed emotion.

Ekene had always been a rebellious child, but the confusion he felt surrounding his sexuality only got worse as he got older. He decided the best way to ward off bullies was to become one himself. He made bad friends and bad choices. Once, he got excluded from school. By the age of seventeen he had run away from home six times. Coming home the seventh time, drunk out of his mind, he dimly heard his mother tell him to stay outside.

He was surprised when Chibuike welcomed him in. Achike's mother had died only a year earlier, and Achike was still finding words for his feelings. And yet Chibuike had allowed him to stay; had given him stability and routine. Had let the two of them finish growing up together.

'I'll owe him for life, Achike. But you need to be realistic. You know he's too proud. I bet he doesn't even like you looking after him.' He looked hard at Achike. 'I bet you had to drag him kicking and screaming out of his flat, didn't you?'

'It took some persuading.'

'So how will this work?' Ekene asked again. 'Are you going to take him with you on location? Have you thought about this at all?'

Eventually Achike said, 'I thought you'd be proud of me.'

'What?'

'It seems silly now,' Achike said. He heaved a heavy sigh. 'I hadn't said it aloud before. But being in Nigeria was ... ' He shook his head. 'It made me think about things.'

'What's Nigeria got to do with us?' said Ekene, before he could think. 'You know what I mean. They hate us there.'

'I know,' said Achike. 'But ... it just made me think, you know? Everything there was about family. For a week of the filming I was staying with this one family that had four generations under one roof. You remember I Skyped you from their house?'

'I remember.'

'It was really hard sometimes. They did have arguments once or twice when they thought I couldn't hear them. It was about the computer, or in-laws. Or about money. And there was no privacy. Everybody knew everything about everybody else. Towards the end of the week I think they started to suspect I was gay. I was worried about it, actually.'

But Ekene saw in his face that there was more to it. Achike's eyes were focused on something in the distance, as if trying to remember a dream he'd had. Ekene knew: Achike had fallen in love with something.

'But they were this amazing family. The great-grandma was ninety years old or something, and she didn't have a pension, but it was okay because her son and his wife and kids looked after her. They all woke up really early every morning to pray together, and then they ate breakfast and talked about their plans for the day, and about what the kids were doing in school. And everybody helped everybody do things, Ekene. Nobody had to cook or clean alone, or look after the kids alone if they didn't want to. There was always somebody home. *The family* was like this big thing that everyone was part of. Nobody was lost or left out. Nobody was ever alone.'

'Sounds great,' said Ekene. 'Wish I knew what that was like.'

'I had no idea, either,' said Achike. 'Being there, it hit me, you know? I'd never seen it before. I'd never had a chance. And I know you haven't either. And I know it was stupid of me to think I could ever have what they have. I know I could never have a family there.' His eyes clouded over for a moment, and he seemed to be contemplating something sadly. 'But I couldn't not try, Ekene. Being there, I felt like I was just on the outside of this amazing, strong, warm, loving, infinite *thing*. After that, I had to try and see if I could have it for myself, somehow. And I thought when I got back, and I brought my dad to live with us, you'd look at me ... ' He spoke hopefully now. Deep breaths. 'You'd see how much I care about him, and you'd see ... I don't know. Something. You'd see what I could do. What I could build for us. And something would change. And we'd be a family.'

Achike finished his last slice of pizza and wiped his hands.

Ekene felt his throat start to close up, and he tried to be gentle. Who had a heart like Achike's? And who, in the face of a love like this, would not quail? Who could bear to stay, and see himself found wanting?

'Achike. What do you want me to see that I don't already see? I've known you since we were kids. I've seen everything about you. I know what your heart can do. I know.'

Achike tried to wave the emotion away. 'It feels silly now. But, yeah. That's what I was thinking.'

Ekene turned his head to wipe his eyes. Pigeons had gathered in the centre of the square, settling and then fluttering away by turns. Somewhere, someone's child was wailing.

'You do too much for me, Achike,' Ekene said, gently.

'I don't think so.'

'And you do too much for your dad.'

'I could give up acting,' said Achike. He said it just as though it were easy to say. 'I could quit.'

But Ekene only looked at him, annoyed, as if Achike had made a bad joke.

'I could,' said Achike. 'I don't have to do this forever.'

'You can't quit,' said Ekene, simply. 'You can't quit. You just can't.'

'You sound like Julian,' Achike laughed.

'Then Julian's right. What would you do? Give up the work you've wanted to do ever since we were kids? Ever since I met you?'

'I could. If I wanted.' Achike sounded almost petulant. Ekene tried not to smile.

'To do what? Babysit your dad? Try to replicate some family you barely even know – a family that would have probably turned on you the minute they saw who you really were? Why can't you just let yourself have this one good thing in your life? Why do you think everything has to be sacrificed?'

'It's not like that, Ekene,' said Achike. 'You know how hard it's been, all the pressure. And it's only going to get worse now I'm getting bigger roles. You know I'll have to have a dietician soon? I'll have someone whose job it is to make sure I never get spots or lose my six pack. I've told you.'

'But isn't it worth it, if you love acting?'

Achike shrugged. 'This isn't where I want my life to be, Ekene. I've seen people like that. I know them now. One film set after another. Premieres, premieres. They can never hold onto anything. I want family. I want something stable and safe.'

'You could have both. You just need to not be so extreme about it,' said Ekene.

'Doesn't sound like me,' said Achike, trying to laugh a little.

'You don't have to give up anything completely,' said Ekene. 'Why would you give up everything you've worked so hard for?'

'Yeah,' said Achike. 'Too hard. I don't want to work this hard at something I'm not really passionate about anymore.'

'You mean you don't enjoy it at all?'

'I *have* enjoyed it. I've had a great time. I love playing these characters. I love that I get to chase this dream. But you were the one who cared about the craft of it. It should have been you.'

Ekene looked at him silently.

'The reason you're not saying anything is because you know I'm right,' Achike said. 'You were always better at it than me. I just had a look a director wanted one day, and now here I am. I'm just lucky.'

Ekene shook his head, tried to smile. 'You've earned it. You're good. You've worked hard.'

'And my reward is ... what? Fame? All I want to do is give it up. I want to be free.'

'Achike. Think very hard about this.'

'I want to live a normal life again, Ekene. I just want to live a bit.'

'You want to trade places with me? You want to teach drama part-time? And then have your job cut because nobody cares enough about what you do to pay for it?'

'I'm not saying I want to struggle,' said Achike. 'I don't and I never did. But you know my life isn't the dream either. I wake up early, I run, I lift weights. I learn lines, I say them in front of a camera over and over again. I fly to this city or that village, I do interviews. I do photoshoots. I don't see my friends for months. I do what I'm told. I go where I'm told. I don't complain. I'm tired of it.'

Ekene wanted to gently trace a finger along Achike's brow.

'I know how spoiled this sounds,' Achike said. 'I know. And I know how lucky I am. But I don't want to be lucky. I want to be happy. Every morning, I wake up and I feel like my life is slipping away from me. If I carry on doing this, one day I'll wake up and everything will have gone. And you ...'

'Me?'

'One day I'll be filming in Siberia, or wherever and you'll call me up and tell me you've met someone else.'

What reassurance could Ekene give, when there had already been so many others? Oskar was the most recent, but he had only ever been someone whose name was not Achike.

Across the square, a restaurant turned up the volume on its speakers and sad, slow jazz started to blare out and bounce across the flagstones. Other music, more fragile, emerged alongside it: somewhere, somebody knew some of the words, and that was enough for them. Achike closed his eyes and let the music and the alcohol sway him a little. He looked like he could be happy.

'What would you do if you gave up acting?' Ekene asked.

Achike shrugged. 'I could move into directing, maybe? Maybe I could write scripts. I don't know. This latest film is paying me well, so I could take a bit of time to decide. And Julian could probably sort something out for me, once he came around. He could get me started. Or maybe he'd find someone who could. I don't know.'

Ekene said quietly, 'Do you want me to move out?'

'What?' said Achike. 'No. Don't be daft.'

'I just thought—'

'Ekene.'

'I just don't want to be in the way.'

'You won't ever be in the way,' said Achike.

Who, in the face of love like this, could fail to return that love? Ekene saw Achike look down at his shoes again, saw his lips fall into an unthinking pout. He wanted to kiss them. He wanted to put his arm around Achike and help him do this impossible thing. There was nobody in the world like this man.

'I want to help you, if this is what you want. I do,' said Ekene. 'I don't want you to do it alone. But you've gone and done this bloody stupid thing ...' He shook his head again, exasperated. 'And you know I'm not like you. I'm not good with people. And I can't look after him the way you can – the way I already knew you could, Achike.'

'Thank you. I mean it.' Achike looked like he wanted to say something else, but he didn't.

'So what happens next? What happens tomorrow?'

Achike thought for a moment. 'I don't know. I guess I'll try to talk to my dad about his drinking? I should wait till he's sober, shouldn't I? It'll be difficult.'

Ekene nodded. 'I'll be there.'

'And it's not all bad,' said Achike. 'Tomorrow's the wedding, right?' He sounded very tired now. 'Oskar and his new man. It was good of them to invite you.'

'Yes.'

'You don't think?'

'No, I do.' Ekene smiled, weakly.

'Odd that they're getting married so soon, though. Nobody gets together that quickly. This new man must be some sort of rebound, surely.'

'No idea,' said Ekene, neutrally. He hoped he sounded forgiving and mature. 'I think maybe it's someone he knew before me. Maybe when I left, he realised what he really wanted.'

'It's his loss, you know.'

Ekene shrugged.

'Are you sure you want to go to the ceremony?' Achike said.

Ekene gave a determined nod. 'Yes. I want to.'

'I know you think you have to. They've reached out and invited you.'

'I guess.'

'But will you be okay, watching your ex get married to someone else? I know things weren't great in the end. I really don't want you to suffer through it if you don't want to go.'

By way of answering him, Ekene brought Achike's head down to rest on his shoulder. It was almost all he wanted. 'I do care about you, you know.'

'I know. That's what's so confusing. I thought things would be different after Berlin.'

Ekene let his body go still, his lips resting on Achike's head. 'Things are different. I just need you to be patient. I need time. I don't know what we are yet, Achike.'

At times like this, when Achike came back to him from somewhere else in the world, Ekene sometimes wondered if Achike missed LA, or felt the pull of New York. He wondered if Achike thought that even London felt small now, like a childhood bedroom. Somewhere further on in the city, new high-rise blocks joined the skyline and red lights perched on cranes.

'Are you sleepy?' Ekene asked. 'Do you want to go home?'

'No, no.' Then Achike yawned. Then he laughed at himself.

'What time did you get to bed last night?' Ekene asked.

'This morning, actually. About three.'

'And you went to get your dad as soon as you got back to London?'

'I slept on the tube, a bit.'

'Achike,' said Ekene, almost reproaching him. 'You must be so tired.' He ran a hand over the soft hair on the back of Achike's neck. He asked himself, *Why do I do this?* Achike's skin smelled like sweat. Ekene breathed in deeply.

'Let's go home,' he said.

'No, no,' said Achike again. 'You're here, I'm here. My dad's probably still at home. Let's stay out. We could go dancing.'

'Dancing? Achike, you're exhausted.'

'We haven't been out in so long,' said Achike, sadly.

'Yeah, but we can do that any night. We don't have to go out right now.'

'That means you really want to,' said Achike, wryly. 'Come on, let's stay out. We never get to do this.'

'What about your workout?' Ekene mimed doing barbell curls.

'I'll fit it in before we go to the wedding. Let's do it,' he said, sing-song, promising Ekene more music, feeding him more dreams. 'Let's find somewhere where the music is terrible and nobody knows how to dance. I've missed you.'

Chapter 2

Achike moved slowly at first, unsure of himself, and forgetting that Ekene had seen him at his worst. Embarrassment clung to his heels and dragged his movements.

But then Ekene was pulling faces and laughing, and Achike was buying drinks. And then Ekene was pulling Achike further into the dance floor, and then they were together. Nobody could touch them. Achike loved the way Ekene danced; the way his body moved was exact and pure, showing how the music should be felt. He understood rhythm, and how to bend and shape himself into it. His movements were intuitive and fluid, but precise. Achike's were quick and easy to miss, but his feet knew work. When they danced, it felt like home. And then they went home.

And then the air was shining. It was the aura – the frightening kaleidoscope that hung before his eyes before a migraine. It put ice in his veins.

Then there was the anxiety. Even though he knew what was coming, even though he knew exactly what would happen. The blinding headache would not be far behind, and the nausea.

The fear squatted in his chest and wouldn't budge. He felt

his breathing shallow and his heart rate increase. Somehow, knowing what would happen only seemed to make it worse. He knew that there would be pain, that he would spend hours in his bed, powerless, helpless.

'I can't see properly,' Achike said. 'This light, it's—'

Then there was Ekene.

'I know, it's okay. Let's get you into bed. Come on.' His voice was soft and certain. His hand was on Achike's neck, the tips of his fingers on his skin, in his hair. 'Migraine? It's a migraine, right?'

Achike closed his eyes and nodded slowly. If he moved his head too much, it would erupt. If he just let him, Ekene would look after him.

'It's okay, it's okay,' came Ekene's voice. 'Don't move. I've got you.'

Achike considered resisting but he couldn't. 'Okay,' he said, quietly.

'Don't worry, I'll sort it.'

'I ... Thank you.'

'Don't be daft.' Ekene's voice was brisk and capable. Love was just underneath. He smoothed Achike's face with his hands. Ekene's hands were like Achike's: long, clever fingers; dry skin that was never soft except when, like tonight, he had taken care to moisturise. Practical hands, Achike thought. Hands for doing, not for touch. But Achike wanted Ekene's hands for both now.

Their bodies differed. Achike's was strikingly lean; there was nothing on his bones except what survived his ferocious metabolism. Ekene's body, Achike thought, was more hospitable: it was softer, rounder; it retained more of what it took in. It hugged you back.

Ekene got up and went to Achike's bathroom. He quickly found the medicine – the tablets were always in exactly the same place, just in case. Even in his hurry, he could not help noticing again how tidy Achike's bathroom was. Everything was correct and in place, everything was tucked away in a cupboard or drawer; apart from the incense diffuser with a white ribbon tied around its reeds, nothing was simply left out in the open to find. This was Achike. You had to know where things would be.

Ekene went to the kitchen and poured a glass of water. Seeing a clean hand towel on the rail as he walked back past the bathroom, he soaked it in cold water before returning to Achike's side. Achike's eyes were scrunched shut. He looked agonised already, like he was going to die. Ekene briefly considered teasing Achike for being melodramatic, but thought better of it. He could not enter in on Achike's pain, so for now he kept a respectful distance.

'Open up,' Ekene said.

'What?'

'I've got the water and the medicine. Open up.'

His eyes still closed, Achike parted his lips slightly and allowed Ekene to hold the cup to his mouth. Achike took in just enough water so he could swallow the pill which Ekene pressed to his soft lips. Achike swallowed, grimaced, lay back.

'I'm sorry about this,' Achike said. His brow was furrowed and it ached.

'What do you mean?' said Ekene. He took the damp towel and pressed it to Achike's head until he saw Achike's face start to relax and his breathing deepen again.

'I'm sorry about this migraine,' Achike said. 'We were having such a good night and—'

'Shut up. It's okay,' said Ekene. He made himself sound bluntly affectionate. 'It's not your fault. You probably just ate something that set it off. Or you're tired, maybe. You've been working so hard.' Achike nodded slowly at this last reason. 'And I don't mind doing this,' said Ekene.

'Okay,' said Achike. 'Okay. Thank you.'

'Stop thanking me. Shush.'

Achike was right, though: it had been a beautiful night. Back at the flat, they'd stepped towards the bed, and lay under the covers, shivering in the cold room. Achike was certain that, if the night had gone on longer, Ekene would have finally told him what he had been telling Ekene without words, all this time. He knew it. Ekene would not get away from it. He was sure that, finally, Ekene would have told him that he loved him.

And then the migraine had started.

At first, Achike hadn't wanted to say anything. He hadn't wanted to break the spell, fearful that Ekene would think again, that he would run away, the way he had run away with Joe, and Arthur, and Wei, and Joe again, and then with Oskar. At first, when he knew that the migraine was coming, Achike had tried to hide it. In his kitchen, when the blind spot appeared slightly to the left of Ekene, he tried to look only a little distracted. And when he was unable to bear the harsh lights, he turned down the dimmer as far as it would go and said something about his eyes being tired. When the sound of the stereo began to grate on his mind, he switched off the music and said the only voice he wanted to hear that night was Ekene's. But then they were in bed together, and they were closer, and Achike couldn't hide it.

Even now, the pain had not started yet but it would soon, and when it did, it would make Achike feel as helpless as a child. The medication was a strong prescription-only tablet that dizzied him. It took the edge off the pain if he took it in time, but he knew the headache would still press on him, insisting above his left eye.

He found, however, that if he focused intensely, he could almost slip out from underneath the pain, out of himself; he could dream that it was happening to someone else. But it was exhausting, and the whole thing would last for five hours, sometimes six or more. Sometimes, the pain overwhelmed him. On those occasions he could only writhe, rocking backwards and forwards, his head in his hands, until he fell asleep. As Ekene tucked him into bed, he hoped that it would be one of the easier times, when he could dream it away.

'Ekene.' His voice was too faint to hear at first. 'Ekene,' he said again.

'Yeah? Yeah? What is it?'

'Will you stay with me?'

Ekene looked at him, concerned now. Achike got migraines all the time. He'd been getting them since they were both in school. So why was he so afraid?

'Of course I'll stay. Can you move over a bit?'

'Yeah. Come on,' said Achike. He shuffled up and made room for Ekene, lifted up the duvet in invitation.

'You'll be okay, you know,' said Ekene. 'You're not dying.'

Achike laughed. 'You always say that.'

'And you always get so anxious. Why? You know how it goes. Aura, migraine, sleep. Aura, migraine, sleep.'

First light, then pain, then rest. He knew this.

Achike took a few deep breaths. Ekene guessed that he was trying to keep from vomiting. 'You'll be okay,' Ekene said. 'You're fine. You'll be fine, soon.'

'I know,' said Achike, impatiently. 'I know,' he said again, more softly. 'But it's one of the symptoms. Anxiety. I can't help it. I just get like this.'

'One of the symptoms, eh?' said Ekene, softly.

His hands were on Achike's skin again, and they were the only thing that Achike's body could stand. It was so hard to be touched by someone when the pain was setting in, when he was so afraid. Ekene's skin on Achike's skin felt like a threat, like a mistake. But not being touched by Ekene was worse. Achike moistened his lips, and they were smooth again, and pink, and brown, and soft.

Idly, Ekene wondered if Achike had any conception of how

beautiful he was, or if perhaps he had got used to looking at his own face in the mirror, his impossibly beautiful face on screen.

'Yeah,' Achike nodded. 'One of the symptoms,' he repeated, weakly.

'Well, come here,' said Ekene, pulling Achike into a hug. And then the hug pulled them both closer, and then they started to kiss, and then they were kissing. It was happening.

'Mmm,' said Achike. 'I didn't want it to be like this.'

'Shh,' said Ekene. 'It's okay.'

'No, I didn't ...' Achike breathed deeply and swallowed. 'I just wanted it to be ...'

'I know,' said Ekene. There was silence for a long time, while he let his fingers trace the delicate lines on Achike's face. How wonderful that felt, like observing art. Also, like making it. How could they ever have failed to see that this was what they were to one another? Friends did not do such things. Even many lovers, maybe.

'Does this hurt?' Ekene said, after a while.

'No. It's good,' Achike said. His voice had a comfort in it.

'I want to kiss you again,' Ekene said.

'My migraine,' Achike frowned. 'And ...'

'Yeah, your dad. I know.' Instinctively, they both listened out for him, awaiting his footsteps like an inappropriate gift.

'I'm sorry,' said Achike.

'Stop apologising. It's not your fault. He's got nowhere else to go, right?'

For a split second, it was the two of them wishing Chibuike away. He'd been drinking beer in the shower in the mornings since Achike was a teenager. He took a bottle of wine to bed every night.

'Nowhere else to go,' said Achike.

Achike hurt, now. Everything hurt. He hooked his leg around Ekene's waist and pulled him closer. He could smell Ekene's breath. It was not exactly pleasant – he could smell the cocktails from earlier, like stale tangerines – but it smelled good, because it was Ekene. His breath was warm. Could Achike be in it entirely? Could he live in Ekene's breath?

'I don't have anywhere to go, either,' said Ekene. His voice took on a note of sadness as he remembered. He'd not been teaching drama at the high school very long before they'd made him redundant. Insufficient uptake in the subject. Insufficient funds.

'Yeah, but that's okay,' said Achike.

'You sure about that?' said Ekene. 'It's not exactly sexy, is it? Me sponging off you like this, on top of your dad.'

'When were you on top of my dad? I turn my back for one second . . . '

'Funny.'

'I like you being here,' said Achike. On 'like', he prodded Ekene's chest gently with an index finger, his touch behind the sheets.

'You do?' Ekene kissed Achike's forehead.

'I do.'

'Well, I'll be out of here as soon as I'm back on my feet again,' he said, as though this were the answer to being wanted. 'I mean it. I don't want to be a burden to you.'

But Achike shook his head. 'No. Don't. You're not a burden.'

'You should write a letter to the school and tell them that.'

'Maybe I will.' Achike smiled, then winced as the muscles in his forehead struggled into life.

'The medicine'll kick in soon,' said Ekene. Before he knew it, he was whispering. Somewhere in the large flat, he thought, Chibuike was unhappy, drinking, pottering about in his slippers. The thought of the old man's presence chilled Ekene. But Achike was too close now. Ekene felt his dick harden against Achike's thigh. 'Very soon,' he said.

'Not soon enough for that,' said Achike, without opening his eyes.

'What?' said Ekene, innocently.

'No,' said Achike. 'Not ready.'

'The medicine—'

'It's not about the medicine.'

'We've known each other for more than twenty years,' said Ekene. 'And it's not like this would be our first time.'

'But this,' said Achike, slowly, 'is different. It's not like in Berlin.'

'Well—' Ekene began.

'And it's not my fault that it took so long, either.'

When Ekene didn't say anything for a few moments, Achike opened his eyes again. Ekene had turned off all the lights and Achike could see only the outline of his features. But he could tell without looking that Ekene was sulking. Why did he do this? Even when Achike felt closest to him, fear was always closer. The smallest thing could dispel Ekene entirely and drive him far away. Hadn't they had a beautiful night? Wasn't the distance between them as thin as the sheets?

'It's okay,' Achike said, trying to placate. 'I'm not angry with you.' And then, because he couldn't not say it – because he felt it, and because it would burst out of him – he said, 'I love you. I still love you.'

He had thought that this would make things better, that somehow this time it would bring Ekene closer. But Ekene closed his eyes and smiled a pitiful smile, as though Achike had crossed some sort of line. Why must Ekene do that?

'You should get some rest,' Ekene said. 'You'll feel better in the morning.'

Achike watched, lost, as Ekene extricated himself from the sheets. In a moment he was gone again – his body too, this time – and Achike could only close his eyes and wait for the pain to get worse.

*

'Maybe the pain won't be that bad? You should try to be more optimistic,' Ekene says. There is ample cheerfulness in his voice. They are twelve, and Ekene is distracted, rifling intently through his backpack for something that has eluded him for the past few minutes. His backpack is covered in drawings and doodles, some done with thought and purpose, most just idle moments that persist; his parents refuse to buy him another bag until he learns to treat his belongings with some respect. Like his parents, Ekene wonders when this will be.

They are at the school gates. Everyone else has gone home. But not them: Achike stayed behind to do extra homework; Ekene stayed behind to do detention. Again. They are alone, together. The school is almost empty, the street is quiet. The whole world could be for just these two.

'How many of these *migraine* things have you had before?' Ekene asks this with some scepticism.

'A lot,' says Achike, tersely. He has had three, but he does not feel that this number reflects the severity of his problem. He looks around to see if there is someone, anyone nearby who can be more helpful than this boy. This boy seems a little ... feckless. He has strange drawings on his backpack that look like ancient runes or symbols of witchcraft. Achike has seen him around before, and he is not entirely sure he likes what he has seen. There is a carelessness about the boy. His clothes are no cheaper than Achike's, but they are scruffy and unironed. And not on purpose: the popular ones in their year are the rich ones, and they are deliberately messy. (Achike, with his love of reading, observes the popular children from a distance, and does not like them.) But Ekene does not work this way. Achike can tell he doesn't know how to look after things. Achike doubts, therefore, that Ekene knows anything about looking after people, either.

But Ekene is just as different from the poor students: his trousers are not too short; his blazer is not too long, bought knowing he'll grow into it. His shoes are scuffed, but there are no holes in them and he has a couple of different pairs. (Achike has noticed this, too, without noticing.) Achike feels a tide of frustration rise in himself. Why can't the boy just fit in with one group or the other? Why can't he just ... do things on purpose? Doesn't he know how things work? Doesn't he know where he belongs? Achike is not sure if he wants to fix the boy, but he wants him to be fixed.

'I've been having migraines for ages,' bluffs Achike. He sounds haughty, as though having migraines is one of the benefits of belonging to an exclusive club (a club, perhaps, that requires its members to iron their clothes). 'I know how to look after myself. I'm fine.'

'Don't you have any medicine for them, then? If you get them all the time?' Ekene frowns slightly but remains focused on his backpack.

'I ... left it at home.'

'Right,' said Ekene.

'Whatever,' said Achike. 'It's fine, I don't live far away.'

'I thought you lived on Range Road?' said Ekene.

Achike frowns and turns back sharply to face Achike. 'How did you know?'

Ekene feels the blood rush to his face. He feels grateful that his skin is far too dark for a blush to be apparent except at very close range, but he continues pretending to look in his bag anyway.

'We get the same bus sometimes,' he mumbles.

Achike frowns. 'We do?' And before he can think, he says, 'That's weird. I think I'd have noticed you.'

There is a silence, in which Ekene pauses his search. His hands are still. It is as though he has found something.

Then Achike collects himself and says, 'You're quite scruffy. That's quite hard to miss.'

'Oh gee,' says Ekene. 'Thanks, Mr Perfect.'

'What?'

'Mr Perfect. That's what people call you, you know. You're always so . . . ' Ekene shrugs. 'Well, you know.'

'Who calls me that?' Achike raises his voice. He is offended. Appalled. Somehow, he is surprised.

Ekene changes tack. 'You wouldn't have noticed me on the bus. You always have your head in a book. Sometimes even when you're walking. I don't do that.'

'Maybe you should,' says Achike, still stung. He wonders how many people have been making fun of him behind his back, and if there's any chance 'Mr Perfect' is a roundabout way of showing admiration.

'Forget about it,' says Ekene. 'I'm just trying to help you.'

'How was that supposed to help me?' demands Achike.

'You're pretty tightly wound, you know,' says Ekene, with an infuriating calm. 'I bet it's just because you always take everything so seriously. *Migraines*.' He pronounces the word like a transparently fake name, his suspicion clear. 'Still don't see any sign of it, by the way.'

'That's because *you* can't see the signs,' says Achike, losing his temper. 'It's not like the plague, you know. I don't burst out in boils or anything. Other people can't see the signs.'

'Like what?' says Ekene, unruffled. He is good at this – winding people up to get them to show their true colours. He likes to sit back and watch the colours explode, like fireworks.

'At first, I just get a blind spot – total blindness in part of my vision, a total nothing – then I see some flashing light thingies. Then I get a headache – but,' here he speaks quickly to pre-empt interruption, although Ekene is listening intently, happy with anything he can drink in, 'but it's not like a normal headache. It's severe. *Acute*, actually. And then I start to feel very nauseated. And I become very sensitive to light and sound. But all those symptoms are internal, so you wouldn't see them. It's not like you can see inside my head, you know.'

There is a pause, while both of them take a moment to absorb this wisdom, as well as Achike's astronomical nerdiness. To move the conversation along as briskly as possible, Achike says, 'Besides, you've been pretending to look for something in your bag for the past ten minutes, so how would you ever notice?'

'Aha!' says Ekene, pulling his pencil case out of his bag with a triumphant flourish.

Achike only said that Ekene was pretending because he wanted to change the subject, but now he knows for sure. He wonders why Ekene was pretending.

He looks at Ekene carefully. Ekene steadfastly maintains his performance. 'Found it,' he says, in fake relief. 'Really glad I won't have to go back into school to look for it.'

'Yeah,' says Achike. 'Now you can do all the homework you're not going to do.'

Ekene feigns indignation. 'What makes you think I don't do any homework?'

'You never put your hand up in Science,' says Achike, quickly. Too quickly.

'I thought you hadn't noticed me,' says Ekene, slowly. A smile spreads across his handsome, confident face like first light. Achike, unused to this, turns away from it.

'It's a small class,' says Achike, embarrassed. 'Everyone in that class stands out.'

'I thought you hadn't noticed me,' says Ekene again. He is enjoying this, and Achike does not know why. Is this a trap? He knows that there are boys in his year, straight boys, who think it's funny to do this, to trick boys like Achike into revealing themselves. It's humiliating. His secret could be everywhere by tomorrow afternoon. Is that what Ekene wants? Or does he desire something else? Achike doesn't know which possibility is more dangerous.

'Look,' says Achike. 'I need to get home. I've got a migraine starting.'

'I know,' says Ekene. 'So you'll need some help.'

'What?' says Achike. He looks almost stung.

Ekene is not surprised. He has noticed this boy plenty of times at school, the only other boy in the year with an Igbo name. Achike is always pert and ready at the front of the class, his school jumper always tucked into his trousers. Most of the clever kids don't like Achike because he isn't nice to them. Achike isn't nice to them because he knows they are lazy and complacent while he is diligent and anxious. Ekene wonders if this boy knows how little he fits in anywhere. He seems like the kind of kid who'd like to pick a side; the kind of kid who might not do so well in the grey areas. But maybe, he reasons, the grey areas could be a little more fun if he had some company. And Achike is not grey. His colours are ... different. Ekene cannot name them. But he likes them.

'You'll need help,' says Ekene again. 'You can't see, remember? Here, give me your bag.'

'I don't need—' begins Achike, but Ekene takes his bag and Achike does not stop him. Nearly half his vision is gone. 'Thanks,' he says, meekly.

'Come on, then,' says Ekene. His voice is cheerful, as though they have finally agreed on something. 'Let's get you to the bus stop. I'll go with you, if you like.'

'You will?'

'Yeah,' says Ekene. 'I know where you live. And I don't do homework, remember?'

Achike laughs, and then winces as the muscles in his forehead struggle into life. 'Thanks,' he says. 'That's nice of you.' The truth is the only thing he can think of to say.

Ekene is too happy and excited to say anything. He brushed the boy's hand when he took his backpack. As they walk along the road to the bus stop, he fights a battle of wills with his erection.

He nudges Achike gently, affectionately, with his shoulder.

'Ow,' says Achike.

'Headache?' says Ekene.

'Yes.'

'Already?'

'Yes.'

'Sorry.'

Achike looks at him, then realises something. 'Where do you live?' he asks.

'What?' Ekene says. His body seems to freeze, as though he is trying to avoid detection, as though he does not want to be seen.

'Where do you live?' Achike says again. 'You know where I live. Where do you live?'

Ekene shrugs. 'Near you.'

'Where?'

'A few stops after Range Road. Near you,' he says again, but there is a vagueness about him now, where there was specificity a moment ago. A moment ago, Ekene was immediate, the spark of electricity. Now, he is sparks in moving air, diffuse, dispelled, everywhere, wild to hold.

Ekene is directly in front of Achike, and yet Achike wonders where he has gone. Achike is confused – has he offended the boy? He looks for words with which to apologise, but finds none. He apologises with everything else, instead. With everything else he can find, he apologises: his body language speaks towards Ekene, the softness of his voice calls for the boy. He wants him back, the boy who was here.

Then the bus comes. It's just before rush hour and there's almost nobody on it, only a few passengers who glance lazily at the two black boys getting on, one of them holding two backpacks. A few of them wonder silently if the backpacks are stolen.

Ekene seems to return to himself, and he makes Achike climb the stairs with him and sit at the back; they are both, silently, relieved that all the seats on the upper deck are unoccupied. They have the space to themselves.

Achike closes his eyes and tries to sleep, somehow trusting that Ekene will wake him up when it's time. For the next three stops, Achike allows his head to loll on Ekene's shoulder. And for each of those three stops, Ekene inhales the smell of Achike's hair and imagines how it would feel if he reached out and ran a finger through it. He thinks it would feel very good. He thinks it would make Achike feel good. He knows he has been elsewhere; when Achike got too close, Ekene went away. He hates himself for this, already, so young. When will he learn to look after good things?

Then the bus stops outside a shopping centre and people get on. They bring their noise and their friendships and their eyes; their own conversations and their separate laughter. Had Achike and Ekene been hand in hand, they would have unclasped quickly, so as not to draw attention to themselves. Instead, they move slightly apart, knowing that it takes only an inch of daylight between them to designate what they have – this thing of theirs that they will spend decades trying to understand – as only a common male friendship. Nothing to stare at, nothing to be remarked upon. Only silence; only stoicism. Only a little distance.

But Ekene is still imagining how it would feel to hold Achike's aching head in his lap and run his fingers through Achike's hair, soothing the beautiful boy's pain with only his touch. And in Achike's mind, they never did unclasp: in his mind, they are walking hand in hand into this strange, too-bright world in which they must make their solitary way.

Chapter 3

It was a measure of how long Chibuike had been in England that he no longer minded the cold. He could do it now, this country. He'd finally learned to see the weather coming before it came, and to know how bad it could be. He liked knowing which layers were best when it rained, and which face to wear. He liked steeling himself. He liked to get on with it. He had shoes that didn't let the rain in.

He liked being on the overground train. He'd taken to the nights, now, and there were pleasant journeys he made, out of Peckham and in again. He'd started when he lost his job at the hotel. He was still living in the flatshare near the estate on Cleaton Road at the time, and he found himself going out to drink, only allowing himself alcohol in his room on the rare occasions when the flat was empty. And he found he had to go out, to leave behind the cramped, damp little flat, if only for a couple of hours at a time.

Staying in was too much to ask. Bad enough that a man his age had to share his home with strangers, there being nobody left in his family who he could bear to live with, whose disappointment in him would not be so cruel. But worse – those strangers had eyes, and questions they asked with their eyes.

Questions about the vodka on his breath, about the time of morning he'd had his first drink, about the friends he always mentioned but whom nobody ever saw. His answer was to leave the flat whenever he could.

So it was shame that hooked a finger under his collar and led him outside; but outside he found a world, and he fell in love with that world, and love made his addiction seem softer and somehow friendly to him. On those days and nights, Chibuike was on an adventure, and his addiction simply came with him and held his hand. He found an off-licence that was open late, where he could pick up spirits and have a drink on the train or in a side street if he felt afraid to risk being seen by someone who might recognise him. He'd drink, and be alone, and watch the city lights. And then he'd wash his mouth out with the miniature bottle of mouthwash always in his pocket now, and go home to the Cleaton Road flat, his head bowed, the key turning slowly in the lock.

And the trains! There was life on the trains. People of all sorts. It could be rowdy on Saturday nights and he felt at home then, hiding in plain sight, especially if there'd been a football match that day, or if nothing good at all had happened for a while; or if the weather was warm and dry, or if the weather was cold and wet. This was England, all of England on a train. Once, a woman in her fifties had swaggered up to his window, lifted her skirt at him and waved her hips from side to side in an ungainly, unequivocal dance. Chibuike had smiled and given her a thumbs up. He'd felt a blush of pride when she'd smiled back at him, knowing that he really spoke the language of the land now.

Sometimes it was the opposite, and that was fine, too. Sometimes, a ghostly silence wafted through the tube like a draught, chilling one conversation, then the next. If you went late enough on a weekday, there were plenty of nearly empty trains, and he liked those times just as well. On busy services he wondered if the people around him could hear his mind, hear the things the drinking tried to keep quiet. His loneliness. His disappointment in life, looming like tall buildings. He wondered if the people around him cared when he took a bottle and swigged from it publicly, under brash electric lights. Alone in a train carriage, it was different. He could be anyone. He was whatever a good man was, then. He could be coming home from a late shift at the hospital. He could be a good father, reeling from bad news about his child.

The tube was its own oasis, a porous bubble moving through the city. When the whole heavy machine got moving, it made a kind of otherworldly whirring sound. Mike, the only other hotel porter he'd had the courage to attempt friendship with, said he hated the sound. Said it made him think of aliens. But Chibuike loved it. So what if it made him feel like he was travelling through space? He could be. He could be moving through stars, if he could see them.

Dark, difficult city. He loved it. He loved being on the tube as it climbed. He loved to let it climb onwards; the onward push had become close to him, dear to him, now. On such nights, his undergraduate studies and his engineering work came back to him. It had been years since he'd been able to hold down a job in engineering – he would probably never experience such responsibility again – but Chibuike longed for it. He could hold a longing in him all his life, and every now and again it broke the surface and breathed. Sometimes, when he went over Battersea railway bridge on the train, he would visualise its structure in his mind, and he would be a man that wasn't lost.

The bridge, he knew, worked by compression, held together by the weight of itself and of each passing train that pushed down iron onto iron, brick onto brick. As the train passed, the arches spread this pressure along themselves and then out to the ends of the bridge. How marvellous that each component, each molecule worked this way, sharing the burden of pressure, of travel, of change. It was the opposite of a chain: easily pulled apart, constantly pushed together and, being pushed together, stronger for it. He liked to think of this on each journey, and think of each journey making the next one possible.

England! He'd never thought he'd come to love England as much as he did. He loved its idiosyncrasies: the accents, and the music. He could wail Queen. He might dance to The Smiths when he thought nobody would see him, his body ducking and bouncing, never quite on the beat with the jangle-pop guitar. He didn't mind. When he was not alone, he put on Fela records and complained about new music.

And he loved the things about London that were harder to love because they were easier to miss. The silences, the short-comings. He loved a lot of those, too. He didn't need the city to be perfect.

He'd been a long time getting here. He'd moved to Manchester first and raised his family there. His friends had told him to move to London sooner: more opportunities awaited down south, and he could always move back out to a smaller city later. People did that. You didn't have to like London, they said; you only had to be there.

But London was a gaping maw to him, then. He was only just eighteen when he came to England, and the capital was too eager to swallow him up. His sister Amaka had studied for her medical degree there and hated the place. It only made her miss Lagos more. She used to phone him from the university halls and tell him about her life; she said it was a big ghost town, bursting with ghosts. Full, but empty. He'd shivered when he heard that.

But now, London had his heart. It should have seemed ugly to him, like a lover who has been unfaithful. It should have become something worse. But it never did. There was some-thing pure and faithful and untouchable at the heart of the place. It never left. These days, he didn't recognise the city his sister had described.

Maybe it was all in his mind. The stars were all him, after all; they were not in the sky to see. London had a way of hiding good things and he enjoyed tunnelling the sky with his eyes, looking for light. Most nights he never found it. He had to think of the stars instead, keeping them alive by remembrance.

Maybe it was only these journeys. When the train went between Clapham Junction and Imperial Wharf, going over the water somehow always felt like a thrill, like a risk. As if his voyage through the stars might end abruptly. As if he might find that the iron and stone underneath the big machine of the train were not underneath him anymore, only darkness and pinpricks of light in his mind.

Sometimes, by the time he started to make his way back home, he'd be too drunk to notice anything. No space travel. No movement upwards, only onwards. It was like that, some-times. At first, he'd drunk to get away from sadness; now he did it to silence joy, or the pain that was the cost of joy. He hated to think of his son's stubborn love for him, or to remem-ber his father's dedication to his family. What could be worse? He knew he'd had enough to drink when he took his eyes out of the sky and stopped looking for the stars. What, in the night-time, hurts more than light?

Chibuike was out again tonight. Looking in the train's window, he caught his reflection. The concave surface skewed him; any curved, mirrored surface might make more of him, make him more of a man, and for a moment he would believe it. He hated to look at himself; he got dressed each day without checking his reflection for more than half a second, just to see if there was toothpaste on his mouth, shampoo in his ears. Didn't he used to be handsome? Women had told him he was. He'd hardly believe it now. He hated his face. Waste of a face. Stupid man. Weak man. Failure of a father. What kind of father had to be moved into his son's home like this? What kind of father was he, to have to accept money from his own child whenever he lost his job? He could see his future, bleak, in his low brow, his jutting chin. The bags under his deep-set eyes made him think of his mother, frowning at him for not sleeping properly, letting himself get too thin. Stupid boy. He picked at a stain on his trousers, as if that would do anything.

No wonder his wife had stopped loving him. No wonder their son, part Chibuike, was unlovable to her. No wonder Chibuike had married a woman like that in the first place, a woman who didn't know who to love, or how, or when to show it.

Yet, it was in moments like these that he was caught by curiosity – had he changed, somehow, just enough for him to care for himself again? There were pinpricks of light in his mind again, despite everything. They wouldn't stop. Was he bearable yet?

He was not. He looked away.

His son loved him, but didn't like him much. Chibuike had known for some time; for years, really, if he was honest with himself. He'd lived with it. Now, losing his job, losing days to drink, missing rent, then seeing Achike's face at the front door, his expression set and responsible as though there had never been any question that it was Achike's job to look after him . . . Achike's disappointment in his father was cruel because it was so soft, so fleeting. As though to expect anything more from Chibuike would be to live with an optimism that was simply impractical.

Chibuike had watched his son go from a bright, brave child to one who was confused by the very concept of affection. Threatened by it, as though he could not distinguish between love and trouble. Then Chibuike watched him grow to a man who cowered in front of him. He shared his food and his home with his father, but – no matter how much he was trying, no matter the vision he had of himself as the good son – absolutely nothing else.

Chibuike had given him that. He'd never been good for Achike. He hadn't even noticed his son being abused in secret. Achike was only a child at the time, a young boy. It went on for months before Chibuike saw what was happening. Achike's own uncle. The brother of Chibuike's wife, Ndidi. The man was never convicted, never even tried. Insufficient evidence. The police had wanted to interview Achike, but Chibuike refused absolutely. He'd not known they would demand this of a child. Hadn't thought the thing would require anyone else's courage but his own. How naive he had been.

So the man was still free, somewhere. On his worst days, Chibuike thought he could feel the man breathing, feel the man uttering knives into Chibuike every time he breathed.

And if the man had been tried and found guilty, what would that have changed? It would bring nothing back that had been lost. The mere attempt had made Ndidi leave – what would a trial have taken from them? She'd begged Chibuike not to tell the police. She'd pleaded and wept. She had actually *wept*. She wanted to see to it herself, she said. She wanted to let the family handle it. He'd only stared at her. Was this what family was? Was this what family was for?

He'd stormed downstairs to the living room and picked up the phone. No, she'd said. She would leave him if he called the police. She would divorce him, and Achike would never see her again.

She knew him well, and there was nothing of his that she would not use to get her way. The shame alone froze him: he didn't know anybody in his community who had divorced, and the word was like a curse.

Divorce. It sounded like the end of something, but it was not. It was only a starting point, and Chibuike could see no well-worn path forwards from it. What is a boy whose parents are divorced? He did not know, he could not see. Nor was Chibuike safe. What is a man without a mother, even his child's?

But if he stayed with her, he knew it would be the end of something more essential. If he acquiesced now, there would be nothing upright in him, no steady thing with which to raise his son.

By the time he had finished dialling, Ndidi had started to pack her things.

No wife for Chibuike to love, then. No mother to conceal Chibuike's shortcomings. After Ndidi left, they ate over-boiled pasta for a week, sauce out of the jar, don't ask, don't complain, don't make me slap your dirty mouth if you complain one more time. Had Achike been so disappointed in him, in those days, or was it Chibuike's disappointment in himself that he sensed? One or the other had caused Chibuike to drink more and more. He'd lost his job at the engineering firm soon enough.

On the train, Chibuike hugged his bottle to himself, and then remembered it was colder than him, but did not set it down. He wondered if his son would ever find someone who would love him the way he deserved to be loved. Chibuike sometimes wondered if he had had his turn; if he should move aside and let some better man try. He wondered if there *were* better men. Deep down, he hoped Achike would find someone, anyone, who could love him better than he had done. Maybe then he wouldn't wake up every morning with the weight of guilt on his chest like an infection.

When Chibuike was in school, his father had died suddenly with almost no fuss. Chibuike had never really understood his father, a disciplinarian who had shown love by putting food on the table and his belt on Chibuike's back. Perhaps it was his father's fault, then. Perhaps one inherited such things. Perhaps Chibuike should have transcended the way he had been raised. People did that. So why not him?

Chibuike had not hugged his son since the boy was old

enough to walk. He had never told his boy he loved him. And yet, to his own surprise, there was love in him to give. When his son was born, Chibuike Okoro had cried for long minutes, quietly, happily, the tears petering out and then raining down again like a Manchester afternoon, drizzling just when he'd thought he was safe. The crying had surprised Chibuike. It had terrified his wife. Nobody had told her that men felt this way about their children. She'd looked at him askance, almost afraid, and he found the tears had dried. And something else retreated back inside him, too.

His wife had died when Achike was sixteen, and when the cancer took her there was no room for the smugness he had thought he'd feel. He'd met Ndidi at university in Manchester, years ago. It had been the two of them, and then Achike. When she died, he felt more alone than ever. There was nobody else. Friendships, at his age, were slippery things that didn't last. The few men he knew had families. They had children to love, and what love was left over was meagre. Only Chibuike was left, lingering outside of love, a mirage on the periphery of its vision. And where did a wifeless, loveless old man go? How did he find his way back to his only child?

There was no way back through such mistakes, no tracks laid down for the wheels to grind. It simply wasn't what you did, or what anyone had done before. Decades had gone by, and not a single hug for the boy. He ached to do it, but couldn't find a way.

There was a window open somewhere on the train, and a breeze that nobody wanted blew through the carriage. On the day Chibuike realised his son was gay, he was picking him up from drama club after school, and he was early for once, waiting in his car. He was thinking about Ndidi again, wondering about visiting her grave, when Achike walked out with his friends. His son was wearing makeup. There was makeup on his skin, clumsy and bold.

Was this for the school play? Achike was in his school uniform, but he moved as if he'd never worn a uniform in his life. He moved like no-one else in the world. He wasn't playing a character. But he was unfamiliar to his father: Chibuike had another child, then, who was not Achike. This child took exaggerated steps, and he took in the globe with each one. His arms curled in the air and made swirling patterns as he recited some lines Chibuike could not hear. He made people laugh. There were two girls laughing at him, doubled over laughing at him, and there was Ekene, staring at Chibuike in his car, Ekene patting Achike on the shoulder and telling him stop, look, your dad's here, Achike. Stop. He's looking.

Achike froze, and Chibuike felt his son's blood go cold. Achike had betrayed himself. His father watched him try to decide whether he should run back inside, or run to the car; go back to himself, or go back home. Which was safer? His father watched him waver. He chose both, and got into the car. And his father did not speak to him. Except, stopping at a traffic light, to ask, 'Achike. My only son. Biko tell me the truth. Are you gay?' He did not look at Achike. He stared straight ahead. He was a firm man, and his words meant things. He had seen his son rise, green, above the soil; what would happen if his father did not push him down?

Achike looked at him and said nothing because he could not pronounce what he was. In his father's presence, there were no words for him. So Chibuike said nothing also. Achike wiped the makeup off his face but it didn't make his father recognise him any more. But he did not deny anything. In what little space he had, he sat, quiet, unadorned.

Chibuike knew, that day, that his son was not like other people. Gay, yes. But also irrepressible, and this was more dangerous by far. When Chibuike asked his son if he was gay, he did not deny it. Why? Achike acted like nothing in the world could stamp the life out of him. What kind of person did that?

What kind of person refused to be vulnerable? What kind of person, being vulnerable, insisted on also being strong?

Chibuike told Achike never to let anyone know *what he was*. Since he wanted a career as an actor, Chibuike advised, it was best to keep his secret to himself. And try to change, if he could. That was the father Chibuike had been.

He took years to accept his son. He thought often of the time he had wasted, telling himself that he'd wanted to toughen Achike up, to prepare him for the real world. He took years to see how much tougher his son would have been without him.

Now, Chibuike wished he could summon something in himself that could prove Achike wrong about him, and let light in, let life in. But he'd been fired again, and he was living with his son. He'd sounded the depths of himself and heard the hollow sound, again. And there was a silence between the two of them. It wafted through the large flat when Chibuike arrived, settling on one room, then another. Every footstep echoed. Nobody laughed much. No music could ever be quiet enough.

Work was no easier to keep than his child. His manager at the hotel had lost patience with him. He'd struggled for months to find and keep a job he wanted, slowly eating through his savings, and then more quickly drinking through them; by the time Achike took him home, he had barely anything left of what he'd saved through years of the frugality his parents had taught him. And the work at the hotel had always been a miracle, so much so that he hadn't really thought it would last: a friend of a friend had called him, needing someone to fix this door hinge, change that light fixture. Chibuike had been surprised to know that he could do these things, and more surprised to learn that the hotel wanted to hire him full time. It was difficult work, tiring his body when it didn't tax his mind, but he welcomed that, feeling redemption in the difficulty. It had been so long since he had hoped to be useful to anyone. And now, who knew how long it would be again?

He tried not to think about the indignity of his new life with his son. That the first thing Achike had done when they arrived was prepare a shopping list, and that *he* had asked if *Chibuike* wanted to add anything. That there would be mornings when Achike woke up early for a jog while Chibuike stayed in bed, hungover and unable to move. That there would be times when Chibuike came home drunk, and Achike was waiting. Or times when Achike was with Ekene. When Ekene was around, Achike was always something short of waiting, and something beyond it. Chibuike had noticed this. Their friendship was odd. Impenetrable.

And Chibuike was hurt by this, but in the small way that such problems hurt: small enough to persist, small enough for the hurt to last a long time. He filed the problem away in his mind, another job to attend to later. A hinge to replace, a light to find. He'd get to it.

The train pulled up, stopped, released a driver from his cabin. The new driver gave the old one a curt nod and took his seat, familiarised himself with the controls. He waited for a signal and then set the tube on its way. Shepherd's Bush. Hardly any stars were visible. Only Orion, and the red lights of cranes above high-rises. Harsh, bright, beautiful city. He felt for it the way he felt for his own child: he could lose his temper with it, and be utterly tender for it in his heart. But how long could things go on that way? The squeak of the hinges had been an annoyance at first; now they woke him in the middle of the night, like the sound of a baby crying. He never got back to sleep.

How he had known and not known! He had stood on the edge of love, as at the farthest reach of land before the drop of cliffs and the wide sea, before flight for creatures who could, or before the long fall. He had stood on the edge, and felt clean air on his skin, and kept back.

He knew now. The light was all Achike. Chibuike had found

his son inextinguishable. But he had fought it for so long before he knew to only try and stand in his child's light.

He would get to it. He would fix what had been neglected and broken. Chibuike did not know how, but he would make his son love him again. It was not too late. There would be another job, and he would find it and keep it. Somehow. As soon as he could. And he would save up enough money to rent a place of his own again.

Next stop: Willesden Junction. A man in a long coat got off; an elderly woman ushered her two grandchildren on. Outside, on the platform, there were two women, loudly drunk, wailing through a Spice Girls song as they huddled together in the cold. Beautiful, wild city. They were bad singers but Chibuike watched them. It was warm for December, but the women were so close together, the way that men would never permit themselves to be, without crossing some sacred threshold. Could there be only distance and sex between men?

Not between Achike and Ekene. The two of them were ... what were they? Chibuike had never had a friendship like it. It was said by some Nigerian elders that this tenderness between men was unAfrican, a function of English life. Men here were said to be different from the men in Nigeria. But Chibuike had lived here and there, and he had always wanted what his son and Ekene had. And were there not men in Nigeria who had to have it?

Achike and Ekene talked about everything. They talked about musicals, and Achike's love of dancing. They talked about men they found charming, or ridiculous. They talked about things that scared them, frustrated them, drove them on. They probably talked about him. He hoped Ekene would be kind when they did, but he knew Ekene had no warmth towards him. He was always with Achike, telling stories, sharing secrets, laughing with Achike. Chibuike wanted to be grateful that his son was not alone, and he was grateful in part;

maybe this was the man for his son. But the laughter always stopped when Chibuike came near. He looked away whenever he saw Chibuike coming, that boy.

Ekene was a man, now, but Chibuike's abiding memory of him was stubborn, as if Ekene was his own child. He remembered Ekene as a teenager, slightly podgy, eyes downcast. Ekene had stayed with them for months in the end, that summer when his mother kicked him out. It was a strange time. In that time, Ekene's laughter was rarely heard and never seen. The day Ekene moved in, Achike had spoken about it like a dream come true. Imagine living with your best friend! Chibuike had never seen him so excited.

But after a while, things changed. Ekene became sullen and withdrawn, hating to leave the house, making ungenerous remarks about Achike, how he was so lucky, how he didn't know he was born. Strange things for a boy his age to say about anyone. He was only seventeen at the time, and should have been too young to have lost anything. Or too young to know it if he had.

Worse than this was the way Ekene looked at Chibuike, as if there were a question on his lips, the words of which he could not quite form. Some unfinished business. Or the way Ekene seemed to evince a hunger, sometimes, that startled Chibuike. What did Ekene want from him? Was it possible he wasn't repulsed by the old man? The thought repulsed Chibuike. He put up a wall between himself and the thought. It wasn't that. Ekene wanted something else. And did Chibuike have this thing to give? Was there only distance and sex?

He felt almost comfortable with this idea, the thought of Ekene in his son's life, a sort of son-in-law. He hadn't always. But Chibuike had grown some, and changed some. He was not so hopeless. He partly hoped that the two of them might get married, one day. Such a thing! Perhaps it was not too late. Ekene belonged with the family. Achike was his son, his only child, yes, but Ekene had partly grown up in his house. Even before he'd stayed there, he'd spent so many evenings with them, making Achike laugh, drawing him out of himself.

And it was true that Ekene had seemed to disappear for a while that summer, and that something bright and gentle in him had never returned. And that, one day, something dark and sullen took its place. But Chibuike had had his part to play in this. He knew. He knew what he did. Stupid man. Failure of a – what was he to Ekene? There was only approximation, or nothing. He was like a father. To Achike, Ekene was like a brother, but also something else entirely different. How could Chibuike possibly express all of this, even to himself?

Worse than this was Chibuike, seeing the question in Ekene's eyes but afraid that his answer would be wrong. The thoughts, the love, unexpressed, sat patiently undefined, like stars behind smog. How could he find his way to telling the boy that he was safe with him? How could he find his way when there was no path? It felt as though no man had ever said those words before. If there were a name for Ekene's place with him, could he be the first to say it? How could he speak a world into being? How could he invent a language for love?

On the platform, the women began a second verse. Chibuike wondered if it were the singing that kept them warm, stirring shared memories of the original song. Or was it the ease with which they hugged, resting skin on skin, trusting one another without question?

Chapter 4

'Why do I still go out drinking with you?' Achike cupped a palm to his forehead. 'I never normally drink vodka. I don't even like vodka.'

'One day you'll thank me for all the good times,' Ekene said, smiling smugly. But his voice was calm and quiet, and Achike let it echo in his mind. He liked this. So often, everything they did or said was ambiguous, and it could be exhausting. Sometimes it was nice to let things be simple. Sometimes it was nice to tread a well-worn path, and fall into their familiar roles: the sensible one and the roguish one, the moderate one and the wild one. They could be in a film. They could make sense.

'You'll be fine,' Ekene said.

'It's not even just the hangover,' said Achike. 'I think I've still got a bit of that migraine, too. You know how they linger.'

'So you chose to remedy this by ... hanging out in a grave-yard?' Ekene was standing straight and proud. He had his hands in his pockets. Achike hit him with the back of his hand, but smiled. Ekene was good to be with. And in his second-hand suit, nobody had ever looked so handsome. It was a brown, light woollen thing he'd got from a charity shop and had adjusted at the dry cleaners. The back vent of the blazer lifted slightly, and Ekene's bum was underneath.

'Alright, genius,' said Achike. He'd not told Ekene how much his own suit cost, and Ekene didn't recognise the label. Ekene frowned at it, only admitting to himself how well it fitted Achike. Achike knew it, and smiled to himself, avoiding Ekene's gaze, which he knew was approving, and steady. Achike's body had got a little broader in the past few years, and the weight he had gained was compact. His body was hollows, now, and concave curves.

The sun was shining on puddles from that morning's rain, creating little pools of bright light that made people squint and look away. There were more dark clouds on the horizon. So it would rain again, and then it would not. And there would be more sunshine on more puddles, and then there would not.

The church, in Chiswick, was Unitarian and performed gay marriage ceremonies, but it had belonged to the Church of England until its congregation had dwindled away to nothing, a few decades ago. Many of its former congregants were laid to rest outside its front doors. Just beyond the graveyard was the street, tiny and cobbled. The sound of cars on a busy road was not far beyond. Guests arrived in dribs and drabs.

The wedding wouldn't start for another twenty minutes and they were dawdling in the graveyard outside. Ekene wanted to wait until more people had arrived, so that they could sit at the back, unnoticed. It was a good day outside.

'Nobody does this,' Ekene teased. He liked the differences between the two of them. He liked to feel the edges of Achike. To be reminded that there was someone alongside him, jolting occasionally.

'You make me sound like a necrophiliac. People do this. I like reading the gravestones. It's interesting. People do this.' He was distracted by the arithmetic of the short lifespan before him.

'You find death interesting?' Ekene said.

'Not death,' said Achike. 'Life.'

Ekene looked sceptically at the graves surrounding them.

Achike sighed. 'Look at all these. I think *all these people* over here died of TB. All of them. Can you imagine? None of them got to be old. Most of them didn't even get to forty.'

'I used to think you got to forty and then you died.'

'Look at this guy – this guy died right in the middle of life. I wonder what they were all doing when they died.'

Ekene watched him and saw the cogs turn in Achike's mind, saw him paint their lives in bright colours. Then he said, 'Coughing?'

'Be serious,' said Achike. 'Look at them. This one: Maria Helena Tyworth, 1850 to 1869. She was only nineteen. Maybe just eighteen. And look, here – her father died just a year later. And then her mother. Don't you think that's sad? You can just imagine their lives, their sad little family, all the people left behind who must have missed them.'

Ekene scuffed a foot sheepishly. 'Well, now I feel like a dick. I wasn't trying to be a dick.'

Achike looked at him thoughtfully, kindly. 'Forget about it. Just look.'

Ekene sighed, gave up on distracting Achike. 'Okay.'

'And they must have been so scared,' Achike said. His voice was breath, it was so quiet. He straightened up, put a hand on his back to soothe the pain of bending over. His muscles always felt a little tight after a migraine. 'The people who survived, I mean. All the aunts and uncles and cousins ... They must have spent every day of their lives wondering if they would be next. And maybe they were.'

'They probably had no idea what caused TB until years after these people died,' said Ekene, wanting to say something helpful.

Achike nodded. 'Can you imagine?'

'No,' said Ekene, 'I can't. But life here is very different, now. It's not so ... fragile.'

Achike looked over at him. 'Do you think so?'

'I don't know,' said Ekene. He shivered a little. 'I hope so. I don't know. I don't like to think about it. It's all a bit morbid.'

'But it doesn't feel all that morbid to me. I suppose because it all happened a long time ago. And I never knew these people. It sort of just feels like I'm being told a story.'

This was what Achike did best, of course. He could be far away from anything.

'All these people ... ' said Achike, still lost in reading. 'So young.'

'But you said *life*,' said Ekene, almost aggrieved. 'You said you were interested in *life*. This isn't life. You're just thinking about all the horrible deaths. You'll make yourself all sad. Look – maybe they didn't all die of TB. And they didn't all die young. Look over here.' He strode over to a grave marked by a stone angel; her body was draped in grief over the tombstone, exhausted. And yet her wings seemed poised, as though about to rise; as though some part of her could resist loss, and insist it hold itself upright.

'Thomas George Allory, 1836 to 1910. He was seventy-four when he died. Way older than any of the others in here. He had the time to really live. What about him? What was his life like?'

Achike followed him and read the inscription. 'It says he sat on the Parish Council. He might have helped look after this church, which explains why he's got such a nice tombstone.'

'And he had great-grandchildren,' said Ekene. He saw then that he was trying to waft Achike's mood upwards. After more than twenty years, he did such things without noticing. 'Let's say he died surrounded by his family.'

Achike smiled at him. 'I like that idea, you know. And

seventy-four ... That would have been unbelievably old, in those days. *Crazy* old. Maybe, when he died, he felt like he was ready for it because he'd lived a really good life. Maybe he'd been married to his wife for fifty years. Maybe they'd got married young and figured out life together.'

'Maybe he was famous,' offered Ekene. 'Maybe he worked really hard at something and never gave up until he was the best at it. Maybe he loved gardening in his old age. He could have grown roses.'

'Maybe,' said Achike, hopefully, 'he was still working at it when he died. Maybe he loved it so much, he couldn't imagine giving it up.'

'Maybe,' said Ekene. 'You see? Not all bad.' From behind, he gave Achike a hug as if to console him. He was worried there might be something concerning beneath all this talk of tombstones.

Achike nodded and took a sip of water. 'My dad was telling me how he wants to be buried, you know,' he said. 'He just ... started talking about it.'

'Did he have a date in mind?' Ekene asked. He gave his voice a cruel lilt, then looked away.

'Don't, Ekene,' said Achike. 'It was really weird, you know. He's never talked like that before. He said he wants to be buried back home.'

'Nigeria?'

'Yes. It made me wonder if he'd be happier moving back there, actually.'

'Why doesn't he?'

'He doesn't have the money,' said Achike, simply.

'None at all? He can't even pay for the flights? He must have people there he could stay with, at least for a bit.'

'I think it's because doesn't want to just go back with nothing. He'd want to be respected, he'd want to have achieved something here, something he could take back with him. And he'd want to have enough money to go back in style. You know. Build a house, hire a houseboy.'

'How much money does he have?'

'I'm guessing next to nothing, if he's staying with me. He had savings, but he spent most of that when he lost his job. He probably doesn't even have much of a pension. He was pretty careful with money when I was growing up, but now he's drinking again ...'

'When did he tell you all this?'

'When I brought him back to my flat. He was drunk, obviously.'

Ekene looked at him sadly. 'Why was he even talking about death? He's not really old enough, is he?'

'I guess it's just been on his mind,' said Achike. 'It was the anniversary of my mum's death a couple of weeks ago.'

'I know.'

Achike took a deep breath, wiggled his shoulders as if shaking off a stretch. 'And you know how he hates leaning on anyone, especially me. He's embarrassed by it all, having to move in with me – so that's something you've got in common with him, at least.'

'Very funny.'

'I actually offered to give him the money to go to Nigeria, give him something to build a house with.'

'Do you even have that much money?'

'No, not now I've bought the flat. But I could get it to him bit by bit, if I get cast in the right roles, which Julian says I will, soon.'

'So you'll carry on acting, then?'

Achike shrugged. 'I really don't know. Anyway, Dad wouldn't take the money. He was so ashamed about losing his job, being evicted, moving in with me ... Taking my money would have just made it worse.'

'Maybe that's why he was talking about all the burial stuff.

Maybe he was taking the measure of his life. That's something people do, isn't it? At his age?'

'I guess. I think about things too, sometimes.'

'You think about your funeral?'

'I drew up a will last year,' said Achike. 'Julian said I should.'

'Jesus.'

'Morbid, I know. I decided everything, though.'

'Achike . . . '

'It felt good to have things arranged,' said Achike. 'I felt prepared.'

'For what?'

Achike shrugged. Ekene frowned, but Achike carried on.

'You know, I couldn't make myself care where I'm buried. Isn't that strange? You imagine your grave as the place you'll be forever. You imagine it as home, kind of. People do. Or I do, anyway. And then I realised it doesn't matter to me, because . . . where would be home? Here?' Achike waved his hands around him, indicating the church, the graveyard, the path to the church door, the city. 'None of this feels like it's got anything to do with me.'

'It's because you're not from London,' said Ekene.

'It's not.'

Ekene didn't need to see the look in Achike's eyes then. He had it. The two of them were alike in this: both alone, both outside of things.

Soon, church bells would ring and confetti would pour down on Oskar and the man he would marry instead of Ekene. Soon, Ekene would watch them walk down the aisle hand in hand, down the path from the church door. One day they might walk back along it, a child between them, for a christening.

Achike was restless. 'You know, I read online about this man in Anambra State, where my dad grew up. This man – some thugs found him, some homophobes. They chased him down and lynched him. I mean they *lynched* him, Ekene.'

'I know. I read the same thing.'

'But doesn't it make you want to cry?' Achike did weep, a little. Ekene took a handkerchief from his pocket and gave it to him. 'He wasn't hurting anyone, Ekene. He wasn't doing anything to anyone. I'm not even sure he was gay. The article didn't say.'

Ekene leaned his head on Achike's. He spoke into Achike's hair. 'Sometimes I don't want to be Nigerian.'

Achike pulled back a little in surprise, and turned to face Ekene. 'Do you mean that?'

Ekene waited a moment, then asked, 'Don't you?'

'I don't know,' said Achike. 'I get angry, sometimes. I do want to be Nigerian. I *am* Nigerian. I just wish ... I just wish they didn't make it so hard.'

'Me too,' said Ekene, softly. He took Achike's hands in his and chafed them softly as a cold wind blew on them both. He regarded Achike a little fearfully. Achike so rarely let himself be angry.

'Nigeria might change the laws one day?' said Ekene, weakly, hopefully. 'Look at us, here. A few years ago, this couldn't have happened, not in a church.' He had wanted to cheer Achike up, but there was no changing him when he got like this. The best you could do was to stand with him. And wasn't Ekene angry, too? What sleep had he got after he'd read the news report? Hadn't he wanted to tell Achike about it, and stopped himself, afraid of upsetting him?

'And how long will that take? And what will laws change? Will it make Nigeria home?' Achike shook his head bitterly. 'It'll never be a place for us. People like us, I mean. That family I was staying with in Nigeria ...'

'I thought you liked staying with them?'

'I loved seeing what they had, but you were right: I'll never have that. Not the way they did. Not in the place my parents grew up, where my grandparents grew up. They don't want me, there. That's why my will only says I have to be buried in England. I wouldn't want my dad to take me back to Nigeria. I don't care about anything else.'

'Achike—'

'I know, I know. I'm not naive. I know I'm not welcome here. I know that. But I *am* here, and that's all there is. It's all I have. Even if England doesn't want me. Even if there's no place for me. I'm here now. It's done. I'm here.'

'Where *is* there a place for us?' Ekene said. 'There's nowhere.'

Achike wondered. Where was a place where they could be black and gay and safe?

They looked out at the sky for a few moments, until the usher directed them towards the church doors.

As they walked, Achike looked carefully at Ekene. Before he dared to say aloud the words that were in his mind, he inspected Ekene's face, steadily, as though he could read the odds of success in Ekene's brow, in the set of his jaw. He examined the evidence of Ekene's eyes – how bright were they today? – and the straightness of his back. He so dearly wanted to be right.

He watched. He waited in his uncertainty, feeling for the way the wind might blow. He might be wrong. Achike had been wrong about love. He had been wrong about Ekene, too. If he could only watch and wait a little longer, he might be right, this time.

Before they went into the church, Ekene stopped Achike at the door suddenly, but his face was calm when Achike looked over, and so Achike did not worry that something was wrong. Ekene did this, sometimes. Maybe he just wanted to admire something he had seen in the nave. He could be impulsive about little things, or big things. Achike was not such an impulsive person and Ekene confused him often, but he liked to feel the edges of Ekene, the differences between them.

The organ music began, and Ekene let his hand settle in the

small of Achike's back, and Achike knew that nothing would change his mind. Nothing could. Ekene was beautiful, and that was that. That was all. Ekene was beautiful. Still.

Achike had known for a long time that Ekene was beautiful in great, extraordinary measure. Ekene's beauty did not depend on circumstance. It was immune to changes of time and place. It was in Ekene's face, in his smooth, dark skin, in his eyes, which had a watery, almost otherworldly quality. His beauty was absolute, and final. Should Ekene gain or lose weight, should his hair fall out or should scars find their way across his skin, nothing would really ever change, not for Achike. If Ekene's eyes clouded over milky white. If he lost every tooth in his head. If his hair went grey tomorrow – still, everything would remain, untouched, like a butterfly long ago pressed in paper but still somehow able to lift its wings into miraculous flight.

And yet Ekene's beauty was, at the same time, particular. It was specific. If you were to ask Achike what was beautiful about Ekene, he could explain. He could explain Ekene's arms that were long and slender, although longer and slenderer than Ekene himself would have liked. He knew Ekene's lips that were ... not 'full', no. Achike thought hard about the right word, feeling strongly that Ekene deserved a precise account, even only in his own mind, of what made him remarkable. Ekene's lips were *heavy* with beauty. Yes. Everything about Ekene was like this. Like a leaf in a rainstorm, cupped as if by a delicate, invisible hand to hold cool water.

He knew that Ekene didn't think of himself this way. Ekene had never really been happy with his appearance. He looked too much like his father. And Achike knew, just as he had always known, that Ekene would have liked to be taller, broader, tauter, other. But this was immaterial to Achike. Achike could see Ekene with absolute clarity. He could observe Ekene's mind, his face and his body with a kind of scientific objectivity that told him yes, this man was the most beautiful man he had ever seen, or would ever see.

For years, now, he had been in love with Ekene, and for years there had been almost no hope. Ekene had always been unavailable, uninterested, distant, with someone else. Ekene had dated guitarists who couldn't pronounce his name, actors who couldn't commit, models who had cut Ekene out of their lives abruptly and with surgical precision. Ekene had been with strangers, with ex-boyfriends from years before, with older men, younger men. But not Achike. Never Achike, not really, not properly. Ekene was a closed door made out of glass, with everything Achike had ever wanted on the other side. And, looking at him now, Achike was a child again, his nose pressed against it, wondering.

So, for a moment, he allowed himself to wonder. He allowed himself to hope beyond the parameters of logical hopes to dream beyond what was sensible to dream. What he could afford. He wanted this: this church, this music, for them. He wanted it to be the two of them getting married, today. Yes, Achike and Ekene, about to walk out into the world as one, in matching, fitted morning suits. In Achike's dream, they would be the perfect couple. They would divide the wedding planning equitably so that neither one would end up yawning over flower arrangements or rushing the seating plans. Achike might help Ekene reconcile with his parents, or remonstrate with them, or help him live without them; Ekene would have learned to think of Chibuike as family.

Ekene would be better. He would clip his toenails without being told. He would make new friends and believe in himself. In the evenings, they would cook each other's favourite foods, give each other's favourite films a chance. They would dance spontaneously in the kitchen and then laugh at themselves adoringly, make coffee and appreciate jazz.

Maybe Ekene would think about moving again. Bolstered

by his domestic bliss, Ekene's career could find new life and breathe deep from Los Angeles' air. They would succeed together. Young Nigerians – young queer people who might have despaired – would see their faces and see hope. This would be the beginning of grand things they had deserved. It would be the two of them, Ekene and Achike, Achike and Ekene, walking hand in hand down the aisle of life until some day, decades from now, when they would exit into the dark beyond. And neither of them would ever be alone again.

Maybe it was time for it to start, now. Achike hesitated when he thought about their night in Berlin, unspoken of since. It hung in the air, a whip before the crack. It had been more than sex. Neither of them knew what it was, yet. Or they both did.

But Achike was not the man he had been. He had grown some, and changed some. He was not so hopeless. And he was looking after his father. He was proving that he was kind, and capable, and strong.

So maybe it was time. After all, Ekene seemed different, lately. A little less restless. And they were thirty-seven now. Both men, both grown. This was it. This was all there was. He listened to the organ music swell and rise; he recognised the melody.

And Ekene was single. Hadn't Achike noticed, ever since Ekene had come back from Berlin, a sense of calm? And, in spite of everything, hadn't he also detected ... hadn't he suspected—?

'Achike? Achike? You in there?' Ekene said, half a smile rising on his face.

Achike was doing that thing again.

Achike had been a choirboy. It had only been for a few years, when he was a child. He'd given it up when he enrolled in acting classes; his father was delighted to encourage one artistic pursuit as a distraction from the memory of his abuse, but could not stomach two. Achike was made to choose, and he chose acting, the thing that made it easier to be distracted, the thing that made it easier to be far away.

But Achike could hold a longing in him all his life, and every now and again it broke the surface and breathed. Ekene knew that Achike missed singing. Sometimes, when he heard a familiar piece, Achike would mouth the words. Ekene wasn't sure that Achike knew he was doing it. It was like a reflex, inherited from a forgotten time. It was strange – Achike looked like he was in some sort of trance, actually, or casting a spell, but Ekene didn't mind. He liked seeing Achike this way. He liked to watch the magic happen.

'I'm fine,' said Achike, coming to himself. He spoke slowly and calmly. Maybe he hadn't noticed anything was wrong. Maybe Ekene was worrying over nothing. Maybe he was not being cruel, after all, to have Achike here with him.

'We don't have to go inside,' Ekene said. 'If you're bored, I mean. We can go somewhere. Get some food. Nobody will know.'

'Don't be daft,' Achike said. 'You've been invited. We should be here, if he invited you after you broke up.'

'True.' Ekene smiled faintly. Oskar was a fifty-year-old entrepreneur from Berlin. He'd been distant and cold for weeks before he finally told Ekene that their two-year relationship was over. At first, Oskar had refused to give anything but the vaguest reasons: they were growing apart, they wanted different things, it couldn't last any longer than it had.

But that wasn't enough for Ekene, and he'd pressed Oskar. He'd asked him for the truth, even though it was like touching his own wound. He'd insisted.

'It doesn't make any sense,' he said. 'What have I done? Why now?' He could have kept quiet and let it go, since he knew within himself that Oskar was right. But some false fire was alight in him, and it burned him and made him shout as though he'd been wounded. He wasn't wounded by Oskar, not anymore; he knew it had to end. It had ended, even before

Achike came to stay with him in Berlin, even before they'd made love and Ekene had ruined the whole thing. He only felt so foolish for not being the first to admit his relationship with Oskar had ended. He had been the one tiring himself out, holding up its edifice.

Oskar sighed. Why did he sigh, then? Was he tired from his trip to London, the trip Ekene had always known was not for business?

'There's someone else,' Oskar said, quietly. 'And it's serious. I know it's not fair on you. I never meant for it to happen. And I know how much it must hurt you. You've done nothing wrong. But here we are, I mean ... There's nothing I can do, Ekene. It's over. It has to be.'

Ekene had nothing to say to this. Oskar wouldn't have listened if he had. And Ekene knew it: the way Oskar had told him the truth so plainly, so helplessly, to deprive him of any right to reply or refuse.

'How serious?'

'Ekene, please.'

'Do you love him?'

'Yes, I do.'

What good would it do Ekene, then, to tell Oskar that he was hurt by this more than by the end of the relationship? Oskar had used the words of a good man against him, had used words to make himself a good man, and innocent. Oskar was a victim, too, not just Ekene. What could Oskar do? Love had surprised him. He hadn't been looking for it; it had found him out. Ekene could say nothing about that, because Oskar had never meant for this to happen. It didn't matter that Ekene was the one being left behind; that he had run away from Achike for this; that nobody and nothing had found him.

It surprised Ekene that Oskar was having a church wedding. It must have been his fiancé's idea. What kind of God could a man like Oskar believe in?

At the door, Ekene turned to his friend and smiled. Instinctively, he took Achike's hand, pressed it. He felt a pang of guilt at what he was doing. But surely there was nothing wrong in that, nothing terribly unfair? He and Achike were friends. He was happy with his friend, happy that his friend had come with him today. He just wanted his friend, that was all.

'It's good to see you, you know,' said Ekene. And he meant it.

'You too,' Achike said. The string quartet began to play. 'And I think it's a really good sign that you've come here today. And that you were asked. I think it's lovely.'

And it was lovely. The last of the migraine had slipped away without him noticing, and everything in the world seemed to take his hand. There was a relief, and a kind of quiet exultation that followed every migraine, that made him fall in love with everything. The lilies adorning the pews. The string quartet. Even their clothes, the slightly worn-down clothes of the underpaid musician: it was all everyday loveliness, it was all comfort and ease. The children of the other guests, allowed to play in the aisles before the grooms arrived. Their parents, looking on, or playing with them. Frocks, suits, shirts, ties, hymn books, carpets, candles. The photographer made little jokes to get the guests to smile, or he waited as they took gentle poses, or he caught them as they were, spotting honest moments. Achike loved it all, although it was strange that any opening of the heart should follow pain this way; he had often thought it to be the reverse.

Behind them, the church's old oak doors stood open to the day. Achike allowed his mind to slip past the present moment, again: he recast the whole wedding with himself as a groom. He imagined himself shaking hands with the guests, dutifully keeping feuding family members apart, smiling conspiratorially with the best man, and taking a deep breath before he met Ekene, smiling Ekene, at the altar.

Confused, he turned to Ekene again. He turned to Ekene

and saw his eyes on the church inside, as if his own life were on the other side of the door, as if it were about to walk up the aisle, away from him.

'Ekene?'

Ekene started to cry.

'Ekene, what's wrong?'

Ekene already knew a lot about Oskar's groom. He was young. No more than twenty-seven, from what he'd seen online. Ten years younger than Ekene, as if Oskar liked the roundness of the number. And he was another black man: this time fresher, sunnier, easier. The man looked fragile. Ekene wanted to catch him. Or push him and watch him shatter. Where were the grooms now? They must be inside the church somewhere, greeting people. They would be casting vague, unseeing, satisfied glances over the guests as they made their way to the front of the church.

'Ekene. Tell me what's wrong.'

Ludicrous that the false fire should still burn. It wasn't Oskar he wanted now. There'd been no love between them. Ekene was there for the other man. He wanted to cradle the man's heart in his hands and keep it safe from Oskar. He wanted to plunge a syringe into the man's heart, draw out his life and stab it into his own veins.

'Ekene? Did Oskar invite you?'

Ekene looked at Achike as if he were waking up, as if seeing him for the first time in a while. He had only thought that nobody checks invitations at a wedding. He had thought it would only be him that the false fire burned.

Achike strode long steps away, his head bowed. He moved fast, folding his arms across his chest, as though he could wrap his anger tightly inside himself.

'How could you?' he hissed, as soon as they were away from the church doors. Not far off, late guests walked towards the church and Achike didn't smile at them. An hour ago, he had thought that he was part of that world of happy people. When would he learn?

'How *could* you?' he said again. 'You told me you were invited! You told me that Oskar wanted you there. You told me he said you could bring a *guest*. How could you lie to me like that? How could you drag me to that?'

'I'm sorry, Achi.'

'When are you going to grow up?' They'd done this before, on purpose, turning up uninvited to weddings. Years ago, at drama school, they'd spot wedding parties and crash for the free food. But they were much younger, then. Barely old enough to hold down steady jobs, barely paying their bills when they did. But that was for then. This wasn't like before.

Ekene let his hands fall limply by his sides. 'I needed to see it.'

Achike shook his head and dismissed Ekene's words. Not good enough. 'And did I have to be there while you – you ...' He searched his mind for the name of the wrong thing Ekene had done.

'I'm sorry!' Ekene said. He couldn't bear the look on Achike's face.

'Oh, you're always sorry afterwards, Ekene!' Achike sounded very tired, suddenly. 'You're always doing things like this. Ever since we were kids.' Unthinking, Ekene took a step backwards as he saw the scale of Achike's rage. The corollary of the two of them having known each other for so long was that they could recall, at an instant's notice, every wrong done over the last twenty-five years of their lives. They could be brothers, the way they could fight. 'I'm sick to death of it.'

'I'm so sorry, Achike,' Ekene pleaded. 'But don't say that. I'm not so bad. I didn't mean to embarrass you. I honestly didn't think anyone would notice us there.'

Achike scoffed. 'You can't be serious.'

'It's a big wedding. I thought they'd assume we were family. I just had to see it. I just . . . had to see it, that's all.'

'See *what*? What did you have to see, Ekene? What?'

Ekene took a deep breath. He thought carefully. 'I guess I had to see the guy Oskar had chosen over me. I had to see them get married. I had to see it done. I know it seems selfish and reckless and self-destructive to someone like you, and I don't know what to say to that. I can't explain or defend it. But as soon as I knew they were getting married, I knew I had to go. I knew I had to see it. And I don't regret it. I'm sorry, but I don't.'

'You are unbelievable,' breathed Achike.

'Come on, Achi. I'm sorry about what I did to you. I am. I'm so sorry I made you come with me. I should never have put you in that position. Not you.'

'Why did you bring me here?' Achike rounded.

'I just said I don't . . . ' But Achike was glaring at him, furious, impatient. He needed a truthful answer. So Ekene shrugged and said, as though it were obvious, 'Because I couldn't do it alone.'

'Ekene!' Achike's eyes bulged for a moment. But then he seemed to shrink. He crumpled. He teetered between rage and pity, unsure which direction he should take. How dare Ekene use the words of a good man against him?

When Achike spoke again, his voice was quiet and weak. 'I'm not your toy, Ekene. I think you forget that. Maybe because we've known each other for such a long time. But I'm really not . . . You can't just use me.'

'I didn't use you. I just needed you.'

Achike shook his head, refusing to be disarmed. 'Well,' he said. 'You got me here. You got exactly what you wanted. So: are you happy now?'

'Achike. Please.'

'Well? You nearly snuck into the wedding of two people who actually do love each other. Are you happy?'

'I don't know.' Ekene only turned away, his broad back a shield.

'Don't you know how much that hurt me?'

'I'm sorry. Achike, I've said I'm sorry.'

'And you're right, you know. It does seem selfish to me. I can't imagine doing anything like that. But not because I'm some perfect automaton like you obviously think I am.'

'I never said that.'

'It's because I can't imagine loving anyone else but you,' Achike said, suddenly sounding very unhappy. 'And if you ever got married to someone else ...' His voice was so soft. Ekene hated himself, then. This was goodness, and fragility. He only wanted to cradle Achike's heart in his hands. Why had he done this? 'If you ever married some other man, I wouldn't be here watching you. I couldn't do it.'

'Achike,' said Ekene. 'I've said I'm sorry. What do you want from me?'

'What do you want from *me*?' Achike pleaded. 'Don't you know I'd have given you a wedding if you'd asked me?'

Passers-by passed by. They stared and smirked.

The two of them always came back to the same question. Sometimes it was unspoken. Today it was not, and when Achike asked the question out loud, Ekene had already been thinking it, moments before.

'Don't you care about me at all?' Achike said. 'Don't you love me even a little?' But Achike had said this so many times, now, over the years, and asking the question again was like telling a joke that had long since ceased to be funny. It wasn't so easy for him to get the words out now; this time he stumbled, he mumbled. He was ashamed of having to say them. But he had to know. 'After everything I've done for—' He stopped himself. 'After everything we've been through?'

Ekene shrugged and turned away, kicking at some moss on a wall with the tip of his shoe.

'Don't do that,' Achike said. 'I'm still here. You can't pretend I'm not here. Do you know how many times you've touched me?'

'What?'

'Do you know,' Achike said, slowly, doggedly, 'how many times you've touched me since I got back? Don't shake your head at me. The way you put your arm around me, or put your hands on me. But you can't tell me you love me?'

'And can't you touch me back?' Ekene said.

Achike blinked and frowned as if he were dazed. 'It didn't feel . . . safe,' he said, weakly. 'I was afraid of what you'd do next.'

'So was I,' said Ekene.

They were on a quiet road, and this was the nice part of town. The buildings here had solar panels, lawyers, architects. Children galloped unevenly to the park in wellies. People and trees whispered. You didn't get into fights here.

But Achike wouldn't give up. He had to have an answer, this time. 'Ekene,' he said. 'Don't you—'

'Please don't,' Ekene said. 'Please.' Sometimes, what frightened Ekene was not the possibility that he had no love for his friend, but that this was the best love he had to give.

'Look at me,' said Achike. His voice was commanding because of its hurt, so Ekene looked. Achike was beautiful: not only a surface beauty that he could simply take or leave, notice or overlook. Another man's beauty might be temporary or temporal. Another man's beauty might fade or alter, founder or falter. Over the years you could chase another man's beauty through its various stages of decline: through dimming eyes, through smooth skin that crumpled and folded and gave way, through a voice that grew husky with time. But with Achike there was nothing to chase. Beauty ran through him like blood. It was in everything he did; every look, every gesture, every word. There could be no part of him that was not beautiful. And Ekene loved him. Of course he did.

So why couldn't he say that?

'Achike,' he said. 'I'm so sorry, I—'

'For the love of *God*. Not again. Not again.' Achike screwed his eyes shut and turned his face to a nearby wall, his eyes scanning for something. Maybe he had just seen a bright light somewhere.

'What's wrong?' said Ekene. 'Migraine?'

'Yes,' said Achike, giving in to it. 'Migraine.'

'Oh shit. I'm sorry. It's probably my fault,' said Ekene. His face was wrinkled with concern. Achike didn't argue with him, and instead clutched his hand to his head. 'Has the headache started yet?' Ekene asked.

'No,' said Achike. He still sounded angry. 'Just the aura. I need to get home.'

'Have you got your medicine?'

'I left the pills at home,' said Achike. 'I guess I didn't think I'd need them today.'

Ekene nodded silently. It was his fault. The sudden stress must have brought it on. Of course it must have.

The air in front of Achike was dancing in dangerous colours and a large patch of his vision was hidden behind them. Already the slightest sound or bright light made him wince. First the aura – the frightening kaleidoscope that would hang in front of his eyes for twenty minutes – then the blinding headache and the nausea. He normally got these attacks once every few months, sometimes every few weeks. But two in two days?

'I'll have to . . .'

'I know,' said Ekene. 'It's okay. Let's get you home and into bed. Come on.'

Achike considered resisting but he knew he couldn't; he couldn't even see to drive himself home. 'Okay,' he said, quietly.

'Don't worry, I'll sort it,' said Ekene. 'I've got you.'

'I . . . Alright. Fine.'

'Okay.'

'Thank you,' said Achike.

'Don't be daft,' said Ekene.

'I'm still angry with you, you know.' How frustrating, for his body to be weak at the very moment when anger made him feel most strong, for him to suddenly become as helpless as a child. How base, for him to have to lean on anybody now.

Ekene used Achike's phone to call a taxi home, and made a mental note to pay Achike back later; the tube would take too long and Ekene wanted to be alone with Achike, after their fight. It was lucky that Achike's father had left the flat that morning. He hadn't said where he was going but he always stayed out for hours on end.

The cool silence of a taxi seemed fair. They both sat in the back, one seat apart. Achike hid his face from the window, not touching Ekene but turning to the seat between them in a gesture that was part-intimate, part-cautious, part-distanced. Had he or Ekene been sitting one seat closer, he would have been resting his head on Ekene's shoulder, the way he would have liked to. Ekene imagined how it would feel if he reached out and ran a finger through Achike's hair and said he was sorry, he was so sorry.

When they got to the building's entrance, Achike allowed Ekene to walk him inside, holding an arm out just behind Achike as though he might fold over and fall back at any moment. Along the corridor, Ekene opened doors for him and quietly encouraged him through the hallway. He treated Achike like glass, but Achike said nothing, too busy finding his way. He kept his eyes half closed and shielded them from the artificial lights that seemed to be everywhere. He moved on, on towards darkness and rest.

*

When Achike had first moved into his flat, Ekene had offered to help, but Achike declined, already having hired movers. He could afford them. Ekene remembered feeling envious and sad. A few years ago, their lives had been on vaguely similar trajectories: both of them young, both Nigerian-British, both gay, both still in shock at the expense and stress of London, both somewhere between struggle and comfort. When Ekene had decided to give up acting and teach drama, he had had his doubts. But he knew that even if his life sailed on choppy seas for a while, Achike would always be within sight. The two of them, he had thought, would be in it together.

But he didn't think so now. Achike would be famous soon. And he had money, and this meant a number of things. It meant that Achike had achieved everything he had set out to since the age of eight, while Ekene still didn't know what he wanted from life. It meant that Achike was as close to pleasing his father as he would ever be, while Ekene was always so far away. Ekene's mother only wanted him to find a woman and have a child; his father had never really wanted him all that much.

Achike's money changed other things. He had a lot more money than he had ever had before, and a lot more than Ekene was ever likely to see at one time. Even before he moved in with Achike, the small indignities of never having quite enough money continued to plague Ekene. His bike would break, the heating bill would be too high, the rent might go up next year. Still in his childhood mindset, he kept an eye out for vouchers, fixed things himself if he could, took cheap holidays or none at all. He hesitated before spending anything because money, no matter how regularly it came in, might be irreplaceable in a week, in a month.

He lost his job at the school. He had saved a little money, but not more than a couple of months' rent and living expenses, if he was frugal. And if he wore through that, what then? He couldn't go back and live with his parents. The only option, he knew, was Achike.

Achike's life did not look like Ekene's anymore. Over the last few years, money had gradually appeared in Achike's life like a series of romantic gifts from a secret admirer. It had intoxicated him like wine, scented his life like fresh flowers in the hallway each morning.

When they got home, Ekene looked around the flat as if seeing it for the first time. He was happy for his friend. But he wondered how long they could stay in each other's lives. He wasn't the kind of person that people like Achike spent time with. That sort of relationship didn't happen. And if he were to lose Achike, he wondered, what else was left for him?

*

In his bedroom, Achike sat on the edge of his bed, while Ekene closed the blinds. It was finally dark now, but the air felt close. Everything felt close. Ekene stood back as though to admire some work well done. He put his hands on his hips.

'All good?' he said.

'Did you get my medicine?' asked Achike. 'I can't see it to get it.'

'I've got it, it's here. Here you go.'

'Thanks. Err ...' Achike moved his hands slowly over his bedside table, but they passed through thin air.

'What's wrong?'

'I need some water.'

'Oh,' said Ekene. 'Shit. Sorry. I'll be right back.'

Ekene raced out of the bedroom to get the water. Achike let himself fall back into the bed, pressing his hand to his head in anticipation of the pain that had not even begun yet.

He heard Ekene's footsteps. His eyes still closed, he felt rather than saw Ekene enter the room and approach the bed silently, on tiptoe. Had he been asked, he would not have been able to explain how he knew that Ekene was there. Ekene's shoes made little noises as his feet met the floor, but there was something else to it as well. Even after what Ekene had done, would it be too much to imagine that the hair on his arms stood on end when Ekene approached?

'Here you go,' said Ekene. He put the cup of water down on the bedside table. 'And, err, here's the ... other thing. In case you need it during the night.' He left a bucket by the side of the bed, for vomit. After experiencing a few of Achike's migraines over the years, Ekene sometimes showed a kind of brisk familiarity towards them.

'Thanks. The pill ...' Achike reached out blindly for it and Ekene, half smiling at Achike's feebleness, pressed it to Achike's lips. Then he picked up the glass and held it to Achike's mouth while he swallowed. Achike winced at the motion of the muscles in his face and neck, already beginning to tense. He sat back in the bed, tried to relax.

'Drama queen,' said Ekene, mischievously.

'Oh ...' Achike groaned and turned his head away, despite the beginnings of a smile flickering. 'Don't.'

'*I am dying, Egypt ...* ' Ekene said.

After half a second, Achike replied, '*Die when thou hast lived; quicken with kissing.*'

They laughed in whispers, Achike under his headache, Ekene under his guilt. How many years had it been since the two of them, awkward teenagers together, had play-acted the tragic end of *Antony and Cleopatra* so many times that they'd memorised the words? They'd barely even known, then, what they wanted out of it: the gesture towards a recognisable, visible bond, however reckless; the rosy fingertips of femininity touching their skin. The two of them had read out the smaller parts between them; had taken it in turns to play *the man*, Antony, finding scant joy only in his most dramatic lines as he died. They'd relished the freedom of playing *the woman*, a freedom as bewitching as the queen. They let their wrists fall limp, then, and made quick costumes out of bedsheets. It was almost enough.

The bright day is done, and we are for the dark.

'You don't have to stay, Ekene,' Achike said. 'It's not a very interesting place to be, I know. And Oskar's probably wanting to enjoy his wedding night by now, so you wouldn't want to let that go undocumented.'

Ekene laughed weakly, but Achike heard him move sheepishly back from the bed.

'Ekene? Do you really have to go somewhere?' Achike asked. Even speaking was painful. He had already released his friend. But he had to know.

'I was going to head off after the wedding, anyway. I'm sorry to—'

'Are you—'

'I feel a bit—'

'Don't worry—'

They spoke at the same time, apologising and excusing. Ekene broke the pattern and said, 'I'm just ... meeting someone. Just for dinner. I wasn't going to mention anything yet, since it's just a first date.'

'Oh.'

'He seems nice.'

'Oh.'

Achike waited a while, but when nobody spoke, he felt that he should. 'That's nice. I'm glad. That's fine.' He could hear the disappointment in his voice and tried to think of some other things to say but suddenly there was pain after all, as though someone had shone a bright light in his eyes. This would be one of the worse migraines. Achike turned over on the bed.

'Look, come here,' said Ekene. He leaned over Achike and arranged the bedspread so that Achike was comfortable. He thought for half a moment and then decided to tuck the corners of the bedspread in underneath him, swaddling him loosely. He let his hands rest gently on Achike's legs when he was done. 'Will you be okay?'

'Yeah, I'll be fine. Thanks for doing this, Ekene.' His voice sounded so weak.

'Are you sure? I feel just terrible leaving you like this, but I said I'd meet Elliot in half an hour and—'

Elliot. So his name was Elliot. Achike found himself wondering if Elliot was white, if Ekene had chosen a white man over him. Maybe that was it.

It didn't make sense for Ekene to leave now. Achike knew that Ekene loved him. He *knew* it. He had always known it. So why couldn't Ekene just admit it? Why couldn't he just say it? Achike wanted to say it all the time. But every time he said it, Ekene pulled back a little further. Once at a house party as teenagers; once after Ekene had starred in the school play. Twice when Ekene was throwing up, Achike's hand on his back. Once in Berlin, on New Year's Eve, watching the fireworks. Time after time he'd confessed, insisted, but Ekene only shook his head sadly, as though Achike had been trying to solve an equation and kept coming up with the wrong answer. But it was right. Why couldn't Ekene see it was right?

'It's okay. Honestly,' said Achike. He sounded very tired. 'I think maybe we should take some time.'

'Time?'

'Yeah. I mean ... how long can we carry on doing this? You don't want what I want.'

'What are you talking about?'

'When I saw you in Berlin,' said Achike, 'I thought things might be different. After what happened. The way we talked. I thought things might finally have to change. But then you broke up with Oskar, and nothing changed. And I went away and filmed, and nothing changed. And then you moved in, and nothing changed. It's been months and months, Ekene ...' Ekene looked at him and waited. 'I think maybe it's time you moved out.'

'Do you hate me that much?'

'Of course I don't hate you, Ekene.'

'Achike, please. I was a shit today. I was. But it doesn't mean that I don't care about you. It doesn't mean we can't be—' He sounded urgent now. But he still didn't know what to say. 'You really mean a lot to me.'

'And do you love me?'

'Achike . . .'

'Do you love me?'

A breeze had got in somewhere, and it played with the edges of things. Ekene couldn't say a word.

'I think you should go,' Achike said. 'Soon. You'll be happier, too. And there must be some jobs, somewhere. Maybe not in Peckham, but somewhere in London. Or back home in Manchester. Anyway, I might not be here long, either. You said so yourself. So it's fine.'

'Achike.'

'I'm not saying I never want to see you again.' He took a deep, difficult breath. 'I just . . . Jesus, I just need to know what that would feel like, for a bit.'

Ekene waited until he could speak clearly. 'Are you sure this is what you want?'

Aren't you? Achike wanted to ask. But that would be one more question, one more thing Achike needed that Ekene didn't know how to give him. Achike was tired.

'I'm sure,' Achike said. 'It's time. You go. We'll talk about it more in the morning. Have a good time. And honestly, thank you for looking after me.'

'You're welcome,' Ekene said, weakly. He took one last look around the room, as if to check that he hadn't overlooked some object, something out of place that would keep Achike from sleeping and, in so doing, keep Ekene awake, worrying.

'Okay,' said Ekene. 'I'll make a move.'

'Okay,' said Achike. 'Thank you. Goodbye. Don't worry, I'm okay. Don't worry about me.'

Ekene gave him one last, long look. He nodded curtly to himself, and left, closing the door.

What hurt Achike the most? He closed his eyes and thought about it.

Later, Achike made himself lean over to the bedside table and feel around for the water and more pills. It was too soon after the first dose to take another, but he did not care. His head was all pain. The light from the street slipped into his bedroom at night, so he kept his sleeping mask on. He couldn't see and he knocked the pills to the floor.

'Shit. Shit.'

The dancing lights had gone from his vision, but the headache was blinding. It was worse than anything he had ever experienced before, and so was the nausea. He felt his stomach convulse and he vomited into the bucket Ekene had left by the bed. It took long minutes before he had nothing left inside him; there were moments when he thought it was over, but his body forced him over the bucket again, pale streams of liquid issuing from him with startling force.

Eventually he sat back on the bed and tried to look for the pills, but his neck was stiff. Unseeing, he patted the floor until his hand found the bottle. He swallowed the pill, buried his head underneath the covers and waited for the pain to recede, waited to fall asleep.

How long was it until he heard the door to his room open again?

Of course, his father was nowhere to be seen. Achike tried to steel himself to the knowledge that Chibuike would rather be elsewhere, deep in spirits, hating himself, than by Achike's bedside, even for a moment. Was Chibuike still so disgusted by him? In the early days, after Chibuike realised Achike was gay, he looked at him with so much sorrow, so apologetically, as if he had let his son down again. How obvious it was that Chibuike wondered what his son would have been like if his uncle had never touched him, wondered if he might peel back a layer of time and pain and find another son underneath.

Achike tried to breathe steadily. Maybe fathers could explain sons? Ekene had been worse off than he had. How much of a father had been given to the boy? The very best love Ekene's father could give had always been weak, meagre. Ekene was less than an obligation to him; he saw nothing in Ekene that could tie him down, much less lift him up. When Ekene's mother sued for full custody, his father did not contest it. Ekene once told Achike that he had got in touch with his father after the settlement, but the man had turned him away. He had a new wife and new children by then. There were too many layers of time and pain to peel away, and Ekene's father had had no appetite for reliving a past life, going over past mistakes. 'And besides,' he'd said, 'you're a man now. You don't need me.' Ekene hadn't smiled for a week after that.

Achike tried to be grateful for the father he had. Chibuike had spent years waiting for a version of his son that would never exist, but Ekene's father had made his family wait for *him*, and when Ekene found him, had simply shrugged his shoulders and walked away. So Achike tried to be grateful, even though Ekene's father had caused Achike so much pain in his own way, too. If Ekene's father had been a better man, maybe Ekene would still be with Achike now, holding the cool, wet flannel to Achike's forehead and whispering him to sleep. Anyway, so many people had their own story to tell of a father who hadn't been there, or hadn't been right; as bad as Chibuike was, he could have been worse. And Achike's mother had been worse, while she was alive. He knew that, although his father never mentioned her. And he tried to be grateful. But it was hard to be grateful for something he hardly had. He had long felt that Chibuike drank to escape him as much as the world.

He became morose, thinking again about his mother, and how it might feel restful to hear her voice, or feel her press a cool, wet flannel to his forehead. She used to sing to him. And then she left.

He told himself that he only had to survive the pain – to outlast it – and then he would be able to get up again, to open the curtains, to step outside. It wouldn't take long, he thought to himself. Only a matter of hours. Tomorrow, things might not be so bad.

Ekene was home. Every moment he'd been gone he'd been wandering as though lost. On the way back home he'd stepped around pools of yellow light from the street lamps like a cursed thing. How could he get himself to say it? As he'd walked back to Achike's flat, he'd mouthed the words *I love you, I love you, I love you*, feeling his breath curl itself inside his mouth, roll thickly around his tongue. He could never make the words more than this. He came home feeling desperate and lost.

'Achike?' Ekene called softly.

Slowly, Achike turned over in his bed.

'How are you doing? How's—' He stopped, and could smell the bucket. 'Hold on.' He took it to the bathroom. Achike heard him empty it, flush the toilet, rinse the bucket out using water from the tap in the bathtub, flush again. A few seconds later, Ekene was back. Achike could not even open his eyes. Every movement disrupted his mind, setting off tiny red fireworks under his skull. Nothing was quiet enough.

'Achike, it's a bad one, isn't it?'

Achike nodded.

'Oh, shit. Achi, I'm so sorry.' He took the damp towel and pressed it to Achike's head. 'Have you taken more medicine? Or is it too soon for that? Can I do anything?'

Achike nodded, and shook his head, then mumbled, 'Why are you back?'

Ekene overlooked the bluntness of the question. 'I was worried about you.'

'Oh.'

'And guilty. Mostly guilty, actually,' said Ekene, exhaling. He sounded as though he were releasing something other than breath. He spoke quietly. Achike wasn't sure if this was because of his migraine, or because of Ekene's guilt.

'Oh,' said Achike again.

'Yeah. If you can believe it.'

'Ekene ...'

'Shh. No, it's okay. Just ... I couldn't stop thinking about you, that's all. I'm so sorry. I never should have left.'

Achike opened his eyes as far as he could. Ekene had left all the lights off except the bedside lamp, which he had turned away from Achike, and towards the floor so it didn't hurt his eyes so much. Achike couldn't make out Ekene's face. He could only keep his eyes open for a moment at a time, but he knew that Ekene was very close to the bed. There was the smell of him. Ekene smelled of whisky, which Achike knew he liked. Achike hated the smell of the stuff, hated the thought that Ekene had been drinking it with someone else. But he wanted Ekene there, the whole of him, every drop.

'I'm so sorry, Achi,' Ekene went on. 'You didn't deserve that. None of it. I know how much you care about me, and for me to just leave like that, I don't know what I was thinking. I must have been ... Jesus, I'm such a shit.'

'You're not a shit,' said Achike, tiredly.

'I am. Look at me!'

'You're not a shit, Ekene. You've just ... you've been through some stuff.' Achike held his forehead in his hands, but carried on. 'You just haven't come out the other side yet. You will.'

Ekene refused the tears that approached. 'You shouldn't have so much faith in me.'

'Can't help it.'

'But you deserve better, Achi.'

'Then do better.'

Ekene didn't know what to say to this. There was nothing

he could do, in the moment, to respond. He only said, 'This is awful. You just lying here, hating me.'

'I've got a migraine,' said Achike. 'I hate everything.'

Ekene laughed a little but Achike could feel his eyes on him, waiting for forgiveness or dismissal. Achike took a moment to breathe, and his chest rose and fell uneasily with the effort of it.

'It's okay,' said Achike. 'I know you were hurting. I know you loved him.'

'Achi.'

'It's okay.'

'Achi—'

'I love you,' he said. He tried to sound firm, but he was so exhausted, in so much pain, that he sounded sleepy. Why was it that the pain made him feel braver?

'I . . . ' Ekene hesitated, blinking hard in concentration. 'You mean everything to me, Achike. I'm so sorry I did that to you. I'm so sorry I ever made you feel like you weren't important to me. You are.' Achike heard him move a little closer, as though his words couldn't have meaning unless he said them here, right here. 'I couldn't be without you. I hope you know that.'

Achike gathered his thoughts and breath. Neither of them spoke for a few moments, listening to Achike breathe as deeply and slowly as he could.

'Will you stay with me?' he asked. Maybe it was the pain again, making him bolder. Or maybe he was capitalising on Ekene's confession, which he had waited so long for. He was starved, and yet he felt that he was being greedy. Why was that?

He pushed on. 'Will you stay in here, Ekene? Stay the night?'

'Of course. Of course.' Ekene nodded.

'Ekene?'

Ekene went across the hall to his room, where he stripped to his underwear, and he came back with blankets and pillows for a makeshift bed on the floor.

'Looks like we're both in for an uncomfortable night,' he said, spreading cushions on the floor and grimacing in anticipation of the discomfort of a night spent sleeping on them.

'It really hurts,' said Achike. He was crying. 'It hurts so much.'

'Oh, Achi,' said Ekene. He thought for a moment, hesitating as though trapped in an awkward position. 'Listen, I'm going to get into the bed with you, okay?'

'Yeah?'

'Yeah. I think you could use a hug.'

'Thank you.'

He got in under the covers and wrapped his arms around Achike, tucking Achike's head down so that it rested on Ekene's chest. It was so easy to do.

'How's that?' Ekene asked. 'That okay? Just nod if it is.'

Achike nodded.

'It's okay,' said Ekene. 'I'm here. I'm not going anywhere. You're okay. Just try to sleep.'

'Mmhm,' mumbled Achike.

'Do you need anything else? Can I fetch you anything?' Ekene switched off the light.

Achike said, 'No.'

'Okay. Just try to sleep. You'll be better in the morning.'

'Okay.'

'Okay. Goodnight, Achike.'

'Goodnight.'

I love you, Ekene breathed. *I love you, I love you.* He could not make it more.

But then Achike was on fire. He *was* fire: he'd been a man one moment, and he was flame the next. All the heat and pressure and noise that the earth and sea and sky had ever seen had all come to buckle in his brain, and the life in him was being burned away.

Achike was shouting, *shouting* so loudly and urgently. He could not form words, just a long note pushed out, a word that wasn't a word, a word that could have been relief, or a shock that was over in a moment. Achike could not speak; he was utterly inaccessible. He was fire behind glass, fire in the sky.

Ekene's first thought had been to quiet Achike, or question him: how could anything deserve such chaos? He'd never known or seen a pain that could make someone shout for more than a moment, never this growling that could frighten demons. Achike's eyes bulged and then screwed shut, then rolled back and retreated into him. He clamped his fists to his temples and shook himself like a father with no patience could shake a child to death, trying to jolt out of him some awful thing.

But the pain insisted, and Ekene's next thought was with him, and told him that this was more than a moment. It was a moment stretched out and lived forever, a life of agony that should have been over, but refused to end. It was the anaesthetist's syringe going deeper and deeper into the nerve, the needle never-ending, and no numbness for it.

Ekene threw the sheets off himself and placed two hands on Achike's head, firm and priestlike. Ekene did not exist, then. Whatever calm or health he had to give must flow through him, must leave him and become Achike's.

'Achike! What's wrong? Tell me what's wrong. Achike?' Nothing. Ekene looked around, grabbed his phone. 'Hello? I need an ambulance immediately.' The operator transferred him to the ambulance service. Only two small, dark, silent seconds, and then another voice. She was assured, professional, quick.

'I understand you've asked for an ambulance – can I just get the address you're calling from, please?'

'We're at flat 618, 28 Wagfield Street.'

A beat. 'And is the patient breathing?'

'He is, but he's in a lot of pain. It's his head. He was having a migraine, but now it's way, way worse. He's really suffering.'

Ekene quickly told her what he knew: how Achike's bedrest had turned on him; how the sweetness of the night had quickly turned sour.

'Can the patient lift his arms above his head?'

Ekene forced himself to answer the question, though it seemed irrelevant. 'No, I don't think ... I think he'd really struggle.'

'Can the patient smile?'

'Smile?'

'Yes,' the operator said, steadily. 'Can the patient smile? And is the smile even on both sides?'

Ekene recalled hearing something about strokes that made sense of the question, and he turned to Achike. 'I don't think he can smile,' he said. 'The pain's too bad. But he's grimacing, and both sides of his face are the same.'

'Okay. Now I need you to check if he can talk. Can he form any sentences?'

'Achike?' Ekene stepped closer to Achike, then knelt by his side. 'Can you say something for me?'

Achike's eyes bulged in Ekene's direction. Sounds came only through Achike's teeth, pushed over his tongue.

'And can he breathe?' said the operator. 'Is there anything obstructing his airway?'

'No, I don't think there is.'

'Can you check?' she asked.

He looked into Achike's mouth, which was still open, screaming.

'His airway's clear.'

'Okay,' said the operator. 'And exactly when did the symptoms start?'

'Just a couple of minutes ago, right before I rang you.'

'And has the patient ever had a stroke before?'

'No, he's only young.'

A beat. 'Okay. I've dispatched an ambulance to you, and

now I'm going to ask for more information, so I can relay it to the paramedics while they're getting to you. You say the patient is young – what age?'

'Thirty-seven.'

'And you say the patient is male?'

'Yes.'

'And what's the medical history? Any long-term conditions or allergies? Is the patient on any medication?'

'No, nothing, there's nothing. He's healthy. He should be healthy.'

'And can you give me any more information on the patient's condition? You say he's in a lot of pain in his head: has he hit his head recently?'

'No, nothing I know of. I've been with him almost all day. I'm sorry, he's really in a lot of pain – when's the ambulance getting here?'

'The paramedics will be with you as soon as possible. It won't be long. Please stay with the patient until the ambulance arrives, okay?'

'Okay.'

'I'm going to end the call now, but if he gets worse before the ambulance arrives, I want you to ring 999 again, okay?'

'Okay.'

Ekene was alone in the room again. Achike was still shouting but intermittently now; he'd exhausted himself. There was so little of him left and he could only whimper. Were the neighbours out? Hadn't they heard the screaming?

Ekene tried to be useful again.

'The ambulance is on the way, okay?' he said. 'You'll be okay.'

Nothing, only more pain.

Maybe a cold, damp towel would help? But surely the woman on the phone would have told him that. What if cold made it worse? But doing nothing might also make it worse.

Ekene reached over to an old jumper folded on an armchair,

and put it on for when the ambulance came. There were joggers hanging over the wardrobe door, and trainers by the bed. He put them on.

The doorbell buzzed for two full seconds and Ekene ran to the receiver to let the paramedics in. After a few moments, he heard their footsteps on the stairs and there was a knock at the door.

'Ambulance, yeah?' said one paramedic.

'Yes, yes, please come in. He's through here.' There were two men, both tall, one fair-haired and one red. Neither of them had looked at Ekene, their eyes moving past him to where the emergency was.

'My name's Aaron,' said the one with red hair as they walked. He gestured behind him: 'This is Greg.' Ekene nodded.

In Achike's bedroom, Greg stood back while Aaron kneeled by the bed. 'What's his name?'

'Achike.'

'Achike, can you hear me?'

Too much had ebbed out of Achike, now. He had been silenced. His eyes were unfocused, his breathing shallow.

'Achike. Can you hear me, sir?'

When Achike did not respond, Aaron nodded to Greg, who pulled up the stretcher, and together they lifted Achike onto it. But Ekene watched Achike's face as they moved him, and there was nothing. Did he even know he was being taken away?

'I'll show you the way to the service lift,' Ekene said. It was through a fire door and around a corner. 'It's slow—'

'How slow? Slower than the other lift? That was pretty slow on the way up.' said Aaron, quickly. Of course. Ekene should have thought about this.

'A little slow.'

'Should we take the stairs?'

The lift came just then, but only Aaron could fit in with the stretcher. 'I'll meet you downstairs,' said Greg.

He and Ekene raced downstairs and waited by the lift, which seemed slower than it had ever been. Greg did not try to talk to him. He just watched the numbers on the display above the lift doors while they both breathed.

The doors opened. 'Right,' said Aaron. 'Let's go.'

Ekene followed them outside to where the ambulance was waiting, its lights still flashing. The emergency had not stopped.

The paramedics opened the back of the van and wheeled Achike inside, but when Ekene made to get in, Greg looked at him sharply.

'Are you next of kin?'

'I'm . . .' He knew he was not. Ekene looked for what to say instead, but nothing came to him.

'We have to follow the rules,' said Greg. 'I'm sorry, mate. And I can stand here talking to you, or we can get your friend to hospital.'

Ekene nodded. Whatever he was to Achike, it wasn't enough. Achike would go out into the night alone, nobody he knew to hold his hand and whisper sweet dreams to him.

Greg was already inside the ambulance again, bent over Achike's body. Aaron was in the driver's seat. Ekene stepped back onto the pavement. Behind him, neighbours were looking out through their windows. So, they had heard.

The doors shut and the siren went back on. The ambulance sped down the road. And that was all.

Which hospital were they going to? Ekene didn't even know how long it took to get to the nearest A&E department, or if Achike would be alive when they got there.

He ran back into the flat – he hadn't thought to lock the doors – took his phone from the bed and called a taxi. He waited ten long minutes for it to arrive, and in the car he ignored the driver's attempts at conversation. He looked out of the window. It was beginning to rain lightly. Until Achike was safe, nothing else existed but the sound of the engine, and of the drizzle on the window.

The journey took fifteen minutes; they had no siren to speed them on. At A&E, Ekene rushed to reception, appalled that there should be a queue, even one that moved. He looked around: he was not the only one with problems. After a moment, a woman to his left closed her eyes and slid off her chair, falling to the floor. Someone gasped. People came and carried her away.

By now, Ekene was almost frantic, but found he could not let it show. What about everyone else's problems?

When his turn came, he spoke quickly and clearly to the receptionist, but she asked him the same question.

'Are you next of kin? Are you family?'

'No,' said Ekene. But he'd had time to think, now, and added, 'He must have my name down somewhere, though. We're like family. Please. My name's Ekene Nnamdi, if you could just look—'

The receptionist shook her head gently. 'I'm sorry, we can't give out any information except to next of kin, and we can't let you see him if you're not. Do you know if the next of kin is here? Did they come with you?'

'No, he didn't.' Ekene looked around the room, but couldn't see Chibuike anywhere. Would he even know Achike was here?

'Are you in touch with him?'

'I don't think I have his number.'

'Someone from the hospital will have called. I'll take your name, though, if you could spell it for me?'

Ekene went through the steps robotically. He knew the ways to avoid confusion, knew which letters to enunciate in case they were missed or misheard.

The receptionist made a note, and nodded. 'Alright. I'll let the doctor know. I'm afraid I have to ask you to step back, though, I'm sorry. Wait till the next of kin gets here.' Ekene nodded. Who was he, after all? He looked for a seat; there were not many free. Everyone was in pain, or waiting for someone's pain to be over. There were a few children there, all of them quiet; they were afraid or sleeping. He wondered what had happened to the woman who'd fainted.

But Ekene had seen it all. Such things he had seen, and nobody to tell. Achike had been on fire, and the life in him had gone up in smoke. Ekene hoped they would take care of Achike, but he feared ... He'd seen Achike's face as they set him on the stretcher, as they wheeled him into the ambulance, as the doors closed. Achike was gone. There was no way back from where he was now. Ekene had seen it.

His mind was on Achike, and yet, of all things, Ekene wished for his father. He almost never did; it was too much of a betrayal of himself, to admit to a longing he could not address. Acknowledging it only made it worse. Only an emergency could make him confront it. He confronted it now. He allowed it; it was fair. He so wanted to be held, to be enveloped by the presence of someone older and more solid than he was. He closed his eyes and thought about his father, who would never think about Ekene first, or think of Ekene at all. He thought about Obiajulu Nnamdi, then, who'd walked away so easily, and stayed away so long. Could he ever see his way back to his boy?

Ekene wondered whether his father would come if he called him now, if he knew how much Ekene needed him. He wondered what would happen if he could find his father's phone number somehow, or if he would know what to say when he did. Or perhaps his father's new family was so precious to him that he could not spare even a moment to remember his son, who was alone, and afraid. Obiajulu's new family was his new self. Ekene only represented his father's past, the mistakes he had made, the woman he wished he'd never really loved. It was not worth Obiajulu's time to go back to all that.

Ekene opened his eyes, and was exhausted. He'd been so silly. There was no point in reaching out to thin air, to someone so far away. Ekene knew what his father would say to him, even now, if he were to call and ask for comfort, for presence, or an embrace. He would say that Ekene was grown. He was a man, now. He shouldn't need such things.

Chapter 5

Chibuike was waiting in the tiny Relatives' Room of the Intensive Care Unit. He didn't know for how long.

He tried to think reasonable thoughts. He tried leashing his mind to logic to keep his thoughts from the intolerable, the impossible. He told himself the doctor would explain, and that he could see Achike soon. He must be still, and let the future come to him. He tried to focus his mind on the wait, as though there were something he could do now, as though waiting were something he could do, instead of the absence of doing something. The failure to do something. His son was in hospital. Where had he been?

There was only a small space in his mind still governed by logic and free of panic, and it seemed to shrink as the moments passed. Beyond that space was a dark night sky and a large hospital, beeping machines and nurses with worried faces and terrible things that could happen.

On the phone they'd said it was important. They'd said that his son had had ... 'a serious bleed'. Is that what they'd said? He hadn't heard them properly at first. Or he had heard them, but he had been so stunned by what they said ... 'Can you come in as soon as possible?'

He'd been away on the tube again, well on the way to being drunk. He'd just got out of the ticket hall when he got the call on the phone Achike paid for. Would Achike know? That he'd been drinking when they called? He'd got off at the next stop, taken a taxi into the city centre, and thrown away his bottle, half full. Did it matter that he hadn't even thought to finish his drink?

But the craving came upon him now like the holy ghost, powerful, irresistible, awful. He buckled under its weight, but there was nothing to be done; he had nothing on him to drink. Besides, he wasn't here to help, after all. He wasn't here to save the day. He wasn't here to save Achike's life, if that was what was needed now. Chibuike was here to wait. The most he would be able to do was call a taxi and ride with his son on the journey home. He could do that. He could hold off his addiction long enough to do that, surely?

And maybe that would be something. *A serious bleed ...* Maybe Achike had only fallen and cut himself. Maybe he had been mugged. He was always telling Achike not to walk around with his phone out at night. He was always telling Achike to be more careful, to avoid certain streets. Someone might recognise him and know he had money. He'd thought to tell his son that people do terrible things – but he'd never said that. Achike did not need telling.

Still, maybe it was only a mugging. Yes. He thought Achike might emerge from the double doors at the end of the corridor with his arm in a sling. He'd be disoriented, and a little embarrassed. He'd take one look at Chibuike's worried face, and he'd laugh, and they'd go home.

Or maybe it would be worse. Chibuike's mind untethered itself. Hadn't they said it was serious, on the phone? Achike might be unconscious somewhere, with wires going in and out of his skin.

Or maybe—

Chibuike crossed his legs and uncrossed them. Surely it would be no more than a mugging. It must not be. Did it count for anything that he had waited in the rain for the taxi to arrive? Did it count that he hoped it would crash, that he would die rather than hear the doctors tell him his son was—

He watched the ceiling light flicker. He smelled the room's hospital smell – something that seemed to arise from every surface, plastic that had been wiped down so many times it had started to break down on a molecular level and release itself into the air, particle by particle.

Time stretched out – he could see bright light between its straining fibres. Was it only his mind? What was it that made the room seem like the only one he'd ever known? If there was bad news, the doctors would surely take him into a morgue to identify the body, not to this windowless room in the ICU. Or perhaps in a moment he would be by his son's side in a hospital room that was lonely, no flowers, no hope, no beeping machines, no wires needed now.

Chibuike was familiar with bad news. His father had been dead when his body arrived at the hospital, but Chibuike's wife had been diagnosed with stage-four cancer before their divorce was finalised. Chibuike remembered the doctor's attempts to arrange her face as she prepared to give Chibuike the news that his wife had died, that his son had lost the only person in his life who knew how to look after him, if not love him, who could get him to school on time, meet his friends' parents, put on the show required. Ndidi was good at that, at the motions. The mechanics of parenthood. Chibuike remembered the shock, the numbness, the way grief eventually became banal, a silent shriek in the heart's dark night, every night, every night, every night.

He couldn't do it again. He felt himself wishing the worst on himself in the hope that somehow, some cruel, beautiful, merciful deity of hospital smells and harsh strip lighting and lost love might see his suffering and take pity on him and give Achike back to him, unharmed.

The doctor walked in. Chibuike examined his face eagerly, trying to absorb some sense of what had happened before the doctor broke the news in words. He had no patience left now. Was the doctor shuffling? Did he clean his glasses for longer than he should have? Chibuike begged the man's face for a head start but nothing moved. Or perhaps the doctor's face was as clear as day, relief in his eyes, but Chibuike was too upset to see it. Yes, that might be it. Yes. If that meant Achike was only lying unconscious on a ward; if it meant he was only sleeping. If it would bring Achike back to him.

The doctor breathed. He blinked, he looked at the floor and then at Chibuike, and then he introduced himself. Dr Patel.

'Are you Mr Okoro?' Still, Chibuike was able to notice the mishandling of his name. *OWE-ko-row.*

'Yes,' Chibuike said.

'Do you know why you're here?' Dr Patel's voice was gentle.

'Yes,' said Chibuike. 'I got a phone call. I came as soon as I could. Someone said my son had some sort of bleed? Is he okay? Can I see him?' There were thorns in his throat. He swallowed hard and the doctor asked him if he would like a glass of water. Chibuike refused politely; everything else could wait.

'What's happened?' he said. 'Where's my son?'

'Mr Okoro,' Dr Patel prepared his face. 'Your son suffered what's called a sub-arachnoid haemorrhage. It's a very serious bleed in the brain, as you were told on the phone. Your son would have experienced it as a kind of terrible headache. We did everything we could, but I'm afraid we weren't able to revive your son, and he died just under an hour ago.' Dr Patel spoke slowly, steadily, and his words were like high tide: big, heavy waves. Chibuike felt cold, suddenly, and he had the sensation that he was plummeting somewhere and would be lost. He grasped the arm of his chair.

'What? No. Please.'

'I wish there was something we could have done.'

'I can't ...'

'I'm so sorry to give you this news,' said Dr Patel. 'I know this must be very difficult for you. Please take all the time you need to process.'

'Wait, wait, *wait*!' Chibuike scrunched his eyes shut, held his hands out, palms down, as if to calm a child that was running too fast and might hurt someone. 'This isn't right, it can't be right.' His voice came to him weakly as he looked down at the tiled floor. 'This ... bleed ... what caused it?' He searched frantically for the next right thing. 'He doesn't smoke. He never smoked a cigarette in his life, do you know that? He's never been in hospital before. And he's so young.'

Dr Patel nodded understandingly, and forgave the man's use of the present tense, the way he appealed as though the death had been the doctor's decision. 'I understand that this must be very confusing for you. It's obviously very sudden, but it wouldn't have been caused by any lifestyle choices, sir. Please understand me: this was not your son's fault. Or anyone's fault. He's never been an in-patient, as you say. And there's no record of him ever coming in for brain scans, no medical history that would be relevant here, so there's no way he or you could have known that this would happen. I know this must be hard for you, but I hope that can give you some kind of comfort ...'

But Chibuike was silent for a very long time.

'The most likely cause,' said the doctor, 'is a blood vessel malformation that he would have had from birth, but even that—'

'From birth? All this time?'

'It's possible, yes.'

'Why didn't you know?' asked Chibuike. 'Why didn't you know beforehand? Why wasn't something done?'

'We don't routinely scan people for this sort of thing, because the chances are so small. So there was never any reason to suspect that your son was in danger. You'll know as well as I do that he never would have shown any symptoms or warning signs. For all we knew, and for all anyone knew, he was going to live a long and healthy life. I'm so sorry that he didn't.'

Chibuike was well out of the sky now, and alone in deep water. He let himself float for a while. It didn't matter if he was cold.

'So ... so what happened to him? You say he would have had a headache?'

Dr Patel nodded, readier for the fair question. 'Yes, that's right.'

'Like a migraine? He has migraines sometimes. Could the migraine have caused this bleed?'

'No,' said Dr Patel. 'The migraine and the bleed that happened tonight are very different things. The headache caused by this haemorrhage would have been much more severe. It would have been the worst headache he'd ever had.'

'Oh.'

'We call them "thunderclap headaches": the pain would have been sudden, and I'm afraid it would have been extreme.'

'Oh.'

'I suppose it's possible that he mistook it for a bad migraine at first, especially as he would have experienced some similar symptoms, like vomiting. But it's likely that he would have soon realised that something was wrong.'

'Did he call an ambulance?'

'An ambulance was called at about 00:30 this morning. Your son was rushed in as soon as possible and every attempt was made to resuscitate him on arrival, but unfortunately the bleeding was very fast and it spread through the brain very quickly, and there was really nothing more we could do. None of our attempts to revive him were successful. I'm so sorry,

Mr Okoro. Once it starts, this kind of haemorrhage is very difficult to treat.'

Chibuike tried to steady himself. Deep breaths. Big kicks, brave strokes.

'My boy,' said Chibuike. 'He was a good boy. He was good.'

Why must it feel as if Achike was in the room with him? The world had changed and not changed; it was empty, now, yet it felt no different from what it had been this morning. Hope still lingered with Chibuike, as if it didn't know where else to go. It fed dreams to him, telling him Achike might walk through the door now and comfort his poor father, and laugh at the doctor's mistake, and they could both go home. How unfair it was that Chibuike should be left with the least bit of Achike, only the parts he could not see, could not embrace.

'You say he was in a lot of pain?' Chibuike said.

'I'm afraid so.'

'Are you sure? There's no way he might have died before he felt the pain?'

Dr Patel made an uncomfortable face. 'Yes, I'm sorry to say he would have been in a great deal of pain. When this sort of thing happens—'

'So it happens a lot?'

Dr Patel stumbled a little. 'Well, it's not unheard of, no, but your son was of an age where it does sometimes happen, sadly.' He frowned, hearing the inadequacy of his words. Then, as an offering: 'I can give you some things to read, when you've had some time to process all this. You know – websites, leaflets that can explain the research done into the causes of this sort of thing.'

'Yes. Fine.'

'And, although the pain would have been really quite ago-nising, I would hope that it would not have lasted too long.'

Chibuike looked at Dr Patel properly, as he spoke. As though, if the proportions were correct, he might be able to exchange this young doctor for the son he had lost just that morning. Chibuike's grief grew nimble fingers, pulled apart the threads of the universe and rearranged them for him so that, perhaps, yes, he could exchange one young man for the other. And after all, the doctor was about the same age as Achike had been. It seemed unfair, cruelly unfair, that this one should remain while the other was gone. Was there no spirit, no god of his ancestors who might right this wrong?

'And I can put you in touch with grief counsellors, of course. Many families find it beneficial.'

'I just don't understand . . . ' said Chibuike slowly, eventually, 'how something like this can have happened. It's so unfair.'

Dr Patel watched Mr Okoro carefully, but the man did not seem angry. He seemed cheated, yes. Bereft. But it wasn't vengeance he wanted. Only direction.

'Sir,' said Dr Patel, 'I understand that this is terribly difficult for you. Especially if you were very close to your son.'

Chibuike hesitated for a moment, then nodded.

'Are you sure there's nobody else you'd like me to call?' said Dr Patel.

Chibuike shook his head quickly. 'No. Thank you. I . . . Not for now. Can I see him?'

Dr Patel nodded. 'Of course. Although if you'd prefer to wait, we can bring you back tomorrow? When you've had some time?'

'I think I need to see him,' said Chibuike.

Dr Patel nodded. 'Follow me. The bay is just through here.'

The ICU was not far from the Relatives' Room, and Chibuike and the doctor walked through to it. The first thing Chibuike noticed was how small it was – there were only six bays. So few people were this unfortunate. Only six people for miles around needed this much care.

Each bay was closed, some bad luck lurking behind a blue curtain. From one or two, doctors and nurses emerged, walking quickly towards their stations or to other wards or rooms, checking facts and figures with one another in hushed voices.

'Which one is he?' Chibuike asked. Without thinking, he reached for the blue curtain nearest to him, then withdrew his hand quickly. Whatever was behind that curtain might not belong to him. And if he saw even a glimpse of someone else's child, he might not be able to see his own.

'It's this bay, here,' said Dr Patel. He gestured towards the bay at the far end of the ward.

Of course. This was the only silent bay. The machines had all been switched off.

'I must ask you to prepare yourself,' said Dr Patel. 'It won't be an easy sight.'

'I need to see him,' said Chibuike.

'Of course. Please just be prepared. I'm afraid there are still tubes in your son's body.'

'Oh. Okay. Yes.'

'It's from the treatment we gave him. We had to keep it all in, in case we had to do a coroner referral.'

'I understand.' Deep breaths. Head above water. 'It's fine. I understand. Please let me see him.'

The doctor drew back the curtain gently and showed Chibuike his son's body, lying still on the bed. Everything was so quiet, suddenly. No machines monitored Achike now. No nurses checked his pulse. Chibuike nodded sadly, as if confirming what he had hoped he would never know. What should he do with his tears?

'I'll leave you alone,' said Dr Patel. 'I'll be just at the other end of the ward if you need me.' Chibuike did not turn towards the sound of his voice, but heard his footsteps retreating. He closed the blue curtain.

He walked up the bed to Achike's side and held his hand between his own two. It was as though the life was not quite gone from Achike's face; he looked as if he might wake up at any moment. It had been years since Chibuike had watched him sleep and now, looking at Achike's lifeless body, he felt somehow as though he were intruding on his son, seeing a thing a father should not see. He stayed very quiet.

The ventilator tube was strapped to Achike's mouth. Even if he were to wake up, if his eyes were suddenly to start open, made bright and tender by what had happened to his body; even if Chibuike's every wish were to be granted; even if Achike were to be with him again, in the room, only waiting to be taken home safe, there was the ventilator tube. Such things were not for sleeping sons, not without the machine switched on to help them breathe. But there was no need for all that now.

Chibuike had stopped believing in God when he was just a child; his father's death seemed to point to a world beyond fairness and order, beyond praying and hymns. He hid his unbelief from his mother at the time, knowing it would only hurt her more, but it came to him now, his lack of faith. He knew that he was all alone in the room, and the only thing towards which he'd ever raised his eyes was gone. There was no heaven he could see from where he was.

On the way back to the Relatives' Room, the doctor tried to say consoling things. 'The circumstances are nothing short of ... tragic,' he said, after a moment's pause to see if the word was right, if he was entitled to it. 'I mean, this is a rare thing to have happened, and there really was nothing anyone could have done. But at least he wasn't alone when the rupture occurred.'

'What?' Chibuike started.

'I understand someone was with him.'

'Who was with him?' said Chibuike. 'Who was with him?' But he knew. It must have been Ekene. It had always been Ekene.

Ekene had been with Achike in his last moments, but the

gratitude that Chibuike knew he ought to feel was out of reach. He felt jealousy, and spite. Somewhere, Ekene held the memory of his son in his final moments. Somewhere, Ekene had a piece of Achike that Chibuike did not have. Chibuike had clinical notes; he had statistics and a cold hand to hold. It was not enough.

'I was told a Mr Nnamdi came to the hospital to ask about him,' said the doctor, slowly.

'Where is he now?'

'I'm not sure, I'm sorry. We normally don't let people ride with patients in the ambulance unless they're next of kin, so I'm not sure where this person will be now. Not far, probably. I can get someone to check for you, if you'd like to speak to him?'

Chibuike nodded, returning to himself. He found that he wanted to see the building crumble. He wanted to take it apart piece by piece, the whole shambolic pretence at aid.

And yet, he wanted to sit still. He wanted to die. Not loudly, but quietly; he did not want the rush and fever of doctors over him. Chibuike wanted to fade, slowly, away into nothingness. He wanted simply to stop breathing, he wanted to slow, and then stop the organs and mechanisms in his body which kept him breathing, and feel himself return to dust. It was all point-less now. It had all been for nothing.

'I'll see if I can get someone to track him down for you,' said Dr Patel. 'I'm very sorry, sir, I must attend to another patient now.' He paused again, waiting for the anger that surely must come. It did not come. The man seemed to have nothing left in him. 'But you feel free to stay here as long as you need. There's no rush. And if you need anything else, please just step outside and let someone know. There'll be someone here all the time.'

'Okay,' said Chibuike. 'Thank you. Okay.'

'And again, I'm very, very sorry for your loss.'

The doctor stood up and left the room, opening the door briefly but widely and allowing Chibuike to see into the outside world. He cast one sorrowful look at the man before he left, as if Chibuike were to be his patient soon.

Doctors and nurses hurried from place to place, spoke urgently about patients or casually about their plans for life outside of work. Weekends would still come. Phones rang dully or shrilly in the distance. It was all the same now. In the brief moment before the door closed, Chibuike found himself listening out for the happy conversations, only to know that they still existed far from his mind. He wanted to hear what it was like to be unconcerned with death, in that moment. He wanted to know that there was someone nearby who remembered joy.

Dr Patel closed the door, giving Chibuike one last wan smile. He released a heavy breath and then looked up and saw a young man waiting anxiously outside the Relatives' Room. How long had he been there?

'Please,' said the man. 'Was that Achike Okoro's father in there?'

Dr Patel cocked his head to the side. 'What's your name?' he asked.

'Ekene Nnamdi. I spoke to the receptionist. They told me to come here.'

'Yes. Alright. Wait a moment.'

Dr Patel stepped back into the Relatives' Room, and there was a brief pause while the doctor spoke quietly to Chibuike.

Ekene had been reliving the nightmare ever since he'd got to the hospital. His mind played it back and forth, running his hands along the smooth wall of his memory for a chink, a hold. What had happened? There could have been some underlying condition that Achike had never known was there, a monster waiting in the dark ocean of his body, ready to rise up and bring about the end of his little world. And could Ekene have caught such a thing before it struck? He kept thinking that there had to have been a chance, a moment when he should have acted faster. He kept thinking that he should have known that it was no migraine.

Achike had said 'goodnight'. Ekene had that, at least. But everything that happened afterwards seemed to drown out that soft word. He wished he could snatch the moment back, clutch its hem and draw it in, hold it tight this time, before he had to let it go.

Chibuike appeared at the door, shuffling a couple of steps towards Ekene before standing still. Dr Patel walked quietly away.

'Ekene,' said Chibuike. 'Bia ebe a. Come.'

Ekene did as he was told, knowing the news must be bad. Chibuike's voice was raspy, tired. There was a stale smell coming off the old man as Ekene walked past him into the Relatives' Room: the smell of a night without sleep.

Once they were alone in the room together, they both seemed to hesitate. Ekene sat, but Chibuike stood. And Chibuike said something Ekene had never expected him to say.

'I wish my father were here. He would know what to say.'

Ekene blinked and watched him. How bizarre that, at this moment, Chibuike should choose to be vulnerable. How bizarre that Achike's death in the absence of a father – for surely it had been death – should put Chibuike in mind of the absence of his own. Achike had once told Ekene that his grandfather, Chibuike's father, had died in a road accident when Chibuike was very young, and that Chibuike had been raised by a step-father he never spoke about. Chibuike was not young anymore, though, and neither was his grief; his father had been dead for fifty years. Fifty years, and he was still waiting for his old heart to learn to be strong.

But the moment passed, and Chibuike was himself again. Ekene watched as Chibuike's eyes examined him with faint disapproval, clearly taking in his rumpled clothes and trainers, obviously chosen in haste. But Chibuike was no better off. The clothes seemed to hang off him like old skin.

And yet, miracle or sacrilege, they had both survived Achike's death.

'Sir,' Ekene began. But Chibuike held up a hand for silence, for time to compose himself. Chibuike's skin was dry from the disinfectant gel in every doorway, and he rubbed the ashy space between finger and thumb. Beyond, in the waiting room, people came and went, their footsteps dimly audible.

'Ekene,' he said. 'You were with Achike tonight?'

'Yes, sir. I came straight here. They wouldn't let me in the ambulance, but I got a taxi as soon as I could.'

'What caused this?'

'I don't know. Didn't the doctors tell you? Can't you tell me? Can I see him?'

Chibuike seemed to hold the moment in his hands. Was it kindness or cruelty to keep Ekene in suspense this way?

Ekene glimpsed his reflection in the glass of a framed print on the opposite wall. His face was set, but he looked no less fragile for it. He had never thought there was much of the child in him, but now? He was whatever a man was.

Then his eyes met Chibuike's, resting on them for a moment that communicated no understanding, no peace. Instead, his sight roved over Chibuike's face for a trace of the boy he had surely lost. Ekene found it: the way Chibuike pursed his lips when he was nervous, the way his beard seemed to skirt his cheeks as if by design. Maybe it was this that made Ekene stand up and ask what he had not thought, a moment ago, he could dare to ask.

'What happened? Where is Achike? I know he might have . . . I saw him so . . . Please tell me.'

There was no cause for Ekene to hope. And yet he did. He could not defeat it. Hope was still there, in the dark ocean of his body.

'Achike died,' said Chibuike. 'Not long ago.'

Ekene's legs started to give way and he sat down again without thinking. He began to cry, but how he hated crying in public. The box of tissues in the corner was empty – what should he do with his tears? They irked him. He hated that his own self could be so disobedient, that his heart was not his own. Why must he get upset when he'd already known what Chibuike would say? He had seen the life drain out of Achike's face.

Seeing Ekene cry, Chibuike took a step towards him. He was the doctor, now, and he could administer kindness if he chose to. Something in him chose to – perhaps one of the impulses within him that had been operating without his say-so since he got the phone call from the hospital. He told Ekene what he had been told: that there was nothing they could do, that the doctors had tried their best. That Achike's death might have looked innocent when it came. Something told him that a hug was right for this moment, that it was not far off, like the spring, like the new year. But he held back. Instead, he stood close, ready on the periphery of Ekene's distress, holding back its borders.

When Ekene finished crying, Chibuike asked, 'How was he? What was he like before he died? Can you tell me? I know you probably don't want to talk to me.' His voice failed him many times while he spoke. He forced it on. 'But I need to know.'

Unthinkingly, Chibuike put a hand on Ekene's shoulder to steer him towards courage and speech. Ekene, startled at the contact, looked up to see Chibuike's face and judge the intention. But Chibuike only withdrew his hand and shrugged as if asked a question he could not answer.

'We'd been at a wedding in the morning,' said Ekene. 'And we'd had to leave early because ... ' He winced at his guilt. 'Because he was having a migraine.'

'Yes, I know. The doctor told me.'

'He did?'

'He told me that might have happened.' Chibuike heard his own voice: it was bullish, and louder than it needed to be. His voice was surly, suddenly. He did not want it to be. He wanted to know how to be gentle now. He wanted to see a way to being kind.

In the end he'd raised a gentle man, and a loving one. Even if he knew that he had never given Achike those gifts, he'd had them in the end. Only yesterday, he'd begun to hope that his gentle son could raise a kind of gentleness in *him*. Now, without Achike, he must see a way to being kind alone. He sat down a safe distance from Ekene, a couple of seats in between them. By way of encouragement, he said, 'The doctor said something about this kind of bleed being easily mistaken for a migraine.'

Ekene had to know. 'And did the migraine cause it?'

'No,' said Chibuike.

'Are you sure?'

'That's what the doctor said.'

Ekene nodded, and thought through his memory of the night. What came to him was tears, and panic. He tried to remember Achike at his most alive, to recall Achike's dazzling light that seemed to come from nowhere; he could not reach it.

It struck Ekene that he would have hugged anybody else by now. Instead, the two of them sat, separated, as if touching would be unthinkable.

But Ekene thought about it. He could not remember Chibuike ever hugging him. Chibuike was not cold by nature; there was something in him that could not make himself be unkind in a direct sense. But at the same time he struggled with warmth, hesitating and stumbling with it, as if walking on new legs, and Ekene had seen him shrink from it, unfamiliar and daunting. Chibuike kept to himself. He'd had few friendships in his life, and less love. He'd never hug Ekene. He could never do it. Never lay a firm hand on the nape of his neck, and let Ekene feel his tears roll down his face. He could never look Ekene in the eyes, and keep his hand on his shoulder, and say that he, too, had nearly died tonight, hearing the news. Chibuike might know words of comfort, but they would be disjointed and few. If Chibuike expressed love in any form, it was forced from him. If such a thing ever came from Chibuike, it was because he had nothing else to give.

But hadn't he laid a hand on Ekene's shoulder? Ekene began to think again.

'I'm sorry for your loss, sir,' he said. 'He loved you a lot. A lot, sir. I hope you know that.' He looked up at Chibuike to confirm his words and drive them home. But Chibuike only seemed to retreat within himself, as if Ekene had shared a secret Chibuike had no right to know.

'Thank you,' Chibuike said, gruffly. He waited a polite moment, and then said, 'So what happened next? After the migraine started.'

'We didn't know anything was wrong,' Ekene said, after a moment. He felt like a child, as if he were explaining how he and Achike had broken a window playing football. 'He was asleep, and then he woke up in the middle of the night, in terrible pain. He was in so much pain.'

Only yesterday, Ekene had been arguing for Achike to leave Chibuike to himself. It seemed impossible, now, when Ekene felt so weak.

And weakness made him dizzy with ambition, with hope. Having nothing, he wished for everything. He wished to be in his bed, the whole day discarded like a draft no-one need ever see. He wished to have at least warm weather for the hard journey home he now knew he would have to make. And he wished Chibuike could be a kind of father again.

Strange thought, he knew. But Ekene needed this tenderness, the hand on the nape of his neck. There was nothing else left that he wanted.

Chibuike then felt the need to stand up and walk away from Ekene. He went to the opposite end of the room, in front of a poster about a counselling service that his eyes did not see. He thought and thought and thought about what the doctor had said. Nothing they could have done. No way this could have been foreseen.

'It just doesn't make any sense,' he said, his eyes scrunched shut, as though he had caught someone out in a lie. 'Achike was a healthy young man.'

'I know,' said Ekene, not sensing that blame was directed towards him. 'I was there the whole time. I can't understand it. I'd thought—'

Chibuike turned to face him now. 'Perfectly healthy young men don't just drop dead. Perfectly healthy young men don't get taken into hospital and never leave.'

'Actually,' said Ekene, 'they do.' He tried to keep his voice calm. He could see that Chibuike was becoming agitated, even aggressive. But what right did Ekene have to return that aggression? He tried to remind Chibuike of the logic they had been given, the information. He tried to see it as something neutral to hold on to. 'You said it yourself. The doctor told you that sometimes—'

But Chibuike waved this aside. 'I don't care!' He was shouting now. Ordinarily, Ekene hated being shouted at, was the last person to sit quietly and be told off. But this, he recognised, was a father's love. It should have struck no chord with him, there being no echo of a father's love inside him. But that only made the old man's rage all the more difficult to oppose. He did not know this type of love very well. He could barely remember it, and most of the time he tried to pretend it simply did not exist unless, like now, he was forced to confront it. He did not understand its needs, or weaknesses. It spoke, he thought, few words he understood. But he thought he recognised it. He let Chibuike speak.

'I don't care about the doctor,' Chibuike said again. 'Are you telling me that boy –' he pointed towards the door, as though Achike were waiting outside – 'that good, good boy I had, came here and *died*? For no reason?'

Chibuike hated himself in this moment. Who was he? A moment ago he had been kind, he had wanted to shield Ekene, even, from the worst of the grief, and guide him through to the other side. A moment ago, Ekene had raised a good man in him. Hadn't he laid a hand on Ekene's shoulder?

Chibuike had thought he knew the ins and outs of grief. He'd watched his wife die of cancer, years before. This was not that. He had not been *robbed* of Ndidi. They had all known for months that the end was coming. And even before she left him, before the rumours of her chemotherapy, her hair loss, the doctors' appointments, he'd known that his wife, the woman he'd thought he loved, was long gone. As soon as she chose her brother over their son, he knew. There was nothing left.

This was not that. He had been given no warning. This was much more like his father's death: a decree handed down from a god who gave impossible commands and then left his people to perform them. *Lose him. Grieve him. Miss him.* Achike had been alive until the end, had been bright and good until his last day. When Achike came to pick up Chibuike and take him back with him, his words had been firm, but his eyes were soft. Achike had that sense that Chibuike did not have, about how to do such things: knowing he could not argue his father round by brute force, he had pleaded with Chibuike, as though what he wanted was no burden but a gift. *I want to do this for you, Dad. I want us to have this. We can have this.*

It worked.

And that day, Chibuike had listened to his son play the piano for his friend. He'd wanted to join in and hum along to the tune, as if the joy they shared was not such a private thing. But he hadn't, instead listening silently to his son like a memory, or a dream.

Maybe that was the reason he wanted to hurt Ekene. Ekene had been the one who, moments later, hugged Achike so easily, so simply. Chibuike had seen it from his bedroom doorway. It was only a little thing, but Achike had lit up with it. And Ekene did it so easily. As if it cost him nothing. As if all he had to do to love Achike was try.

'You're his father,' said Ekene. 'You know more than I do. They wouldn't tell me. They told you. They wouldn't even let me ride in the ambulance.' He tried to sound gentle, but he felt so weak.

'I don't *care*!' Chibuike barked. 'There *must* have been something. There must have been some reason why he started to feel ill. What do you know? Eh? Tell me what you know!'

There were tears on Chibuike's face, and it struck Ekene that he had never seen a man like Chibuike cry before. He had known men like him. From a young age, he'd sought them out. Staunch men. Stolid men. Gruff men. They knew their own boundaries and they kept them firm. And Ekene liked that. Such men shook hands. They laughed easily enough, but never cried. This – crying – was not what such men did. But Chibuike did it now. He was crying so hard that he could not stand up any longer, almost falling into a seat behind him, his hands raised and cupped in front of his face as though to catch tears from the sky as well as his own.

'Don't do this,' Ekene said. 'He was my ...' He stood up and, when he eventually found the word, he made himself look Chibuike in the eye. 'He was mine, too.'

Chibuike winced as if hurt. 'He wasn't *yours*. You shouldn't have been with him. You shouldn't have been with him, Ekene. You took what was mine.'

'Please, sir,' said Ekene. He had nothing left. 'I know you're upset, but we can just go home and talk. Please. I can't do this now. I can't fight.'

Chibuike shook his head again – another wrong answer – and turned away from Ekene, his head against the wall as he cried. 'Just get out,' he said. '*You*. You took my son away from me.'

Ekene put his hand on the doorknob. He'd really thought for a moment, earlier, that Chibuike might hug him.

'I didn't know what to do.' He tried to hold his voice steady as he spoke, but it would not come out as he wanted it to. 'From the moment it started, I was scared. I was *so scared*. But I did my best. I really did the best I could. I don't know.'

He left the room, and saw in the corner of his eye that Chibuike's face was turned away. When he found his way out of the hospital, it was still dark, but the morning was fast approaching, on its way from somewhere lighter than here. Birds were singing.

He took a taxi home, took a sleeping pill from Achike's medicine cabinet and slept for nine hours. His dreams were intense, and even in the midst of them he could feel the intense weight of his body, a heavy thing now. It felt as if it wanted to press itself deep into the earth.

When he woke up, the world was still the same.

Chibuike stepped out of the Relatives' Room and looked around. The doctor was gone. Without realising it, Chibuike had learned some of the other faces from earlier, in the waiting room; they were gone, too. It was just him now, and people he had never seen. Silent and alone, he was a cold breeze that someone had let in. Had it always been this quiet? Was it quiet, even now? He felt separated from the world of feeling and noise.

Hours had passed. There was nothing keeping him here. The doctor had told his story, and Ekene had told his. Whatever there was for Chibuike to do now, it would be done at home.

But where was home? Was home his son's flat, where there was nothing for him but a son who was nobody's? Or his old flat, where there was nothing for him but an addiction that gripped him like a bad father? He couldn't pay the rent there, anyway.

Chibuike had been asleep on the sofa at noon when Achike let himself into his old flat. He'd woken up to the sound of Achike's boots on the floor and the smell of his cologne, more expensive than anything Chibuike could ever have bought for him. He'd been confused at first, and he was hungover, and it had taken him a moment to put the scent and the man together. So much about Achike was new, these days.

Achike had been working non-stop for weeks and he'd set off for his father's flat as soon as he got back to London, but when Chibuike opened his eyes, his son looked brisk and fresh. In his stupor, Chibuike had wondered if this was Hollywood at work, if someone had taken his child away and made him new, and certain. Today, sober, he wondered again. Achike had pulled Chibuike's arm over his neck and taken him out of the house. He'd been tender, but strong, as if he was rescuing his father from a house on fire. Who'd taught him to do that?

Chibuike had not. He had given Achike the best of himself, such as it was. But, just beneath Achike's skin, there had always lurked an awareness that he needed things that he could never get from Chibuike. The boy had needed a softer man than Chibuike knew how to be, someone other than the father he had.

After he'd found out what Ndidi's brother had done to Achike, Chibuike had dared to hope that there might be some part of his child left untouched. When he realised Achike was gay, his hope ran out. What little love he'd known how to give was withdrawn, or disfigured by his horror. He looked at Achike differently, if at all. Inwardly, he mourned the loss: his perfect child was gone forever. If only he'd known then that it was he, just like Ndidi's brother, who had chased the perfect child away.

Achike had needed a father better than his father. Chibuike knew that now. And Chibuike felt in his heart that Ndidi's brother would never have got to Achike, would never have preyed on him, if Chibuike had not first made Achike vulnerable. Had he given his child a better kind of love.

Chibuike knew what his own father would say, in his place. Chibuike had fed his child. He'd bought school uniform, kept a roof over their heads, disciplined the boy. Chibuike's father had measured out his love in grains of rice.

But was that the extent of love? Was love enough, if there was no tenderness in it? If there was no patience, or faith?

And yet his son had those things in him. Achike had a kind of strength Chibuike could not possess. Achike had rescued his father. He had dragged him from his sleep, out into the bright day.

In the hospital, Chibuike walked towards a nurse, who gave him a number for a taxi company. Even as he dialled, something inside him leaned on his body, pushed it towards something he could drink. He'd been good, with Achike in the house. He'd liked himself a little more. And he knew where drinking would lead him at a time like this, but he couldn't fight it. Achike was not here to save him now.

PART II

If one should bring me this report,
That thou hadst touch'd the land to-day,
And I went down unto the quay,
And found thee lying in the port;

And standing, muffled round with woe,
Should see thy passengers in rank
Come stepping lightly down the plank,
And beckoning unto those they know;

And if along with these should come
The man I held as half-divine;
Should strike a sudden hand in mine,
And ask a thousand things of home;

And I should tell him all my pain,
And how my life had droop'd of late,
And he should sorrow o'er my state
And marvel what possess'd my brain;

And I perceived no touch of change,
No hint of death in all his frame,
But found him all in all the same,
I should not feel it to be strange.

ALFRED, LORD TENNYSON, *In Memoriam A. H. H.*

Chapter 6

'Do you miss him?' Chibuike talks quietly in the kitchen while he makes Ekene's breakfast before he leaves for college. Chibuike toils at the stove, stirring thick porridge, his muscles striving through the difficult thing.

He speaks casually, even brusquely. But Ekene has been in his house for six months. He knows Chibuike now. Chibuike acts gruffly, but this is the way with men. Ekene is still young – only seventeen – but he is learning. This is the way with fathers: they have tough exteriors, only because the insides of them are unbearably tender, like flesh under fingernails. Men are like this.

But Ekene has never seen his father this tender. The tender parts of his father are scant, and they are bounded off and kept for women, other women, always new women. His father guards his heart's good things watchfully with bright eyes, flaming swords. Obiajulu was never meant for children.

Once every couple of years, when Obiajulu and Ekene's mother are arguing too much, or when he grows tired of his own unpromising life, Obiajulu goes out, takes off his wedding ring and meets a woman who becomes his world for a little while. For a little while, Obiajulu stops existing for Ekene, stops paying the household bills, stops making the getting-ready noises each morning in the bathroom while he shaves. When Obiajulu wakes up from each of these reveries – when the women leave him, or when their boyfriends come home, or when the women refuse to run away with him somewhere, or when he realises that each woman is not a dream come true but flesh and blood and needs and questions – he leaves, and comes back to Ekene's mother as quickly and as easily as he left.

Typically, this does not last long, but last year, Ekene's father left Ekene and his mother for three months. Ever since then, Ekene's mother cannot look her only child in the eye, cannot even stand the smell of him, says he smells like something burning, smells like a crime. After those three months, when his father walked through the door as though nothing had happened, Ekene didn't know whose he was.

And then, finally, Ekene's father left and never came back. It has been eight months, and Ekene has been getting into trouble in school, and with the police, and with his mother. His mother has told him that she cannot live with him anymore. He needs to live somewhere else, at least for a while. Ekene pretended not to understand, but he does. Who would want him?

Chibuike's question is still unanswered. Does Ekene miss his father? He does not know what to say. He examines himself closely, but his feelings will not speak to him. His emotions confer amongst themselves: they are noisy and unclear. There is joy there, he knows, and relief, and a feeling of betrayal. But there are also things he does not know, and cannot read. He resents his father deeply. Ekene feels somehow suffocated by the man's absence: he knows without knowing that he will never be able to be a child as long as his father refuses to be a man.

And always there is something else. Underneath the word 'miss' still moves some wild, insubordinate thing that this language can never hold, some monster ready to rise up and usher in a world he cannot comprehend. There is a longing for something in the shape of a father, and for his father to take that shape. But he has never known his father to be this type of man, and therefore cannot miss him. And yet, he does.

'Yes. I miss him, sir.' Ekene feels very exposed when he says this. He wonders if Chibuike will look at him differently, or scoff, or reprimand him for not being a proper man. But Chibuike only nods, as if Ekene has given him the correct answer to something. Ekene's father is a part of Ekene's family, after all, and the rules of family are simple and unbending. So he says, 'But I'm very happy, here.'

Ekene dares to hope.

He has had hope before: his own father knew a kind of love. Once, his father had told him, *You're not like your mother. Your skin's proper dark, like mine, like your granddad's. You're mine, and don't you forget that.* There was a kind of love in this, Ekene thought. Obiajulu loved him. But he could never say it out loud. Or in any other way. He could never check Ekene's homework, or take Ekene to the local library each weekend. He could never talk to Ekene about his dreams, or insist he drop bad habits.

Chibuike is not like Obiajulu. Chibuike has a utilitarian home – there is very little in it that does not serve a purpose – but for the first time Ekene feels that he wants for nothing. He has learned to live within rules. He has felt boundaries hug him tight. He has never had a bedtime before. He has never had a strict ban on fast food. Nobody has ever limited his screen time, or made him floss between his teeth. Nobody has wanted so much of him until now.

People have expected things of Ekene before, of course. At home, he was to be stoic and gruff. He was not to cry, or complain. But otherwise, expectations of Ekene have rarely been firm and they have never been high. He is a clever young man and he knows how to push most people, how to bend them.

But Achike's father does not bend when Ekene pushes; he only remains cool and firm.

Ekene has noticed that there is no alcohol in the house, anywhere he can see. Ekene has also noticed that Chibuike wakes up early and prepares breakfast for the two boys. Plain porridge, in large, plain bowls. Each morning, Ekene eats it uncomplainingly and then goes to school on time, knowing that Chibuike will follow up any complaints he hears from his teachers. There were a few such conversations at first. Ekene pretended he did not like them.

Achike makes more sense to Ekene now. He always thought his friend was a miracle, and there is still something unlikely about him, especially given who his mother was. Achike has a compassion and a companionable quality that nobody has taught him. He is forgiving in a way that was never learned. Achike can be soft, somehow.

But Chibuike put a lot of himself into his son. Achike has his father's self-discipline, his Protestant horror of indulgence. Chibuike's almost military expectations live inside Achike, and they guide him to wash his face with cold water each morning, and to turn out the lights each night at 10:30pm, even when Ekene wants to talk. This is why Achike asks his teachers for extra work and takes such careful notes in class. This is why Achike checks the ingredients on snacks, calmly refusing anything with too much sugar. This is why Achike cannot bear for anything to be too sweet.

This is the best that Chibuike has. He can only give a love that gives no quarter. The rest of it, he does not know. But this is enough. It has to be enough. Achike's mother has been dead for over a year and Chibuike will not permit this loss to erode even an ounce of his son's character. In a few months, when Achike turns eighteen, Chibuike will send him out into the world, and he is certain that Achike will be ready.

Ekene sees this. He sees that there are things in Achike that he was given. And he sees that there are things he himself was not. Sometimes he wonders how things might have been different, if his parents had been different. Or, perhaps, if he had not needed so much from them. It occurs to Ekene that there is a version of himself that someone might see, and feel for. He knows it is possible, even likely, that he cannot be loved. But lately he has been wondering if there is a side of him to which someone might at least respond with some kindness, or pity, or curiosity. Any of which he will accept. He has been dimly aware that such a version of himself exists just beneath his skin, but it has never seen light before. He wonders how long it will last.

There is no uniform at their sixth-form college, but Chibuike insists that the boys both go to school in smart, ironed shirts, formal trousers and polished black shoes. Ekene considers undoing his top button but decides to leave it as it is. At this point, Chibuike still has an African's contempt for the cold British weather and, in a house where almost every other expense is spared, the heating is usually on.

'Achike will be better by this evening,' says Chibuike, calmly. He doesn't even look up from the stove. A microwave would be an indulgence.

'Yes, sir,' says Ekene.

Chibuike switches off the hob and spoons porridge into a bowl for Ekene. 'You don't get these migraines?' he asks.

'No, sir,' says Ekene. And then, because he is grateful that something about him has been noticed, something individual and separate: 'Thank you for asking.'

Chibuike nods softly. 'I remember how afraid Achike was, when he got his first one. He thought that the world was dying.' Something in Chibuike seems to relax as he says this; the telling of the story seems to massage some muscle in him that never stops working. Ekene wonders if Chibuike wishes his son were here, to hear this story. He wishes he could be that son for him. He wants to burrow deep in someone's heart and bring it ease.

'He told me how frightening it was,' Ekene offers, eagerly. 'He told me how, at first, he gets a blind spot, and that there's a bit of his vision where he can't see things. Like a bulb has blown. He told me sometimes it's big enough to cover whole people, even buildings. It sounded scary.'

'The first time,' says Chibuike, 'he couldn't see *me*. He told me I'd disappeared. We had to take him to the doctor, you know. We thought there might be something wrong with his brain.' Ekene waits for the cloud to pass over Chibuike's face, for the warmth to return. 'But, of course, he was fine. His migraines are nothing to worry about, really. I told him not to be afraid. I said, *the world is not dying. You are not dying. Just because you cannot see something, doesn't mean it isn't there.* I don't think he really understood me, then. He was just a little boy, when it first happened.'

Ekene nods and smiles. He is aware that, in a way, Chibuike has just done something quite significant, or given something. He intuits that Chibuike is not often so sincerely himself.

'I was a little hesitant about taking you in at first, Ekene.' These words come out of nowhere, and Ekene freezes in motion, his spoon just touching the surface of the half-solid, half-liquid cereal in front of him. He is reminded that this is not, in fact, his home. He watches Chibuike.

'Many parents would not have done it,' says Chibuike, thoughtfully. He almost sounds a little generous, a little patient, as though he is giving himself a gentle appraisal. 'But I chose to let you into my house. I chose to let you live with my son.'

'Thank you, sir,' says Ekene. But he knows Chibuike is not looking for thanks. That is not the purpose of this conversation.

Chibuike does not acknowledge what Ekene has said. 'I have been watching you, Ekene. You are becoming a much better young man than you were before, are you not?'

'I am, sir,' says Ekene.

Chibuike nods approvingly. 'You are.' He sits down next to Ekene at the table, but does not bring any food for himself. Instead, he looks at Ekene for a long moment and gestures at him to eat. He wants Ekene to have enough food. So simple, but it is a kind of power he has. Men are like this. Men have power; sometimes, they use it to feed you.

Chibuike likes doing this. He enjoys having Ekene stay in his house. The boy's father has never been up to much; the community knows this. Chibuike has heard how Ekene's father left Ekene and his mother for another woman half his age, for three months. Chibuike has heard how, when the younger woman left *him*, he went back to his wife as if nothing had happened. Chibuike has met the man a few times: he does not like him. The man smells like something burning. He smells like a deep injustice.

After a while, Ekene eats, conscious that he needs to leave for college soon. But he wants to tell Chibuike something. He wants to tell Chibuike that he is gay.

He is aware that this might seem absurd. But he has been thinking about this for some time.

He knows who and what Chibuike is. He knows a little about his background, and about his beliefs. He knows that there is a tension between him and Achike. He knows that Achike flinches from his father's touch. He knows that Chibuike has not completely stopped drinking, as he has claimed. He has kept this from Achike. And, most of all, Ekene knows that Chibuike is not his father. He knows this.

But Ekene has never been looked after like this before. And it is doing something to his heart, every time Chibuike checks that Ekene is in bed after lights out, every time he wakes up early to make the boys breakfast. It is doing something to Ekene.

What it does is nothing familiar: he has no desire for Chibuike. He does not want the man's flesh at all.

And yet.

It is almost like falling in love.

Ekene cannot keep it to himself. What if, on the other side of this utterance, lies paradise? Ekene knows who Chibuike is. He labours under no illusions about the man's likely beliefs. He has seen Chibuike say and do things which are far from gentle. He has seen Chibuike lose his temper. He has seen him beat Achike for tiny, inconsequential things. He has seen him take a belt to Achike's back, and he has seen him beat Achike harder when he cries out in pain. He knows that Chibuike suspects Achike is gay, already. He has seen it. And he has seen what happens next.

It could happen to him, too. Or worse, Chibuike could throw him out on the street. He could stop Ekene from ever seeing Achike again. Ekene knows this. Chibuike could beat him unconscious. He could do it.

But what if he doesn't? What if Chibuike sees something in him, bright and strong as a ring on a finger? What if Ekene has something inside him like that? What if he can declare what Achike can only whisper – and what if, instead of shame, Chibuike sees in him courage and light?

What if men can be different?

He needs to know.

So the words rise in him like hope. The words have been waiting in him, just beneath the skin, a monster waiting in the dark ocean of his body.

'I'm gay, sir.'

And Chibuike stares at him, levelly, and then looks away. He gets up and goes to the counter. He slowly stirs the pot of porridge.

There is so much silence.

Ekene wonders if he said anything at all, and what is to be done now. Nobody else has ever done this. Surely, nobody has ever done something like this. There is no way forward now. There is no language for what happens next.

So he repeats himself. 'Sir. I'm gay. And—'

'I heard you,' says Chibuike. His back is still turned. Ekene watches the man take heavy breaths. He watches the heaviness and the breathing move the man's shoulders up and down, up and down. He watches the man hold something in.

Eventually, Chibuike speaks again. 'You don't have to keep saying it. Did you think I would be happy to hear it?'

'I wanted you to see me as I am,' Ekene says, but the words sound stupid and naive, like a thing one would only say to oneself. Was honesty so valuable, in the end? Was closeness such a good thing? He looks around him, conscious that this moment is not the one he imagined, but the one he naively dismissed. He has asked for love, but he sees only trouble.

Chibuike turns around. Has he been crying? He speaks again. 'I brought you into my home. I wanted you to show Achike that this gay thing is not the way. I wanted you to set an example. I thought you could teach one another.'

Did Ekene hear the man's voice crack?

How can all this be? Was Ekene only there to set an example to Achike – to alter him? Ekene can already see that there is almost nothing about Achike that he would alter if he could. He can understand a parent's wishes: if Chibuike had taken him in, for example, because he could offer more self-discipline than Achike, or better manners, or more ambition. But Ekene's heart tells him that Achike has more of every good thing than Ekene has ever seen. If his purpose was to improve Achike, he has been given an impossible task, a pointless task. So he does not feel he has failed. And yet he feels he has failed Chibuike.

'I'm sorry, sir. I didn't mean . . .'

Chibuike waves his wand, dismissing him. Ekene quickly picks up his bag and leaves the house. His porridge is half finished; he cannot tell if he is hungry. He only knows that he is empty.

But he should be empty. He needs to shrink to the size of a

pinprick, if he is to come back to this house. If he is to live here any longer. And he must live here; he has nowhere else to go.

For as long as he is living with Chibuike, this is never spoken of again, and Ekene will always feel that he has lost not one father, but two. There will be distance between them, now, and silence.

Ekene woke up feeling hopeful this morning, but he has learned how quickly things can change, how foolish his instincts have always been. He will look at himself warily now.

When he woke up this morning, he never would have known what Chibuike has shown him, but he knows now. Men are like this. Love is like this.

Chapter 7

Chibuike was perfectly fine.

He liked to pour himself a glass of wine and sit in the living room. He would burrow into the armchair and wait for the electric heater to massage the temperature to something comfortable. It was not a warm flat, but after enough time, he could feel the European air relax its tight shoulders for once, and give in. Things weren't so bad. Did the world outside fall away? Or did it lean in closer, a new friend? He would pour himself a glass of wine and put some music on. Things weren't so bad.

Achike was never home anymore. Why was that? Where had he gone? Sometimes, Chibuike forgot. He liked that.

And Chibuike had the living room to himself. He unfurled in it, like a teenager home alone. The night was his. No sneaking out to the shop and travelling back slowly, his mind slowed down by drinking. No sneaking in like a teenager after his parents had gone to sleep. For one night, there was no guilt, no shame. Such time was so precious. He could put on some music: maybe Sam Cooke, this time, crooning 'Just for You'. He could pour himself a glass of wine, and feel the wine massage his shoulders.

Sometimes, he found himself dancing. He moved the

furniture out of the way and kicked off his shoes. He danced with his eyes closed. He felt the wine burrow into his hips and tuck itself in. He felt the warmth begin its slow journey through his body. He remembered that he knew how to dance, after all. He remembered that his body knew how the music should be felt. He'd forgotten, but his body reminded him. He would twist, shimmy, dodge the chill that was settling on his bones now. He would step, duck, slide through the thicket of himself, in search of joy. Sometimes, he found himself.

He was quick on his feet, this man. Sometimes, Chibuike felt himself electric. On evenings like this, he could move like ball lightning through cold air. Things weren't so bad. His grief was never home on Sunday evenings. It would go out, taking long journeys out of the city and travelling back, slowed down by drinking.

He needed this tonight. Things were not so good. Sometimes, his joy kicked him off like an old shoe. He remembered, then, that Achike had begun his long, slow journey outwards and would never come home. Then, he couldn't move properly, and he would hurt himself and fall over onto something soft. Maybe an armchair. Sometimes he would fall over onto something hard and angular that left the shape of itself in his skin. He was an old man, and he bruised easily now. He wasn't a teenager anymore. But would it be too much to ask that he might ball himself into something soft, and light, and welcome?

Achike would be back. Eventually. Achike would come back to him. Achike would be at the piano and play some music. He would move this cold, cruel sadness out of the way. He would sit at the piano and play one of the songs he played for Ekene, and Chibuike would listen from his little room, and kick his shoes off, and joy would travel back to him slowly, and he would dance, and hear the two of them talking, and not be jealous anymore because his son was home, and Achike would be a teenager again, and Chibuike could start over and make everything right. And his son would come back to him.

And his son would come back to him.

And his son would come back to him.

Chapter 8

His name was not Achike.

That was what Ekene remembered most about the man. That was what he wanted. His name was something else; something ordinary. The man's name was not something precious to him; that was what mattered. Ekene had forgotten it now. As he trudged past the concierge, he made vague efforts to recall it, but it was gone. The name had died on him before he'd even left.

Was it grief? He asked himself the question, like a father coaxing answers out of a child he knows is being bullied. *Did grief do that to you?*

And had grief driven him out into the big, lonely city? Had grief stolen into him, rearranged every atom inside him and magnetised them, pushing him towards the nearest warm, young body? Was that it? That wouldn't be so bad, if it were grief. He had, after all, been laying under a sad blanket, something heavy on his heart, his heart heavy in his chest. Had he tried to shake it off too soon? Had he only been too good, too brave? He had been lying in Achike's bed since he came home from the hospital. He longed to be in someone's arms. Even if it felt like cheating.

He had always thought that grief would be different: that

the entirety of grief would arrive at some later threshold of his life, unfamiliar but recognisable. He had thought he would know how to make room for grief because it would arrive in a definite and immutable shape.

But Ekene himself was new, now, and unused to himself. Grief had burrowed into his heart and made its labour strange. His longing for Achike made each contraction tiring and alien and uncertain. There were moments when he cried miserably for his loss, and moments when he was silent and numb. At times, his entire body knew only Achike's name; other times, like tonight, he had eyes for everything, anything.

The man had been younger than Ekene. He was barely a man – perhaps twenty or so, only an undergraduate. But he looked so jaded. He'd looked almost defensive when Ekene arrived at his door, as though Ekene wore trouble on his face. Ekene had seen the man relax slowly as they sipped wine. He'd seen the young man – Karl, he recalled, finally – begin to smile and flirt and find his place in the strangeness of their meeting. Before Oskar, Ekene had met strangers for sex countless times, and he could see that Karl had not. As Karl poured a second glass of wine, Ekene noticed him convince himself that this was the beginning of something. He knew very well that Karl (surely too old a name for someone so young?) thought that Ekene could be something he had no intention of becoming.

So, then, why did he pretend? Why did he let such a young man, laughing, a little drunk, take him by the hand and lead him into his bedroom? Why did he make love to him – it was love-making for Karl, fucking for Ekene – in his tiny room, photos of university friends pinned to the walls? Why did he laugh at Karl's awkward jokes and pretend not to mind the mess? And kiss Karl tenderly on his little lips as he came inside him? Did he have to do that? Did he have to say a long, slow goodbye, as though, if he saw Karl in the street, he would ever acknowledge him?

Where had all this come from? Was he so alone? Did he have
to make the boy smile, that way? Had he been so desperate
to believe in love that he had given it – or its semblance – to
a stranger, only so he could feel its reflection on his skin, like
moonlight?

Ekene turned the key in the lock and pushed open the front
door to Achike's flat. He braced himself for the silence on the
other side.

It was dark. Karl lived only a few streets away, but Ekene
had walked and walked around afterwards, trying to shake off
what he was feeling. He could hear Chibuike snoring in the
living room, asleep in his chair by the heater. The curtains
were drawn, and streetlights showed him a bottle of wine on
the floor by Chibuike's chair, and an empty glass.

The overhead lights were off. It was cold: the electric heater
was on, and still pumping out heat, but the window was wide
open and winter was here. At the sight of Chibuike with his
arms wrapped around himself protectively in sleep, the blanket
half falling off his legs, Ekene breathed in sharply, then held
his breath as if he could take back the sound. But Chibuike
did not wake up.

Ekene closed his eyes. There was something in him, under
his skin. Was it grief that made him do what he did next?

Chibuike seemed so weak now, so much in need. And Ekene
had not seen his own father in so long, and his own need gave
no quarter.

Still, Chibuike was not Ekene's father. Ekene held himself
back for a moment, sensing himself on the threshold of something unfamiliar and perhaps dangerous. He teetered on it,
uncertain what was best or what was safest.

How to wash away the heart's old habits? He could not see
how. He wanted so much to be free of whatever unfair bond it
was that tied him to Achike, or to his own father, or to Achike's

father. He wanted so much to be free of whatever had made him do his heart's harsh bidding this evening, and was bidding him even now. Silly heart. Maybe it would never learn. He had tried to teach it. He knew how this worked: he had met countless father figures in his life – teachers, mentors, older lovers – and he knew that the thing was to ask for just a little less than you wanted. Just enough to keep the pain at bay, but not enough to cause alarm, never enough to make it known that he could never be satisfied. He had done this before, and he knew the rules.

But he could not obey. Nothing – not old betrayals, not disappointment, not distance or death – would show him some other way, or that now, now, now was the time to let go. His heart was not his own. He was Achike's tonight, more than he had ever been; he was his own father's, even if his own father would never claim him. And if there was a love in him that needed somewhere to settle, he must give it a place to be.

He did it. He pulled the blanket over Chibuike's chest and shut the window. He was careful not to touch the old man himself. He wasn't sure why; there seemed something too intimate about it, without permission.

Really, he thought, he should wake Chibuike and help him to his bed. But that would mean talking, explanations, the desire to help and care spoken aloud. Chibuike might misread the situation, might accuse him of being inappropriate, which perhaps he was. Ekene did not have the words to explain what he was doing; he had only the need to do it, the need for some kind of closeness, for healing, and for things not to be so cold.

He retreated, watching Chibuike sleep as though he were inspecting his handiwork, some new thing he had wrought. He was pleased, in a way he had not expected to be pleased, and in a way he did not remember ever having been before.

He stood by the heater, his hands behind his back as if open for a gift. He waited until the temperature was something he could bear. He watched Chibuike sleeping. He watched Chibuike earnestly, even fervently, as though this hurtful man were his own child. Ekene liked seeing him this way, the man's softness uncovered, like the flesh under fingernails. Ekene needed to see this. His eyes stayed on Chibuike's face as though his dreams were feeding him.

Ekene considered returning to his room, but there would be nobody there. Instead, he eased himself onto the sofa. It was just warm enough for him to drift off in the moonlight.

When Chibuike woke up, the world was still the same. But there were a few cruel moments in which he forgot that it was. The wine was still a thin film between himself and the truth, and while it remained, Achike was with him again, asleep in the next room, quietly breathing.

Then he opened his eyes, and in front of him was not his son, but someone else's. Nobody's.

Ekene's eyes were still closed, but Chibuike started as though a trap had been laid for him. How long had Ekene been there? Had Ekene pulled this blanket over him? Who had given Ekene permission to do something like that? Chibuike recoiled inwardly, but he did not move the blanket. He was still warm underneath it, and from the memory of his father in his dream. He was not ready to let go.

And why should he? His son had died only last night and he could not summon the energy to push away anything that looked like tenderness, like closeness. And here was Ekene, ready to give it, despite his better judgement, despite how much Chibuike had let him down, let everyone down. Could there be more than distance and sex between men? Chibuike was not ready to leave the warmth, yet.

Ekene woke up slowly, turning over in his sleep several times before opening his eyes. When he did, he looked not at Chibuike but straight ahead, at the wall opposite. Chibuike watched the realisation dawn on him, too, that Achike was gone. He watched Ekene lose his son, again. And, almost alien to him, he felt his heart break for Ekene. Was there nothing he could do for the boy? Was there no warm, soft thing he might lay over Ekene, to help him find comfort?

'I'm sorry,' said Ekene. 'I just really needed not to be alone in that room. I couldn't go back there, on the first night afterwards. I'm sure you wish I was anywhere else, but I couldn't do it. I'll get out of your way now.'

'It's fine,' said Chibuike. Most of the kindness had been stifled and strained out of the words before he spoke them, but not all, and it was enough to make Ekene freeze as he was getting up. 'I don't mind.'

'Okay,' said Ekene. He looked at Chibuike for as long as he could bear to, but could not understand him.

'I'm sorry. If I was talking in my sleep, I'm sorry,' Chibuike said, eventually. He fought against the thing fighting his words. He tried. 'I think I was dreaming.' And then he was quiet for a long time, and Ekene watched the dream wash over him again, and he watched Chibuike long for the dream to return.

'What were you dreaming about?' Ekene asked. He hadn't thought how strange it would sound to ask the question. It was a kind of intimacy into which he would only have ventured with Achike.

But Chibuike answered him. 'I was dreaming about my own father. He died a long time ago. But the dream felt very real.'

Chibuike spoke, and it too was a kind of intimacy. He spoke, not because he already knew what to say, or because he was practised in love of any kind. He did not even know that this was love. He did not know its language. His childhood, and his manhood, and the whole wide world fought him as his tongue formed unfamiliar words.

He did not speak because it was easy. He did not love Ekene because it was easy. And while grief untied the strings of his repression, it did not produce what he felt. He loved because, painful as the expression was to him, he could not do otherwise. He loved Ekene because Ekene needed him, and because Ekene, too, had been brave, and lonely. He loved Ekene because the impulse to love was part of something infinite and strong, in the face of which he, only a man, was helpless. He loved Ekene because his child, his only child would never come back to him now, and still he had love inside him, and it must out.

Ekene stared in amazement at the man. Chibuike had been a child, once. It hardly seemed possible. And it seemed even more unlikely that Chibuike would ever admit to such a fact. But Ekene basked in it, like light and heat. And he asked for more.

'What was your father like?' he said.

Chapter 9

In the dream, Chibuike is with his father again.

Chibuike is nine years old when Albert Okoro is run over in the street on the way to a job interview in Onitsha. The driver doesn't even stop to see if Albert will live; he speeds off into the distance, his motor howling in panic as he flees. As the life bleeds out of Albert on a busy street, the last things he sees are a thick cloud of dust, and the hands of kind strangers reaching down to help him. They are too late.

In the years since his father died, Chibuike has dreamed his father's death a thousand times. More. More. He dreams himself into his father's place: he is his father, but also himself. In the dreams, it is not his father but Chibuike who steps out of the car onto a busy road, and he evades oncoming traffic to make it to the other side. It is him in the headlights, this time, and he never dies.

Chibuike gets right what his father could not. Chibuike always jumps out of the way, just in time. He does not abandon his family when they needed him most. He does not leave behind Chibuike's childhood, a fable with no lessons learned.

Chibuike jumps out of the way because that is the right thing to do. He jumps because that is what he must do. He can twist, shimmy, dodge the car that wants to break his bones. He can step, duck, slide through the thicket of traffic and fumes. Sometimes, he jumps on top of the offending driver's car, stamping on the bonnet. Sometimes, he jumps over the car, and lands, cat-like, on his feet. Sometimes, he dances out of the way, laughing with relief as he steps, and twists, and lives.

He always lives.

That is what his father should have done, and night after night Chibuike rewrites history to make his father do the right thing. He wishes it could be enough that he, years too late, has the right thing in his heart.

It is not enough. There is nobody to accept any such exchange, nobody to even the score. His father was dead in a moment and his loss will echo through the rest of Chibuike's life, a wrong note played too loudly and never lived down. There is nobody who can make this right.

Chibuike tries to contain his excitement: as his father dies, he is coming home from school on the last day of the year.

He will tell his parents that he scored full marks in his maths exam. Top of the class! For weeks he has been languishing in fourth, or fifth, while his mother purses her lips and his father shakes his head helplessly as though his son is sweating out a fever. *Fifth?* All this money to send him to a good school, for *fifth?*

Little Chibuike has been studying every night, with his father leaning over him, his eyes fixed on his young son's expression so he might catch any nascent mistake before it is made. Chibuike is young, but he must know bad habits from good. He must work hard. He must learn. He must not answer back.

Chibuike will remember these times, and dream about them often: heat of the lamp on his neck; bright, hazy light on an old desk; rough paper under his pencil. He will remember his father's stiff nod when he gets things right; the blunt instrument of his impatience when Chibuike makes mistakes. He will remember the way his father takes off his work shirt and wears only his vest and smart trousers, as though simply rolling up his sleeves is not enough. He will remember the smell of his father's aftershave, and the musk of his body underneath. He will remember the seriousness on his father's face, towards which he cannot be seen to smile without being admonished for lacking focus. Except every now and then, when things are going well and his father forgets his own rules. Every now and then, he gives Chibuike a wink, gives him bright, hazy light.

Chibuike will remember that Albert Okoro works hard; Chibuike will always remember that. But he is very young, and he has only ever had a dim concept of his father's work at the construction company, and his father rarely talks about his work, in the house. Albert prefers to be with his family when he is at home. He loves to 'bother' his wife, Chibuike's clever, funny mother, while she cooks in the small kitchen with the window open for steam to escape, or to quiz his three daughters on their schoolwork. Chibuike's father insists that Chibuike take turns with his sisters to wash the dishes. He is not a feminist; nor will he allow his son to forego any labour that must be done.

Albert hates laziness. Chibuike remembers that. In his dream, his father's contempt for laziness is an invisible, physical thing that sits on Chibuike's chest. The way his father scorns lined paper for writing out homework, dismissing it as the crutch of the illiterate and insisting that the paper be plain. The way he finds out the hard way of doing things. The way he raises the bar impossibly, unnecessarily high, and insists his children jump, *jump!*

Albert Okoro is proud of his family; Chibuike remembers that. He tries to treat his children as equals, spending no more time with any one child than another. He gives the same brand of school shoes to each child every Christmas.

But he beats Chibuike more.

His sisters do not envy him this; they pity him quietly, when their father is gone, believing Albert is disappointed that his son has not turned out differently, somehow, suspecting that he wants to beat out of Chibuike some perceived trace of inadequacy. This does not stop them reporting him to their father, of course, when they think he deserves a beating.

And how he beats his son. When he purloins food from the kitchen. When one of his sisters complains that he used a swear word in an argument (neglecting to mention that they, too, had used a similar word). One day, when Chibuike was left alone with his sisters while his parents went to see a sick relative, his sister tells his father that Chibuike answered the door to a complete stranger who was delivering newspapers around the neighbourhood. His father looks at him, aghast. As though he, Chibuike, has betrayed him. He looks at him as though he, Chibuike, is the stranger whose very presence threatens the safety of the children. Of his only son. Then, without warning, he takes off his shoe and beats Chibuike until he cries, which he almost never does, knowing how his father refuses to allow any of his children to show such weakness in the face of hardship.

And that is how Chibuike knows he is his father's favourite. It is never spoken, but it is no secret. Chibuike's skin, like his father's, is lighter than the others'. And Chibuike has Albert's father's face; everyone knows it. Chibuike is his father's father, come back again. They do not tolerate traditional Igbo beliefs at the school but, at home, Albert knows who his son is.

Certainly, there are times, under the belt or the quick backhand, when Chibuike thinks that his father hates him. There are times when Chibuike, even as a child, wonders what kind of love this is, a love that hurts so much, so unfairly. As a much older man, he will still wonder.

But, whatever kind of love Chibuike's father has to give, he gives more of it to his son. He beats Chibuike more because he loves him more. He beats Chibuike more because, in his other children (who resemble him less in countenance and character), failure would be a disappointment; in Chibuike, it would mean heartbreak. He makes Chibuike work harder, makes him jump higher. As few excuses as he accepts from his daughters, Albert accepts fewer from his son. They spend long, unforgiving evenings together at the desk, putting numbers together, taking them apart. Learning. Men are like this.

But every so often, if Chibuike looks at his father at the right moment – if he catches him at just the right time – his father smiles. And gives him a wink, just for being himself. Sometimes, this is enough.

And today, it will be worth it when they hear about his score in maths. Top of the class! Chibuike will remember his excitement. Will the school have called home already? He does not know. He has never come first in the class before. Good boy. Stars will shine for him. There will be lights in the sky for him.

He walks through the door and finds his mother weeping, her body leaning heavily against the wall. He has never seen her cry before, but he can see that she is shaking with sadness. He can see that crying just makes you sadder.

He stands at the doorway and calls to her.

'Mama?'

She does not move from her position, but her body heaves as she sobs. She is saying something into the wall, but he cannot hear the words.

'Mama?' he calls again. The thought enters his mind that he should go to her, but he cannot move. He does not know how to do this. Where are his sisters?

Where is his father? He is normally home by now. He left early in the morning, long before his children.

'Where's Daddy?'

At this, his mother's legs give way and she slides slowly down the wall until she lands. The floor stops her. Her head is still turned away from him.

Alarmed, Chibuike runs over to his mother, placing a hand on her shoulder. It occurs to him that he does not know what he should do next, before his mother sweeps him away angrily with her arm. He falls back against the sofa.

'Mama, what's wrong?' he yells. 'What's wrong?'

'Your father has died!' She almost spits this at him. She is impatient with him, as if he should have known, as if his ignorance is a nuisance to her, and so is he. He wonders what she wants, if she does not want him.

After a moment, hearing no reply from him, she turns around to see her son, sitting on the edge of the sofa, frowning and staring out ahead as though trying to make out the figure of someone in the distance.

'Come here, oh, nna,' she says, pulling him into her. 'I'm sorry. I love you.' She rocks him back and forth in her lap, grateful for once that he is no taller than he is, lest she be unable to enfold his sadness in her arms. She is grateful that, for now, he is manageable.

'What happened?' he whispers. He is afraid to ask, and afraid to know. But when his mother does not answer, he asks again.

'There was a car accident,' she says, eventually. Her voice is wet, as though emerging from deep water. She gasps for air between short sentences. Deep breaths. Brave strokes. 'He was hit by a car. This afternoon. Your uncle just rang to tell me. He is at the hospital. There was no time to collect you from school. It had already happened.'

Chibuike only nods, still staring out.

She kisses him again and again, but she is crying as she does so, and her grief is a big and foreign thing that Chibuike cannot know and with which he cannot communicate. It spreads broad wings over him, leaving him in its lasting shadow.

His mother asks herself how she will raise him now. She asks herself how she can be two parents in one, and what her life will look like without her husband. Eventually, she notices that Chibuike is not crying, and she takes his face in her hands, looking into his dry eyes.

'What's wrong with you?' she says. She is angry with him again. 'Did you not hear me say your father died?'

He nods, and tries to make the tears come, but they will not; they are somewhere inside him and will not be summoned. He has never cried in front of other people. He hates it. The indignity. In private he weeps at anything, and his heart runs out into the freedom of it, finally allowed to be himself. But not now. He who has cried at a sad ending to a book, or to a film; he who has run to his room and cried in shock at the ferocity of his father's beatings, the shape of them still in his skin – he cannot cry at the news of his own father's death. He cannot. Not with his mother waiting for him.

But his mother continues to examine his face, growing more and more alarmed. Oddly, it is the recollection of his maths test that makes him cry, in the end. All those hours. There will be no lights in the sky for him. And his father will never know that, finally, Chibuike is good enough after all.

The dream shifts; the memory will not.

In the months that follow, things only get harder. Chibuike knows other people, classmates whose fathers or mothers died in the war, and yet he always imagined loss to be something very different from what it turns out to be. Perhaps his friends never properly shared their experiences with him, or perhaps they possess a strength he does not know, but he feels desperately unprepared for what comes. Grief has burrowed into his heart and made its labour strange.

Grief exists stubbornly, insisting on itself at every moment. His father's absence is water in his lungs, drowning him slowly from the inside and pulling him down to places sunlight cannot reach. It is a long day of work every day, every morning, wearying his body before the day even begins. It is a new country, in which he does not speak the language and cannot read the signs. It becomes, too, a finger on his lips, hushing him when he most wants to cry, to scream injustice, or to ask for help. For as his mother, desperate to pull some grace from the wreck of her husband's death, explains to him, he is the man of the house now. And with that comes certain responsibilities. He nods, pretending to understand.

She also pretends. Terrified that the avalanche of grief will crush her boy as it threatens to crush her, she reaches out a hand and tries to pull out a man. But what emerges is an older child: not grown but elongated. No more ready to be an adult than the night after he heard the news about his father's death, when he woke up screaming from a nightmare that he could not bear to describe to her, however much she pleaded.

Soon, a wealthy, distant relative in Lagos starts to visit them. Uncle Amos is ten years his mother's senior and has no children of his own. He is kind, mild-mannered, successful. He has a sharp glance that never stays too long on anyone.

But Chibuike's mother does not love him. Chibuike can tell. She thanks him politely for his visits but never speaks about him when he is gone. Chibuike cannot understand why she continues to invite him to their home for long, quiet afternoons of stillborn conversation.

But Patricia Okoro's family never wanted her to marry Albert, a man with no money and whose parents had no influence. Her mother and father had ambitions for her that were far beyond this man who was barely on the make. She has not heard from her parents since her hasty marriage to Albert: they sent no word when her children were born, and they did not contact her when her husband died. She has no savings, no inheritance, dropped out of university when she got married. Meanwhile, they must eat. And there are the children's fees to be paid, there is gas to pay for. She must find money for rent, uniforms, books.

After a year, she agrees to marry Amos.

It looks like a miracle. Amos has no children, and no worries about children: he has plenty of money and nobody who needs it from him. This is why he can support Chibuike, his mother and his sisters, willingly paying school fees and moving them all into his home without complaint.

Amos's house dwarfs their father's. Their father's home was modest; Amos's is a beacon of loud, manly success. A tall gate of bland and solid steel belies the property behind it. Guarded around the clock, the front entrance gives way to a long-winded driveway, lined with trees. At the end of this journey is the house itself. An architect's daydream, it is a grand, sprawling construction: several square blocks arranged on top of each other, and never quite falling. Inside, it is stucco walls, open-plan living, tall windows. Amos tries to make the house feel warm for his new family, adding carefully co-ordinated furniture and bright lighting. There is a brand-new wireless in the living room, because he knows Patricia loves to listen to music. He wants to give her some happiness.

He wants the same for her children. Amos is not Chibuike's father; he is gentler. He has a way of being firm, while never raising his hand to a child. He has learned that Chibuike struggles with algebra, and is good at explaining problems and solutions. He speaks plainly and clearly, where Albert got confused and muddled in his sentences, taking his frustrations out on his son. Amos spends long hours at work and comes home tired, but seems to shake this off when he sits with Chibuike at his desk.

Chibuike has never been looked after like this before. And it is doing something to his heart. It does something to him, every time Amos does not raise his voice, or take off his belt for a beating. It does something to him, every time Amos does not seek out the hard way of doing things. It does something to him, every time Amos asks him how he feels about something, where his father would insist he should not feel, but only do. It does something to him, every time Amos jumps to kindness, forgets to insist that Chibuike be better than he can be.

But his kindness confuses Chibuike. And his kindness to Patricia only seems to sting her more. In the midst of all her adversity, perhaps, a little bit of good luck is hard to take. Life, for Uncle Amos, is happy in a way it was for her, once, and never quite will be again.

This is Amos's first marriage, and one for which he has waited several years. Chibuike does not like to dwell on the specifics of how his mother and her new husband might spend their time, but they are not the married couple he expected. Chibuike's view of marriage is hazy, but he imagines that a man who has waited so long would dive into love like teenagers do. Instead, Amos spends all his time at the oil company, preferring not to trouble his wife more than necessary. He occasionally socialises with friends. He likes to throw dinner parties, and encourages his new family to mingle, but does not insist. His mother is not unhappy with their arrangement. Chibuike wonders about this.

Before Amos married Chibuike's mother, he was the only unmarried man of his age Chibuike knew. And he was more than fifty when he did marry. He has had no girlfriends, either, no affairs. There are no other women in his life. Amos has a pristine reputation for respectable behaviour. But quietly, questions have been asked.

He fosters friendships with a few men from the oil company, men from the University of Lagos; with doctors, lawyers, businessmen. Always men. They visit the house for dinner on weekends, spend long hours talking quietly in the lounge. Are these men like Amos? Many of them have wives – Chibuike has seen wedding rings on their fingers. But why do their wives never come with them to the house?

Chibuike wonders about this. He wonders, until he is old enough to understand the secret looks Amos shares with his closest friend from work. Ndubisi.

Ndubisi is always the first one to leave the dinner parties, but he is also always the first to arrive, bearing small gifts of beer or chin chin. Amos always says these gifts are unnecessary, but he graciously and gladly accepts. And Ndubisi, more than anyone else, always makes Chibuike's new step-father sad when he leaves. It is a brief sadness that Amos seems to wear lightly, and only for a moment, but Chibuike has been watching him. Chibuike begins to understand that the only reason Ndubisi leaves first is to keep up appearances. And it works; besides Chibuike himself, nobody seems to notice anything out of the ordinary about the two men.

'Take care, oh,' Amos says, whenever Ndubisi leaves. 'The roads, you know ...' He says similar things to all his guests when they eventually leave – the roads are dangerous, and the police do not make them safer – but the look in his eyes is very different with Ndubisi. Chibuike never saw his father look so softly at his mother. Chibuike never saw a man look at anyone that way, so frustrated but entirely content, wanting everything and nothing more.

Chibuike keeps the secret. He begins to rearrange his understanding of the world around this new information. He begins to listen differently to some of the sermons in church. He asks questions of himself, trying to match up what he has heard about these men with the man he knows. Amos is not like those men, the cruel men, the wicked men, abusers, manipulators, liars. But what kind of man could Amos be, doing what he does, wanting what he wants?

Amos. Even after years of the family living in his home, he only intervenes in disciplinary matters to lend a voice of support to Chibuike's mother. He is both there, and not there, and all the time Chibuike is unable to calm the longing for his father. It is like the heart of a dead thing that will not stop beating; the longing persists, always the same, always saying, *And yet, his father is dead.* And yet, Amos lives.

Chibuike wonders if Amos ever wanted a family life of his own, if he feels any sadness at this half-life with which he has been encumbered. A sense of pity dawns on Chibuike. Could Amos not have remained single all his life? If what Amos wants must remain a secret, how can he live with a family in his home, with eyes on him every hour of every day?

And yet Amos lives. Chibuike wonders what Amos was hoping for when he offered them a home. To be loved? That seemed too much to hope for, certainly from Patricia and her daughters: the women in the family, always close, have only grown closer after Albert's death, like singers humming a tune to share memories of a song, like skin closing around a wound. Chibuike, no longer the man of the house but banished from boyhood, finds himself on the outside of his own family, unsure if he likes himself without his father, or what kind of man he can be for his family, unsure if he is flesh or its injury.

Chibuike wonders if Amos feels the same sense of unbelonging. Chibuike wonders how Amos could hold his body to account from moment to moment. How a man could learn to live like a ghost.

He considers offering this discovery to his sister. One night, perhaps, when the others have gone to bed and she is alone. Amaka is older than him by three years, and in the final year of her school studies. She knows, therefore, things which he might not know. She might look calmly on incomprehensible things. To him, she is still the brave girl who was unafraid of the dark. She is what a woman is to him: she is helpful, or too busy, or too proud.

And what would he say to her? He can't pronounce the word

for what he saw. The language of sin arises first in his mind, but its word will not fit; the act will not submit to the word. *Gay.* It corresponds to what he saw, but underneath the word still moves some wild, insubordinate thing that this language can never hold, some monster ready to rise up and usher in a world he cannot comprehend. There is something miraculous about Amos, and what he feels, and what he does: how miraculous it is to be a man who can touch the periphery of his own loneliness and walk away unburned. To be contained within his house, within his time, within the rules, and yet to be a thing that walls cannot contain, that language will never comprehend.

Chibuike tells his sister nothing.

He is sixteen when Amos catches him sneaking beer out of the fridge.

Chibuike takes great care, making sure to take only a single bottle at a time, and only at dinner parties when his uncle has plenty of friends over. He makes sure to slip each bottle carefully into his backpack before the guests arrive.

And then there is the bottle he takes to impress his girlfriend, Nkeamu. He has planned the whole thing. He slips away from the crowd of students at the school trip to the museum, and the house is empty. For once. His sisters are at school, his step-father is at work, his mother is visiting her friends. How nice it will be, on a quiet day, to share something secret in his room, to do with his hands to Nkeamu what other boys can only do with their eyes. The door of Chibuike's bedroom closes with a soft click, and he brandishes the bottle mischievously, excitedly, its brown glass cool on his skin.

But the reality is not the dream. Nkeamu has never tried beer before and, it turns out, she does not like the taste of it. And while the fear of getting caught excites Chibuike, it puts her off the whole silly thing. She wrinkles her nose at the first taste, wondering what is happening to the quiet, shy boy she thought she liked. She makes an excuse, stands up, smooths down her skirt and leaves. Chibuike is alone.

Would he have got away with something like this when his father was alive? He isn't sure. He never would have thought to try.

But here he is: a truant, a thief. His father would be ashamed. And what has Chibuike gained for this? Nkeamu was uncomfortable from the moment she arrived. Even she knew that he wasn't that sort of boy, not really. She clearly saw that he was not the sort of boy to skip school, to run away from his studies, to steal from his step-father. If even she could see that, why didn't he?

He finishes the bottle of beer by himself, sipping slowly, alternating every sip with water in case the alcohol makes him tipsy for when the others come home. He checks his window every few minutes for a car. He notices nothing, only occasional students coming home from neighbouring schools, their uniforms still pristine after a day of doing what they should.

When he eventually comes back downstairs twenty minutes later, it is not his mother he finds in the kitchen, but his uncle and Ndubisi, home from work early. Two truants, two thieves, stealing the day. The two of them are so deep in conversation that they do not even notice Chibuike at first, lingering on the edge of their desire, afraid to be seen, curious about what it might look like to do successfully what he has so badly failed at with Nkeamu.

Amos and Ndubisi are standing at the counter. Ndubisi has a glass of water in his left hand. His right hand is on the marble work surface, a couple of inches away from Amos's long, clever fingers; he has dry skin that retains little moisture except when, like today, he has taken care to moisturise. Practical hands. Hands for doing and, tonight, for touch.

But their hands do not touch. And it is this safe distance,

this hesitancy, which reminds Chibuike that the two of them are not mere friends.

What is it? They are not like a married couple, that much is clear. Every married man Chibuike knows is *familiar* with his wife. Couples like that can laugh and talk easily, with a hand slapped on the arm at a funny joke, an arm around the waist at a party. It is impossible for Chibuike to imagine his own mother and father as strangers, no matter how much they used to love telling the story of how they met for the first time, she a model student at the University of Ibadan, him asking to borrow her lecture notes, delighted when she consented to sit next to him and show him how to do it for himself, only to realise that his note-taking was as precise and deliberate as everything else about him, including his pick-up line. How many times had they told that story? It was as familiar to their friends as their bodies were to each other.

But as Chibuike loiters at the threshold of the kitchen, his body totally still, he sees that his step-father and Ndubisi are not like his mother and his father had ever been. They are more like him and Nkeamu: playful, afraid, their fear electrifying every gesture and imbuing it with a significance that no long-married couple need ever feel. They themselves are only on the edge; they have never been free to set foot beyond.

Ndubisi is exactly the same height as Amos, and he keeps his eyes firmly on Amos's as he speaks, as though he cannot say what he wants to say with words alone.

'You always look well,' Amos says. 'No matter how much time goes by.'

'It's because I never married,' jokes Ndubisi. It is the same joke they often make, but they are alone now and Ndubisi begins to turn his body away, as though the whole of him is ashamed. But then he seems to think better of it and angles himself towards Amos again. 'It's my freedom that keeps me looking young,' he says, quietly.

Suddenly Amos's face darkens. 'Do you feel free? I haven't felt free for many years.' There is a new sadness in his voice. It's true that both of them are wealthy, established men, and they have retained much of their youth, but their eyes look older. There is a tiredness in them that makes sixteen-year-old Chibuike ache with pity for them. He thinks of Nkeamu, with whom he could at least share some kind of privacy in his room, even if she thought better of it. Nkeamu, with whom he can fall in love on his own terms, even if they do not meet hers, even if the two of them will never meet again. Nkeamu, whom he himself may have failed, but at least she has tried him, tested him. He doubts she will speak to him in school tomorrow, or think of him much afterwards. But he will find another girl and she will, perhaps, allow him to sit next to her, show him how to do things.

To Chibuike, in this moment, it is clear that this is a luxury his uncle cannot afford. Lonely Amos lives a half-life, never quite getting what he wants, unable to really want what he has. Even Chibuike, even this child, can see that his uncle's life is filled with the pain of chances never taken.

But now his step-father has turned his head towards the doorway and is looking at him, astonished and afraid.

'Go,' he says to Ndubisi. Amos does not even look back at his friend. They must have been prepared for this eventuality, for the appearance of some intruder on their talk, because Ndubisi does not appear hurt or angry at Amos's bluntness, but slips outside as quickly as possible, using the patio door to flee into the garden and from there to the road. Chibuike knows Ndubisi is hoping that he did not see his face for long enough to be able to describe it to anyone, that Chibuike does not yet know his name, that Chibuike has never watched them before.

'What are you doing?' says his step-father. His voice is firm. Loud, almost. Chibuike is surprised by the man's authority. What kind of person refuses to be vulnerable? What kind of person, made vulnerable, insists on being strong? Chibuike finds himself respecting Amos for this, but he is in a compromising position and he is afraid. He plays for time.

'What do you mean? I just came down—'

'Gini? You came downstairs? Didn't your mother say you had a school trip today? Where have you been? Answer me, osiso!'

'I was ... I've ...' Chibuike stumbles. He hadn't prepared an excuse. He does not have the years of hiding that made it easy for Ndubisi to perfect his exit, for Uncle Amos to switch from teenaged lover to self-possessed man. And the beer, even diluted with water, makes his brain slow. No wonder he didn't hear Amos's car in the driveway earlier. He remembers that he has not eaten since breakfast.

'Chibuike,' says Uncle Amos firmly. How easily he slips into this role! No children of his own. No real relationship with his cousin's children before Albert died and they moved into his house, and yet he knows exactly what Chibuike needs to hear. He needs intervention. Boundaries. Amos knows what a man can be. 'Chibuike, this is unacceptable. What would your mother say? Can you imagine—' He stops abruptly and Chibuike freezes, knowing things have just got worse.

'What is that I can smell? Is that ... *beer*?' Amos sniffs theatrically and his anger is like a knife, now, whispering through the air before it cuts.

'Chibuike,' he says, the reprehension vibrating through his voice. 'What would your father think?'

But Amos has overplayed his hand now, and Chibuike is suddenly angrier than he has ever been, and angrier than he ever knew he was. 'My father?' he spits. 'My father did not die and leave you in charge. He left and now *nobody* is in charge. Which is why we had to move in here with ... *you*.' He says this '*you*' quietly, implying something much more. It is the same kind of quiet, dangerous meaning with which Ndubisi said the word 'free'.

'Who do you think you are speaking to?' comes the indignant reply. And Amos is reaching for his belt. He is not like Chibuike's father, but he will not be disrespected in his own home. Not without consequence. He pushes Chibuike roughly, and the boy falls to the hard kitchen floor.

And for a moment, Chibuike is stunned. Paralysed. His mother's verbal admonishments notwithstanding, nobody has beaten him since his father was alive. Those nights. Long, thorough beatings that made him question his father's intentions, his very heart, until Albert threw the belt down and wept in the corner of the room, fists pummelling the walls. The thought of Amos doing this, the thought of this interloper presuming to take his father's place, seizes him with an outrage that makes the muscles in his jaw cramp.

Just as Amos wrests his belt free, Chibuike reaches up, grabs hold of the leather strap and yanks it hard. Chibuike is only sixteen and he is not yet very strong, but his strength is enough to pull Amos off balance, bringing him to the floor next to Chibuike. Chibuike springs up as quickly as he can and in his rage he rears his arms upward, not knowing what unthinkable thing he plans to do with the belt until he sees the terror in Amos's eyes.

And he knows why his step-father is afraid. Not because Chibuike could hurt him seriously; Amos was caught off-guard a moment ago, but he knows he is strong enough to fight off a tipsy sixteen-year-old boy. He is afraid because he has never seen Chibuike like this. He has never seen *anyone* like this. Bad enough that his step-son – to whom he offered a home without question or condition, whose school fees he has paid for years without grudging, whose food he has bought – has disobeyed the rules of his house. Bad enough that Chibuike has shown him such unwarranted disrespect.

But for Chibuike, this mild-mannered, wide-eyed, inquisitive boy whom everyone knew to be his father's favourite – even

Amos knew that his difficult cousin loved Chibuike more than his three daughters, all equally deserving – for this child to pounce on his step-father at the moment when he was to instil discipline. For this boy to turn an act of discipline on its head. For this child to unhinge himself in such a way widens Amos's eyes and makes him throw his hands up in horror.

And Chibuike stops, just in time. He is angry, yes, and lost, but he will not beat the man for whom only a moment ago he felt a tender pity. To do such a thing is only a starting point, and Chibuike can see no well-worn path forwards from it.

In the silence that follows, while they both catch their breath, he hears the car doors open and shut, hears his mother and sisters emerge. His sisters are chatting noisily, companionably, and his mother is complaining about the prices, hiked up again.

'Chibuike,' pants Amos, slowly getting up from the floor, one hand still held in front of him as though warding off evil. 'Chibuike, my boy. What are you doing? What have you become? This is not you.'

'I know what you are,' Chibuike says, slowly. For a moment, Amos looks at him questioningly, alarmed. But he soon understands.

Chibuike makes his face twist into an expression of hatred, one he has seen many times before – on the faces of people with whom he has silently argued, on the faces of pastors and priests and headteachers and uncles and aunties. He does not hate this man, but he can imitate the symptoms.

And yet, with the symptoms comes the disease. He feels the hatred infect his heart. He never wanted to feel this way towards Amos. But he feels a part of himself die, all the same.

He speaks again. 'I know what you are.'

'I never did anything,' says Amos, hurriedly, and the words sound wrong from him, this pleading for mercy from a full-grown man, speaking to a child. But he says this. He has to. 'You don't know what you're talking about—'

Chibuike, hearing his mother and sisters get closer, interrupts. 'I know. I *know.*'

The two of them look at each other warily. Chibuike throws his uncle's belt down to the ground.

'And you will not tell me what to do. You will not. You will not tell my mother about today. Not the beer, not ... not this. Understand? Or I will tell everyone about you. Everyone. And you know your life will be over. Even if it's not true, like you say. Your life will be over. You know it.'

'Chibuike! My son,' Amos pleads, despairing. He knows he has lost.

'I'm not your son!' he hisses. 'I'm not your son. My father is dead. He died. He is gone. And you are not him. You will never be him. Dirty faggot. So you ... you keep my secret. And I will keep yours.'

Amos has walked, almost limping, to the other side of the room now, and he is as far away from Chibuike as he can be. Sometimes, distance between men is wise. Amos takes a moment to look at Chibuike one more time, as though imprinting a memory on his mind before the moment disappears. And then he nods, putting his belt on. The front door clicks open and Chibuike's mother hugs him hello, his body oddly stiff and unresponsive as Amos stalks out to the garden, where the air is fresh. He walks for a long time before he can re-enter his home. He needs to be somewhere he can breathe.

Chibuike's relationship with alcohol, badly begun, only deepens. Like Nkeamu, he did not like the taste of beer at first, but he perseveres and a partiality for it arrives unexpectedly, like a baby in a Moses basket. Beer tasted bland to him once, and foreign at the same time. Now it tastes familiar.

Most nights, he drinks a couple of bottles before bed, sometimes only one. It helps him sleep. Then it helps him breathe more easily, then it helps him forget how he feels about himself, and then he cannot do without it, and after all there is nothing to save himself for. He comes to hate alcohol for the things it takes away from him. He comes to hate himself for how easily he gives those things away.

His step-father keeps his secret. At first, Chibuike is afraid that the beer will run out, but it does not. Chibuike is afraid that Amos will tell his mother, but he does not. Chibuike is afraid that Amos will try to talk to him again, but Amos does not. Chibuike is nobody's child now.

And his mother does not know. She senses that something is wrong, but it is like a phantom pain whose source she cannot locate. One morning, Chibuike's eyes are bleary and bloodshot. He does not recognise himself. His one bottle was not enough to get him to sleep, but it is too late for that now. It is time to go to school. At breakfast, his mother narrows her eyes at his.

'What's wrong?'

He starts, as if woken from sleep. 'Nothing, Mama.'

She wavers. This is her boy, after all. His voice sounds recognisable again. Carefree. Not the sullen child she has seen slinking around the house, silent during morning Bible study and mumbling through grace at dinner. She does not hear him laugh so often anymore, and never in front of her.

In a moment he is bright again, smiling and laughing off her concern. She relaxes a little.

But still.

She moderates her question. 'Is something wrong?'

'I'm just tired,' he says, bowing his head into his cereal bowl.

'Are you getting enough sleep?' she asks, running a hand over his cheek.

He shrugs. His heart speaks in a language he does not know, begging him to ask for help.

'I'm fine,' he says. 'I just stayed up too late.'

'Studying?' She offers this excuse and he accepts it. For a

few moments, he is back in the folds of his family, a growing boy, guilty of only minor crimes.

Chibuike soon learns that he has been wrong about alcohol. It is not a tool to be used and then put back when he is finished. It responds. It has a mind and a treacherous heart of its own, becoming reticent and ungiving when he needs it most and making demands of him that he fights to fulfil. The more he uses it, the less it works. The less it works, the more he uses it. And just underneath the surface of his mind is his guilt, like a child in his belly, waking him in the night, kicking at his skin, refusing to be born.

Time goes by, and he is almost eighteen. He could do anything, and go in any direction. His grades have fallen, but not so far that he has no options. He is succeeding, in a sense.

His sisters, all older than him, have finished school and gone to university, Nworah and Ekenma at the University of Ibadan, Amaka in London, although she vows to return to Nigeria when her medical degree is complete. His mother has given up trying to understand him. His step-father has not met his eyes for nearly two years.

Chibuike wonders if Amos will ever see Ndubisi again; he has not been to the house since that day. Chibuike wonders what kind of a man breaks something so fragile apart. He asks himself the question daily, but cannot accept easy answers, cannot bear the difficult truth.

When he announces his intention to study in Manchester, his mother is perplexed. Would it not make sense to study in London, as his sister had done? Both cities are too far away from Lagos, of course, but at least she feels as though she knows the capital through her daughter. Amaka is due to graduate only a year after Chibuike would matriculate, but their mother feels it would be easier to keep an eye on him if he goes to London. She hesitates.

He shows her the prospectus again. He highlights the high

educational standards, the successful track record of research. The opportunities for industry. He looks up at her face as he turns each page, checking to see her reaction, checking to see the worry lift. Was she always this old, and did he not notice? Was her face always this lined? Or have the last few years aged her as they have tried and failed to grow him?

He knows exactly what she wants to hear. It's a smaller city, he says, harder to get lost in. Less intimidating for a young person on his own. And there are still many Nigerians there; he won't feel lonely. And it's not that far from London, he reminds her. He could still visit Amaka whenever he wanted. He wonders if he has always been this manipulative, or if drink or grief have made him so.

His mother gives in to his reasons, but his mind is on something else. He wants to be alone. He wants to be free. Free of his family, and free of his past. Perhaps in a new country, in a city entirely his own, he could make a new mould and pour himself easily into it, emerging, finally, a new man. Perhaps, in a new city, he might not so much need the father he will never see again. Perhaps, in a new city, he might not need to drink. Perhaps he might not feel the weight of his guilt so much. He might be able to move out from underneath it.

His uncle hates him, it is clear. Amos barely participates in the discussion, only making it clear that he will pay Chibuike's university fees when the decision is made. And when it is made, his mother nods. He will go to Manchester.

But Manchester is harder than he imagined.

Chibuike refuses to admit that it is worse, or colder, or lonelier, all of which are true. He refuses to define it by these terms because Manchester is more than these things, more than a city; it is a task. Manchester is a project and he will either succeed or fail. And he is determined not to fail. So he will persevere.

He shares a house in Fallowfield, in the south of the city, with a few other international students. There is not much space and every square inch of the house smells like mould, but he likes his housemates.

They're alright. They all spend most of their days studying, determined to make the most of their time here, but living together means that they can at least avoid the worst of being foreign students in a strange land. They can huddle together in this big, beautiful, lonely city. They are on the same courses as the home students – in the same lecture halls, living in the same part of town, sitting the same exams, jealously hoarding the same library books – but they are miles apart. Chibuike and his housemates linger on the hinterland of the student experience like clouds on the horizon. Cold, unfeeling city.

But there is a girl – a woman. Ndidi is a model student. Nothing appeals to her like the crisp, clean page of a notebook, the date and title underlined. She looks approvingly at each blank page before she begins, before she populates line after line with her neat, careful script.

He looks at her the same way. He watches her satisfaction with her own good work, her hand always up in class, her arm straight and slender. She is correct. Surely, she must study for hours each day in the library. He could watch her study for hours each day.

One day, he asks to borrow her lecture notes on thermodynamics; he needs help, he says, with the transfer of heat from one body to another. He is delighted and surprised when she consents to sit next to him and shows him how to do the work himself.

Together they go over her notes, over things he knows and things he did not realise he had forgotten. That life, for them, will not be the abstract beauty of physics but brute fact: metal, stone, brick. That engineering is maths clenched into a fist, and that Ndidi can pull that fist apart, one finger at a time. That nothing is ever created, and nothing can ever be destroyed.

Ndidi's voice is practical and clean. Chibuike looks at her, and understands things.

He quickly starts seeing her very regularly, almost every day. Ndidi cooks for him: healthy food that reminds him of being back home, and of his parents' marriage. She culls his wardrobe. She makes him take better notes.

Chibuike's love for her is a big thing, and striking. Ndidi is beautiful, of course, from her long legs to her sweet-smelling braids, but there is something else about her. Something else that makes Chibuike keenly aware that he is fortunate to be loved by her. Her love is ungiving. Her love is aloof; it is straight and slender. She is exacting. She pours his cheap-smelling whisky down the sink, will not let him drink during the week, or more than one bottle of beer at weekends. When Chibuike is sullen, she is sharp. When Chibuike fails to mention her to his mother, she begins answering the phone at his house whenever it rings.

But Chibuike likes this. She is the thing that will make him better. Yes. He knows by now that energy cannot be created or destroyed, but it can be changed. What if he can change? What if heat, angry and hurtful, can become light?

And Ndidi is used to men like Chibuike. For as long as she can remember, her mother has been the one to manage her father's emotions, working diligently behind the scenes to keep his anger within manageable bounds, constantly monitoring the pressure he applies to their married life, balancing tension and compression. Ndidi does the same for her brother; he is several years older than her but still unmarried. What Chibuike wants from her, men have wanted for years.

Sometimes, she lightly traces his collarbone with her finger, which makes Chibuike feel weak, and strong at the same time.

With Ndidi, he steps into the shape of a big man. He might be a different man, now, and tower over a woman, and not long for his father to hold him. He likes to watch Ndidi's dark eyes shimmer under lights; in these momenst, he feels an urge to hold her, to envelop her in himself. He likes, in moments like these, to put his arms around her. He likes to hold the woman's slender frame, not knowing that in so doing he is reassuring his own most fearful heart. Not knowing that in holding Ndidi by the waist, he seeks to encircle himself.

After they get married, he almost completely cuts alcohol from his life. He finds he only drinks on special occasions now. He wonders why people bother asking for help with this sort of thing.

'Let's do it,' he says again to Ndidi, after supper one evening. 'We should have a child.'

She wrinkles her nose, unwilling to have this conversation again. She knows what is expected of her as a wife. She knows what marriage is for. They have been married for over a year now. And his mother asks questions on the phone.

But her engineering firm only recently started assigning her interesting jobs, after nearly two years of grunt work. And there is something in Chibuike she does not trust. Why should a man want a child so much? He does not simply want to validate their marriage, and she knows his mother does not like her; Patricia would have mixed feelings about any child of his that Ndidi bore. Ndidi does not understand him.

'I want to wait,' she says, finally.

'For how long?' Chibuike says. 'Why? What are we doing?'

'There's no need to rush, Chibuike,' she says, trying to keep her voice calm and light.

But there is a need, for him. Ndidi is the only family in his life, the only friend he still sees. He doesn't tell his mother or sisters anything, anymore. His old housemates all moved away long ago, to London, or back home, or to other cities to continue their studies. He does not like making new friends. Joining in with things. The indignity.

But where else will his love go? Where will he lay it down? It sits in him like a secret he must tell. It has been burning a hole in him.

And Chibuike has been wrong about women. Ndidi will not have his love. He did not know it before, but he knows it now. Ndidi never changed, the way he thought all women must, eventually. She is no softer or more gentle, now, than she was when they met; she is no less withdrawn. She only confides in her brother. He had thought that she would reveal herself to him, and that underneath her sleek exterior there would be something warmer; that underneath what is correct would be something real. But everything there is to Ndidi is on the outside of her. She has never lied to him, but still he has been wrong about her. The look of slight disappointment in life never left her face, after all. Perhaps, Chibuike thinks, this is because she was somehow wrong about him, too.

He needs a child. He needs more life in the house. If Ndidi bears his child, Chibuike will be able to start again. A crisp, clean page for both of them.

'Please,' he says. 'I want a . . . I want us to be a family.'

She looks at him, slightly disappointed again. 'Are you sure this is what you want? Now?'

'We can take care of the baby now,' he says. 'I make enough money. You won't have to work.'

Ndidi contemplates the idea in silence.

'If not now,' says Chibuike, 'when?'

She cannot answer. She wishes she could.

When Achike is born, Chibuike feels that he has birthed a part of himself into the world. When Achike is born, his cheeks swollen and his hair still wispy, Chibuike spends hours staring at this tiny child who needs him, who can fit in the palms of his hands if he holds them together; he truly believes he can heal himself through the powerful, impracticably large love he has for his child.

But Ndidi does not love the baby like he does. She doesn't know how. She can only be strict, and severe. Sometimes she tries to mimic the kind of tenderness she associates with motherhood: she tries to sing to the boy, but she gives up part-way through, exhausted and confused. Sometimes she looks at the baby and is confused, as if unsure of its correct function. And as Achike gets older, he begins to notice this, too.

Soon, Chibuike wishes he had listened more. Ndidi had never wanted children. Why did he think that he could make her want the child when he was born?

He starts to drink more. He hides his whisky where Ndidi cannot find it, tells her he has late meetings and goes to the pub after work instead. He wonders what his father would do in his place. Would Albert know how to love a child enough for two parents? Would Amos have known? Perhaps. But Chibuike is not his step-father. He does not have Amos's softness and his strictness, his authority and his grace, his tenderness and his perception. Chibuike is thousands of miles away from all that. If he'd had those things in him, perhaps he would have noticed what Ndidi's brother was doing to his son before it was too late. Before all he could do was scramble to repair the damage that had already been done.

'How can you defend that man?' he says to Ndidi. 'You think you can be his mother and not his mother?'

'I want to be his mother and I want to be *his* sister,' she says, raising her voice. She is half railing at him, half pleading. 'I cannot give him up! Will you take away my heart? I cannot give him up!'

'Who?' He puts his hands on her shoulders and tries to search her eyes. 'Which one can you not give up?'

But Ndidi only shakes her head. Chibuike stares at his wife

and tries to find words to show his resolve. He wants Ndidi to see his mind in his face.

She was like this when they met, but surely, underneath this exterior there was not only Ndidi? Surely there was something more than this?

Somewhere in the house, their son is pretending he cannot hear them.

After enough time, Ndidi says, 'You know what happens in prison.'

'What?'

'You know,' she says, more slowly this time, 'what happens to men like that in prison.'

Chibuike knows. He has fantasised about it. He has depended on it. In his mind, he has watched an inmate, trapped, furious, himself broken, do to Ndidi's brother what he himself cannot do without being taken away from his child. His love for his son is burning a hole in him. It needs to be spent, and spent in rage. Chibuike would do this, if he could, if nobody would know. Yes. If he could sink a knife into the man, and pull it out, and watch the blood drip down the blade as the man's breath shuddered out of him.

'Leave him with me,' says Ndidi, 'and I will deal with him.'

'Ndidi, you don't know he won't do it again,' he says. 'To Achike or to another boy. You can't stop him.'

'I can,' she says. 'I will.'

'I can't trust that.'

'Then I can't stay. Do you want that? Divorce?'

'Daddy?' Achike appears at the door, a little frightened. Chibuike thinks to himself, not for the first time, that his son is the most beautiful person in the world. The most beautiful *thing*. He is certain, again, that nothing more beautiful has ever been made or seen. He is struck by the bizarreness of this, by the dumb luck of being given something of such indescribable worth. What are the chances? The universe must be a funny kind of place, if even people like him and Ndidi get someone like this. He wonders how long such good fortune can possibly last.

'You didn't need to tell me this,' Ekene said. He avoided Chibuike's eyes and went over to the electric heater, turning it up and standing in front of it, his back to Achike's father. 'Why did you tell me all this?'

There was so much silence.

Chibuike wondered if he had said anything at all. Nobody else had ever done this. Surely, nobody had ever done something like this. There was no way forward now. There was no language for what happened next.

'Because,' said Chibuike, 'I wanted you to see me as I am.' He got up and poured himself a drink. 'I've come a long way,' he said, and tried to let the alcohol soothe back to sleep the part of his soul that was now wide awake.

Chapter 10

Ekene dreamed no such dreams. That night, after Chibuike's confession, he did not see Achike's face in his sleep, and when he woke up he felt bereft again. Once, he might have woken up to the sound of Achike's music in his ears, perhaps Achike's dear breath on his face as he sang some new or favourite song. Now, he woke up alone, and he only heard the faraway sounds of traffic getting louder.

That night, it was the music he dreamed of; not Achike himself, but Achike's inventions and reinventions on the piano, the things he would play when he returned, a kind of welcome for himself, and for the return of their companionship, which had been away too long. In the way of dreams, the music had no form – Ekene could not remember it in the morning, not even snatches of it – but it was recognisably itself, as clear as a silhouette against the sky. In the dream, Ekene was at the front door of the building when he heard the music and, although he went towards it, he never found it. He chased it through corridors and courtyards, masonry and open air, but he never found it. It retreated in waves, and then reappeared in his mind.

He found he envied Chibuike. While the old man had slept,

his father had come alive again for him, and with him, his own infancy, a time before manhood returning to him like a long-lost child. And how strange the effect on Chibuike was! Even the alcoholism had not aged him that night, or not fully, because Ekene had eyed Chibuike's drowsy face and thought that he seemed as though a child had tiptoed into him, and looked out from his eyes. It was a child that told the stories and was resting now, exhausted by his openness.

Ekene did not know what to do with him. What is to be done with a child who walks in out of nowhere? Ekene only had himself to blame: he had started it. But he had laid the blanket on Chibuike because it was the only thing he could do; he did not know what to do next.

Achike might have known what to do. He had taken Chibuike in, after all. He was the reason his father was here. Achike had seen through Chibuike's protests and his problems, and recognised love on the other side, waiting in its strange shape, its labour strange. Achike could do that sort of thing. Ekene ached for him.

Chibuike was not Ekene's father, nor was he easy to love as a friend. Now, Ekene knew all the things Chibuike had done, and not done. Ekene knew the hearts he had broken. He knew how Chibuike had not seen the abuse until it was too late. How clumsy he had been in the years afterwards, and sometimes cruel. How he had blamed the abuse for Achike being gay. How relieved he seemed that he could rationalise Achike's homosexuality as an after-effect of someone's crime. How, for years, he had looked at Achike like a knot to be untangled or cut loose. How much he had tried to undo his son, shaming him for years, separating him from almost all his friends. Except Ekene, whom he had thought would be different. Ekene, who had been so much the same, so lonely and so lost.

And Chibuike, too, had been taken in by a father figure

afterwards. Chibuike had known frightening loss, and he had known shelter in a new home. And then, not recognising the love of a father in its new form, he had spurned it.

But was this all of Chibuike? Or had there been a time, before his betrayal, when he'd brought Amos a kind of peace? Had there only been distance between them? Or had Chibuike, before he knew how to refuse love, accepted it?

Maybe. Or maybe this, here, now, was Chibuike's chance to do what his heart had been too illiterate to do before. Chibuike could be a kind of father, for a while. What else could energy do, but change? What else became of heat, but the transfer from one body to another that needed it more?

Maybe Ekene had started it. Or maybe Achike had, when he had taken Chibuike into his home, and offered his own career as a sacrifice to save Chibuike's life. Or perhaps Amos had started it, taking in a family that was not his, giving them a home and asking so little in return; only the chance to be invisible, only the chance to gesture towards love, when nobody was looking. Or perhaps Amos had known some kind of shelter himself, in his life before Chibuike. Had somebody taught him a language for love? Or was there something in him – and in everyone – that knew, and needed it, and never quite forgot?

Ekene wondered whom he would shelter, and how it would be possible. He had never wanted children, and he had tried to dissuade Achike from taking in Chibuike. He thought he did not have it in him. If there was anyone who did, it was Achike. And his love, and his insistence on love, were gone forever. If there had ever been an unbroken, unerring line of love and kindness, it was lost, now, through hatred and ignorance and mischance.

Unless the love Achike had known was with Ekene, always. And unless now was the time. Unless Ekene had already begun. Unless – unless Ekene had started it again.

*

Chibuike did not want to drink. It was drunkenness he wanted. Stupor. Drinking was simply the way to oblivion, and Chibuike wanted to be there.

He could not find any more alcohol tonight – Achike had hidden it or poured it away – and Chibuike wanted a super-power, the ability to sense alcohol in any room, inside the house, inside the drains. He wanted to be a radar. He wanted to inhale alcohol and exhale grief and loss, and mess and dif-ficulty and awkwardness and figuring things out and getting things wrong and the crawling through broken glass to get past the thing Ekene had put inside his heart when he'd laid the blanket over him.

He wanted oblivion.

But if he got there, how would he return?

Chibuike had been wrong about alcohol. He had hoped that it would shield him from himself and that, for an evening at least, there would be nothing hiding underneath his rough, unfinished exterior. And it was like that at first. As a teenager, he had been almost small enough for alcohol to hold in its large, adult hands, deft and sure as they seemed to untie the knots of his grief. But he was grown, now, and his griefs had grown with him. His addiction, too, had grown, and alcohol scared him; it demanded too much of him, more than he had to give, and then it took more, and more: his home, his job, his dignity. It made him keep secrets and make painful compromises. When he drank, now, it was not his sadness but he himself that was quietly, steadily being undone.

But where else could he be, but oblivion? His only child was dead, and there was nowhere on earth he could go where sadness would not find him.

Unless it was under Ekene's blanket. He hadn't remem-bered that he could feel so much at peace. He hadn't imagined that he, bad father, bad son, could ever again feel *held*. But to be in receipt of kindness from Ekene that night had put something in between them, something that was not sex, but had pulled them close; something that was not distant, but had let them feel one another's edges, let each man touch the periphery of the other's loneliness and walk away somehow warmed.

Chibuike had gone to his bed; he realised he had left the blanket in the living room. Would Ekene mind if he put it on again? If he drew it over his knees this morning in broad daylight, would it mean too much?

Ekene had got out of bed and quietly gone to the kitchen. There were things to do. There were people to be told about what had happened to Achike.

He sat at Achike's desk and waited for courage to descend on him. It would not. He had known Achike's passwords and unlock codes for years, but he hadn't known it would feel so invasive to do this, that it would feel so much like dressing in Achike's clothes, like wearing his scent. He took deep breaths and tried to ready himself. He picked up Achike's phone and started to look through the contacts.

'Good morning,' said Chibuike, coming into the living room. He was wearing the pyjamas Achike had bought him when he moved in, and the tags were still on; he must have changed into them just before getting into bed. Maybe he had hoped for Achike's scent on them, too, and cried when he found only the sterile smell of the department store.

'Good morning, sir,' said Ekene.

Chibuike took a moment for his eyes to adjust to the light in the room, and then his eyes lighted on last night's blanket. He pulled it from the armchair where he had left it and draped it around his shoulders.

'This flat is cold,' he murmured, by way of explanation. Ekene nodded but said nothing, watching for what would happen next.

Chibuike saw the phone in Ekene's hand. He looked confused. 'What are you doing with that?' he said.

'We need to call people,' Ekene said, his voice helpless. He gestured around as if at a mess. 'We haven't told anyone yet. People will need to know.'

'You want to do it?'

'No, of course not. But I have to.'

But Chibuike shook his head. 'I'll call them.'

'I can do it,' said Ekene, trying to be firm. 'I can call people and let them know. I was with him.'

Chibuike saw how Ekene's sharp glance avoided him and everything else in the room. He saw, again, how hard Ekene tried. He saw some of his own father's discipline in the man, the way he found the hard way of doing things, the way he hated laziness. He knew it was an invisible, physical thing that sat, heavy on Ekene's heart. And he took the phone out of Ekene's hand.

'Ngwa, I will do it,' he said, calmly. 'He was my son.'

'Sir ...' Ekene struggled to find polite words to express Chibuike's presumed incapacity, and the horror of his relatives hearing his voice on the phone, slurred, exhausted, then impatient, then gone. 'I just think it might be better if I did it,' he said.

'I'm not drunk,' said Chibuike, tersely. 'And this is not for you to do. Nobody gave that burden to you.'

'Sir,' said Ekene. 'Are you sure you wouldn't rather I did it? Really, I don't mind. And you must be – tired, sir ... '

Chibuike closed his eyes suddenly and clenched his jaw, and for a moment he looked as if he was trying to resist some violent impulse, as if he might raise a hand to Ekene.

'Biko, give me something,' said Chibuike. 'Give me something to do.' He did not shout, but the words came out of him like a strong wave that could break anything in its way.

'Sir,' said Ekene, 'there are other things, easier things.' He eyed Chibuike as if he were a tottering child who sought to hold a newborn, a fragile new life in his hands.

'Give me something to *do*,' said Chibuike again. Was he about to cry? He still could not open his eyes, and he leaned over onto the table as if he could not hold himself up any longer, as if he had been running for a long time and was exhausted. 'I can't do anything,' he said. 'When I think, I think of him. When I eat, I remember he is dead. When I sleep, I dream of him. And I don't want to drink. I need to do something. Ekene, I need to do something simple and good.' And then he opened his eyes, and Ekene saw that this was no child, but a man only half made. Ekene could not imagine anything more frightening: a man like this, unable to fathom his own vulnerability, almost afraid to look at himself. But what did Ekene know of fatherhood? What did he know of what was owed to Chibuike, and what had been denied already? What silent, outraged things inside Chibuike might explode if Ekene intervened now? He was unsure that Chibuike even deserved the right to do this, but he had nothing left with which to bar his way. Though he tried to make himself object, his shoulders only sagged helplessly. Ekene was nobody's father. He could not do this.

He put the phone into Chibuike's hands, and stepped away. When he sat down again, he saw that even this, the relinquishing of something, had exhausted him utterly.

Chibuike took the phone, looking at it with an odd reverence, and a gentleness. He had told the truth: there was nothing else he could do. Sleep did not evade him entirely, but it taunted him and left him exhausted and his dreams confused him. Guilt spoiled everything else.

But there was something more. When Ekene had pulled the blanket over him, it had begun to occur to Chibuike that there was a version of himself that someone might see and feel for. He knew it was not possible that he could be loved.

But that morning, he had been wondering if there was a side of him that someone might at least treat with some kindness, or pity, or curiosity. Any of which he would accept. He was dimly aware that such a version of himself existed, but it had been so long since it had seen light. He wondered how long he could make it last.

Chapter 11

It was lunchtime. They should be eating, Chibuike thought, but he knew that they could not move on until they had done this. Achike's phone's screen had dimmed and switched off four times now. Ekene had told him the unlock code; Chibuike had pursed his lips when he realised Ekene knew another thing that he did not. But he'd said nothing. There was a more important thing to do.

But his hands would not move. He did what he could, holding the phone, trying to imagine what he would say, and how he would say it. Sometimes, he remembered to breathe. He tried to prepare himself. He tried to summon a kind of strength that would support the utterance of the words again. Chibuike wished his father were here, to make him do the difficult thing; he was glad his mother was no longer alive to see him attempt it, and fail.

He tried to imagine himself as the kind of man who could tell his sisters the news, and hear the shock, and stomach the disbelief, and be the kind of man who was sturdy and strong, the kind of man on whom people could depend.

He looked again at the phone in his hands. He imagined the way his sister Amaka would react, the silence on the other end of the line and the suspicion behind it. He imagined her breath stopping for a moment as she forced herself not to ask if Achike's death was, in some way, her brother's fault. And if she asked, how could he say no? Would Achike have died if his father had been closer to him? Dr Patel had said what he had said, but still Chibuike wondered if a better father might have noticed some stray sign in time, the too-slow blink of an eye, or a loss of appetite, or some other echo of the body's quiet cry. It might have been kindness that made the doctor say there was nothing he could have done. And if Achike had to die, did he have to have died almost alone, almost fatherless? Ekene's good heart could not have been enough; he was only the same age as Achike, and young, frightened, helpless. Achike deserved someone who could do more than approximate the role of fatherhood.

Chibuike looked up and saw Ekene watching him, and waiting. Neither one of them felt able to make this first call, make Achike's death seem real again. They had been granted a reprieve for a night, in which they were distracted by one another's kindness; Chibuike was not ready for it to end, and he could see that Ekene was the same. Ekene looked so tired. He could not do this. He was only young, really. He was only another heart Chibuike had helped to break. What sustained him? Who was to say that Ekene would be able to accomplish by himself what Chibuike still hesitated to do?

Chibuike knew that he was not this man's father. But who else was? It would not be enough to step aside, or throw up his hands, knowing he was weak, a failure. It would not be enough for Ekene, and could no longer be enough for him. There must be a part of Chibuike that could resist grief, could insist it hold itself upright and refuse to fail.

Ekene unlocked the phone again and Chibuike shrugged off his offer of help, and when Chibuike dialled the first number and waited for the voice on the other end to sound its last happy hello for the day, it was not because he felt suddenly brave, or capable. It was because, as helpless as Ekene had been last night when he saw Chibuike sleeping in the cold room, Chibuike was just as helpless now. He had no choice. Nothing – not old betrayals, not disappointment, not distance or death – would show his heart some other way, because now, now, now was the time to embrace, to pull the needful man closer and give him shelter. He had failed his own son too many times, and hurt him too deeply. Here was someone's son who could not be failed again. Whatever had made him do his heart's harsh bidding – whatever had made him cry, or confess, or want to clasp his arms around another – he must listen to it. And if there was a love in him that needed somewhere to settle, he must let it. That was all there was.

His sister, Amaka, answered the phone. For the first few moments, she was only happy to hear from him again, after so long. And then Chibuike opened his mouth, and did the brave and difficult thing, and spoke.

Even as Chibuike dialled number after number; even as he repeated the news to each new relative and, through repetition, found his wording waiting for him, readier and firmer each time; even as Ekene reached over to dry Chibuike's tears when someone's shock touched Chibuike's own and words did not hold him up – even then, it was so hard for Ekene to really believe that his friend had died. It did not seem possible that Achike was gone.

But if he was not gone, where was he? Not here, in this flat, where he was too much missed. Not in the coffin his father would pick out for him. Ekene pitied Chibuike, but he was under no illusions about the man's capacity to plan a funeral. Ekene knew exactly the kind of thing it would be: a sermon from a well-worn priest to take up the time, the usual hymns, the usual flowers. That wasn't Achike. Achike would not be there.

Ekene wanted to think of Achike in heaven, where he should be. Ekene had never spent much time thinking about life after death, because he did not really believe in it. But he wanted to believe now.

He did not ask for much: he did not ask for angels, or Eden. None of that. He dared not imagine Achike enveloped into the arms of any God he recognised, because that would have been too much. It would have been too much to ask for Achike to be welcomed home by his grandparents, by ancestors who had watched him struggle through his short life until it ended. Too much, for Achike to be given some second chance at happiness on earth, as in the film he had barely finished making when he died. Far too much, to ask that his friend be granted another life.

So Ekene asked for less. He imagined something more nebulous. Something harder to imagine would, he reasoned, be harder to pierce with logic and disbelief. He wanted something safe from his own cynicism, something he could carry with him, at least until he felt stronger.

For Achike, he imagined a heaven full of things that he himself could understand; things he had known, but nothing tangible. Good things. Safety. Peace. Wholeness. There would be no sorrow, no disappointment. Time would have no meaning. There would be no hurrying for things, and nothing would ever come too soon, and nothing would ever come too late.

Ekene woke from his reverie to find that Chibuike was still there, and still doing the difficult work for which he, Ekene, could not find courage and strength. What was happening to Chibuike? Ekene could not see how it was possible that Chibuike had so much goodness inside him, when he had never seen it in him before. Or how Chibuike was able to show it now. Ekene remembered again the ways in which Achike had sought shelter from Chibuike: with Ekene, in their relationship; with Julian, the father figure.

Julian. Ekene had forgotten about him, and he felt ashamed. Julian had guided Achike, steered him towards things that were good for him, pushed him through things that were difficult for him, protected him from those who would seek to harm him. He had tutored Achike like a son. He had seen a shining future for him, convinced others to do the same. He had plans for Achike. Julian had never lied to him. Julian had been the most consistent presence in Achike's life. Perhaps the best.

Ekene opened up Achike's laptop, and found his contacts. Still there was an impulse within him to call out for his friend, to reach across whatever space divided them and tell him to come home. But already Ekene was learning to take deep breaths, brave strokes, keep his head above water. Even now, he was learning what Achike's absence really was. It was the silence that surrounds music. It was the suspense before the arrival of the first note that never comes, and the memory of what had been heard when the last piano string still vibrated; it was a story that nobody else would ever quite appreciate.

He checked the number again, and dialled.

'Hello?' No secretary, no intern; this was the direct line to Julian. His voice was naturally quite soft, but Ekene heard the edge of steel in it that Achike had always described, the sharpness that cut through directors' scepticism or producers' indolence of mind. His crisp pronunciation made his words spread out and take up space, but also incised them carefully, each one like a carefully prepared piece of paper cut precisely for its purpose.

'Julian?' Ekene said.

'Hello, Achike,' said Julian. Ekene's and Achike's voices had always been similar, both soft but definite. When Julian pronounced Achike's name correctly, fluently, Ekene was surprised, and a little possessive. 'I don't recognise this number – did you finally get a new phone? I'll have to update the system. How's Peckham?' Julian paused here, as if what he said next must be said, even though it would break some unspoken rule. 'And when are you coming to see me, Achike?'

And then Ekene knew. The knowledge arrived like a guest, almost expected. He knew that Julian had loved Achike. And that Achike, somehow, had let him.

He swallowed hard.

'No, Julian. I'm Ekene. I'm his—'

'Oh, yes,' said Julian. 'He told me about you.' And then Julian saw that something was wrong – he had never spoken to Ekene before – and his voice left behind its brighter notes and changed. 'Did something happen?'

'I'm very sorry,' Ekene said. He made himself be gentle; Achike, whatever else he had been to Julian, had also been a kind of surrogate child. A ward. Ekene had not thought, till now, that love could mix with love in this way. But the change in Julian's voice told him this. 'I'm so sorry to have to tell you that Achike has died.'

'What? When?' Julian was made a child, then, the protest in his voice like that of a child who has watched the unthinkable happen and insists he can undo it if the will is there.

'A couple of nights ago. Well, it was very early in the morning. He had a brain haemorrhage,' Ekene explained. 'Nobody saw it coming. We got to the hospital as soon as we could, but they couldn't save him. I'm very sorry.'

'Oh my goodness,' said Julian, and everything that was his – ambition, privilege, accomplishment, impatience, hope – buckled. And crumbled into a desperate, whispered sob.

Some time passed before Julian spoke again. Until then, his presence was detectable only through his unsteady breaths, in and out, on the other end of the line. Other people might have done something to keep the silence at bay, perhaps sigh through the phone, or ask to be excused while they took a little time. Julian only stayed on, his breathing returning to normal over the course of a minute or so.

'He didn't make it?' Julian asked, when he was ready. He sounded almost out of breath, exhausted, and wronged.

'No,' said Ekene.

'A brain haemorrhage,' said Julian. 'What a terrible way to die. Just terrible. You say nobody saw it coming? Or should we . . . should I have known? Were there any symptoms before it happened?'

'No,' said Ekene. 'The doctors say there's nothing anyone could have done. Actually, we both thought it was something else, at first. We thought it was a migraine.'

'Oh dear. Yes, I remember he had those. Debilitating things. I was amazed how well he coped with them.'

'Yes.'

'Agonising. Hours at a time,' said Julian. 'But he always was brave.'

'Yes.'

'So I imagine he'll have been in a lot of pain?'

'I'm afraid he was,' said Ekene.

'And was he alone? I hope he wasn't alone, when he died?'

'The doctors were with him at the end, of course. They wouldn't let me go with him in the ambulance, but I was with him when it started.'

'I see. Well. My father, last year – heart attack took him, he was home, all alone when he died. I wouldn't wish that on anyone.'

'Yes,' said Ekene, feeling helpless now.

And then Julian took a breath and said, as if it were almost too much effort, 'I'm glad Achike had you, even if you couldn't go with him to the hospital.'

Did he know that Ekene knew about him and Achike? Did he consider the two of them rivals, once for Achike, and now for his legacy? Or was Julian mourning, knowing that Achike could never truly be anyone's but Ekene's?

'Thank you,' said Ekene. 'I wish there was more I could have done.'

'When's the funeral? Do you know?'

'No, we're still contacting family. I guess it'll be sometime next week. I'll have to speak to Achike's dad, but I'm sure he'll send you an invitation. Unless it's just close family. You know.'

'Of course, of course. But if it's okay, I would like to come to the funeral,' said Julian. 'And I'd like to meet his father. He spoke a lot about his father.'

'He did?' said Ekene, surprised. He had thought Achike had been building for himself a glittering fortress with Julian, forbidding all thoughts of sadness or want. He had not imagined Achike would invite even a memory of Chibuike inside.

'Yes, from time to time,' said Julian, thoughtfully. 'He was hoping that his father would be prouder of him than he was, I think. The film will be beautiful and he acted very well in it, but of course his father's not seen it yet, and I don't think the mythological element in it pleased him. Achike seemed to think his father looked down on the whole thing, thought that Achike was portraying Africans as pre-Christian primitives. I don't think his father got the hopeful message of it, at all.'

'I've never heard his dad speak about it,' said Ekene, bewildered. How much did Julian know?

'Nor I, to be fair. But I think Achike was very sad about their relationship in general. Then again, I've been given to understand that African men are not often terribly friendly towards homosexuals.'

He paused, waited for Ekene to either correct the assertion or elaborate on it. Ekene did neither, thinking only of the hours the two of them must have spent together, Achike trying to breathe easily in Julian's clumsy, earnest presence; Julian never finding the right thing, the convincing thing to say; neither one ever able to give the other quite enough.

'He and Hollywood have that in common,' Julian continued. 'It's why Achike was ready to go back in the closet when his work demanded it. When I demanded it. Even though there were rumours. Even though it cost him a lot, personally. I know it did. I always thought – well, I always sort of assumed his history with his father was the reason he was so good at pretending. Acting. But you'll know all this, won't you? Will you be speaking at the funeral?'

'What?' Julian's question seemed to have come out of nowhere. Ekene wondered if he did this sort of thing on purpose, at work, to shock people into the truth.

'I just assumed,' said Julian. 'Given how close you were. Achike didn't have a lot of very close friends. And he couldn't have boyfriends in his line of work, of course. Not openly, at least. I just thought you might say something at the funeral. I think it would be rather nice if you did, but of course it's not up to me. And you're still in the process of arranging all that, you say?'

'Yes,' said Ekene, caught off-guard again. How clumsy was Julian, after all? Ekene tried to sound knowledgeable, authoritative. 'Me and his dad. We're sorting it all out. I'll have to speak to him ...'

'Of course. Of course. Well.' Julian breathed softly again. Almost audibly, he decided to let the matter rest. Ekene thought he must be considering his next move. He was. 'I had better not take up any more of your time. I'll draft a statement for the press and send it to the family for approval.'

'The press?'

'People will want to know,' said Julian, gently, wryly, tiredly, 'that a promising young actor will no longer make good on his promises. I shall draft a statement. If the family doesn't like it, I can tweak it, of course, but it won't be anything sensational or out of the ordinary. I'm sure you can guess the kind of thing I might say.'

'Yes,' said Ekene. He gave Julian his email address, for the statement.

'And I'll keep his secrets.'

'Yes.'

'And the production company will want to know, so they can prepare a statement of their own. I'll tell them.' Julian sighed. 'Right. Well. I had better be getting on with it, I think. Thank you for ringing.'

'You're welcome,' Ekene said.

'I appreciate you letting me know,' Julian said. 'And I'm sorry for your loss. You must be taking this very hard. I hope you've got people around you who can help you.'

'I ...' Ekene didn't know what to say. Who did he have around him? A drunk? A patient? A friend? A father? 'Well. Thank you.'

'Alright. Goodbye, Ekene.'

'Goodbye.'

He was gone. The phone bleeped its indifferent dialling tone, and Ekene set it down.

Alone again, Ekene sat in silence and reflected. Who knew what the two of them had had together? Ekene could not believe that Achike had found any true thing with this man, but who could say that he had not been happy in the lee of his love? Julian might have been the one who sustained Achike through the trials of his Hollywood life. Nobody else could have understood Achike's work the way Julian could.

But Ekene could not let his resentment subside. Something burned in him still. He tried to think what the nature of Julian's interest in Achike had been. How real was his love? How pure? Was there some other young client he would turn to now? Even if there were not, even if Julian knew that Achike was one of a kind, was Julian, like Achike himself, drawn helplessly towards anyone who could approximate satisfaction?

Worst of all was the realisation that Achike had lied to him, even if only by omission. He had never said how Julian really felt. That Julian had loved him all along. That this was what had made them so close. That this was the nature of the shelter Julian was able to give.

You shouldn't live in Peckham much longer. I need you here.

You need a building with real security. I'll sleep better if I know you're safe.

You should be in Notting Hill. With me. Stay with me.

Chapter 12

'It's a lot to take in, I know. It always seems a very daunting task, Mr Okoro,' said the assistant from the funeral home. 'But I want to reassure you: it can be done and it will be done. Once everything is arranged as your son would have wanted, you'll see it and you'll feel much better. I can say this from personal experience, sadly. If you're ever unsure, just try to think about what your son would have liked. Try to imagine what he'd choose for himself. That's what helped me. I know there are lots of decisions to make . . .'

Decisions. Achike had never expressed any preferences about which music he would want played, and if he cared whether it were played live or on a stereo. Did he like the organ? Chibuike didn't know. He had never said how he felt about roses. Or discussed a strong affinity for one colour over another. Or had he? He had never told his father whether he wanted a traditional funeral service, or a celebration of life instead. Had he?

'Now, can I ask,' said the assistant, 'is there anyone who can help you with the funeral arrangements?'

Ekene walked into the room. His eyes were red and teary. Why was it that crying, something which had brought him relief, left him looking so sore? Ekene avoided Chibuike's gaze, but he nodded curtly to indicate a difficult job done: Julian had been informed. Ekene pulled out a chair and sat down heavily at the dining table. He put his head in his hands.

'Er, I don't know. It's complicated,' said Chibuike into the phone. 'Maybe. But I don't want ... Do I really need someone to help me? There must be people who do this by themselves, when they have to.'

'Do *you* have to?'

Her question was asked innocently, but Chibuike heard it as an accusation.

'I need to call you back. There's something I need to do. Can I call you back later?'

'Of course. You just dial the same number, and my extension is 46. Okay?' So much concern for him in her voice, all over an extension. Did she think he was deaf? Did she know he was weak?

'Okay. Thank you. Goodbye.'

'Goodb—'

Ekene looked up, tired. 'Was that the funeral home?'

Chibuike nodded. There were questions he needed to ask.

Ekene took a bottle of beer from the fridge. It was not yet time for lunch. He opened the bottle, hesitated, drank. 'What did they say? Do you have a date for the funeral? Is it sorted? We should plan ... '

There were questions Chibuike needed to ask, which only Ekene could answer. Chibuike did not know his son. Achike's favourite music could be anything. An improvisation, perhaps. Who was that singer he liked? Or it could be something Achike had listened to on the way back from yet another place that wasn't home, something that would make everyone think of fresh air and cool evenings after long, hot days. Or a piece of Achike's own composition?

Ekene would know. Chibuike should ask. With his help,

Chibuike might get it right. And it was more than getting it right, more than simply clicking the right things into place: the right funeral, properly arranged, organised, all done well, could recall Achike once more before his long journey onwards. If Chibuike could choose as his son might choose, he could bring his son home to him, if only for one rainy afternoon.

He should ask Ekene.

And Chibuike wanted to ask him. But, despite the fact that Ekene was not far off forty, Chibuike had a father's sight of him, unable to move on from the youngest he'd known him. The man was an illusion; the boy had never tiptoed out, and one did not burden children with such things. He wished only to be a comfort, to sit in a warm room with Ekene and massage the boy's grief into something he could bear.

Would this cross a line? He thought so. But he was almost at the line, and if it could not be crossed, how could he retreat?

There was love in him that needed a place to settle. If Ekene had been a woman, it might have been lust, which was easier to dispel. Chibuike might have fantasised about her body. If Ekene had been female, Chibuike might have taken thoughts of her to bed and lain with them, touching himself to satisfaction. And then he might have rested.

Yes, lust would have been easier. Lust had things to do. Even after Ndidi left, even after she died, Chibuike would masturbate to thoughts of her body beneath his, her taut and clever muscles working while he worked, and worked, and then gave in. He thought of her still, and thoughts of her interrupted his daily life at unexpected moments. The oddest things reminded him of the way she smelled, or the feeling of her mouth on his skin. His lust for his wife had outlived both his love for her and Ndidi herself. It lived, and it pleaded with him. And then he dismissed it, and it was gone.

But this was not that. Chibuike wished to soothe Ekene. He wanted nothing from him, and he wished to be a man who could have nothing, and give everything. To empty his bursting heart for this little boy, who had also been brave and alone. And kind. Ekene had lain a blanket on his sleeping form, and Chibuike had heard him calling Julian. Chibuike should not have allowed him to do such things, things that belonged to a parent.

And there was his pride. How much of Chibuike's son had been left to him, in the end? Ekene had been the last one to see Achike alive, had been there when the haemorrhage began. He knew Achike more deeply than Chibuike did in many ways, and he knew how badly Chibuike had failed his son. It was not to be expected that Ekene's resentment of Chibuike had died last night, as well.

'Did you know?' Ekene said. Chibuike had been lost in thought and now Ekene's face was angry, determined.

'Know what?'

'About Achike and Julian. They were together.' Ekene did not believe that they were in love, not mutual love. But love would wound the old man more, and that was what he wanted. 'Did you know?'

Chibuike thought for a moment, then shrugged. 'Yes,' he said.

'You knew?'

'I knew. And I thought you knew. The way Achike talked about him. The amount of time they spent together. When I heard you speaking to him, I thought ... that you were being kind to me.'

Ekene looked at him sharply, but did not reply.

'Did Julian tell you?' said Chibuike.

Ekene shook his head. 'I guessed.'

'And you're angry with Achike.'

'I understand that people ... It makes sense that he would look for whatever he thought he'd found with Julian. Given the circumstances.'

'Achike would have loved you, if you'd let him,' said

Chibuike, softly. How he wished to enfold the little boy in his arms and shush his fears. But he could not deny Ekene the truth, either.

'He didn't know *what* he wanted!' Ekene said, finally bursting out. Rage, when white-hot, feels like truth. 'He spent his entire life confused.'

'I know,' said Chibuike, quietly.

'He hated himself. And you know why, don't you?' Ekene was gruff now, and examining. He wanted to know how far Chibuike would let him go.

'I know,' said Chibuike. Was this love? Was this a father's love, to let a child crush your bursting heart?

'It was because of you,' Ekene said. 'You are the reason Achike *thought* he loved that man.'

'Ekene—'

'No!' Ekene rose from his seat, anger powering him. He set his bottle down and strode around the room, building up momentum as if for flight. 'You think he and Julian were a *couple?*' He tried to laugh. 'They never even told anyone! Achike never even told me. What kind of relationship is that? It was nothing. He just wanted to replace you, that's all. And if you'd been there for him, if you'd been half the dad you should have been, it never would have happened.'

'He did tell someone,' said Chibuike. 'He told me.'

'What? But he never said—'

'Achike told me that he and Julian were seeing each other,' Chibuike repeated. 'I used to ask sometimes if he was seeing anyone. I was trying. I really was, you know. And he said nothing, most of the time. But on the night he moved me in here, he told me about the two of them.'

Ekene stared.

'Why?' he said. He spoke before he knew how weak it would make him sound.

'I think he did it to hurt me,' said Chibuike.

Ekene said nothing. How much did Chibuike know, after all?

'Julian was almost my age. Achike told me that, too,' Chibuike continued. 'I think he told me because he knew I'd see their relationship as desperate, or wrong. He knew I'd see it the way you do.' He glanced at Ekene purposefully, honestly; honesty felt like white-hot rage now. And it was, but directed inwards. 'And he was right. I didn't like it. Julian is a good agent, but he's nearly twenty-five older than Achike. Imagine that. *Nearly twenty-five years.* Maybe it would be different if I thought they loved each other. Maybe ... But I can't see it. What was a man that age looking for in a man like Achike? Achike was very young for his age in some ways. Very young. He didn't have a good upbringing. I hadn't given that to him, I know. So he was vulnerable. Not weak, but vulnerable. So when he told me, I knew he was punishing me. I'm not stupid. When he told me about Julian, the way Julian guided him, the way he could trust Julian, he was only telling me how much he needed someone to look after him because I never did. I knew. I knew.'

Ekene struggled. Seeing Chibuike lay his faults bare this way muddled him. There was triumph and defeat in it. He tried to scrutinise this man who was aware of all his faults. He ran his hands along the words Chibuike spoke, looking for a point of attack, but there was no weakness to a defence that had already given way. Ekene didn't know what to say.

And he had never known Achike to be vengeful in this way. Achike could be competitive, yes, or even petty sometimes. But this was not the friend he knew. And how could he mourn someone he did not know? The task lay before him, a chasm he could not pass.

And he was the only one who hadn't known. Why?

'You thought I didn't know?' Chibuike said. He watched Ekene's crestfallen expression. He could never ask Ekene for anything, now. How could he ask him for anything after the shame of this? 'You thought I didn't *know*? I've always known!' He laughed as if it were a joke, as if his life were a joke. 'I have known for a long time that I failed my son.' He reached out and took the bottle from Ekene's hand, and Ekene saw the light shake in his eyes when he tipped his head back to drink. He emptied the bottle and set it down and wiped his eyes.

'Because he was gay,' said Ekene.

'Because he was gay. I never understood him. How could I understand that? You know where I'm from. I told you how I grew up. I'm not like you boys. I thought there was something wrong with him.'

'There was nothing wrong with him except the mistakes you made,' said Ekene, relieved that Chibuike had started to defend himself again.

'I'm not explaining it properly. Wait – Ekene, don't go, wait. Please. I need you to help me—'

Ekene moved quickly. Before Chibuike could stop him, he went into Chibuike's bedroom and came back with a large plastic bag, from which he took out an unopened bottle of Montepulciano d'Abruzzo. Chibuike's favourite. He unscrewed the bottle and poured it down the drain. It should have been an act of mercy.

'What are you doing?' Chibuike rose, strode over to the sink, but Ekene pushed him back roughly.

'Sit down.' He was surprised by how little force it took. Surprised by how little thought it required. Chibuike fell back into a wooden chair, and Ekene could tell it hurt. He didn't care. Who was this man, to him?

'Sit down,' he said again. 'You're going to make me listen to this? You want to tell me how alien I am to you, how alien your son was to you? Fine. Sit down.'

He went back into Chibuike's bag and found whisky: dark, expensive, half-finished. He poured it down the drain. It took a long time, and Ekene's arm felt a little tired halfway through.

'You don't understand,' said Chibuike. His body was frozen to the chair. He could not advance, could not leave. 'Please. I need that. Don't hurt me.'

'Hurt *you*?' Ekene shook the last of the whisky into the sink and threw the bottle on the floor. 'Hurt *you*?'

'I know everything I've done wrong,' said Chibuike. He pleaded with his voice now. He pleaded with his confession. 'I've had years to think about it. You're young. I'm not. You have friends –' Ekene turned his head away – 'I don't have friends. I've no wife, my son barely even ... All I've had is time.'

Ekene took out a bottle of vodka. Cheap stuff that would have tasted like paint-stripper anyway. Down the sink. Chibuike watched.

'Do you know what an addiction is?' Chibuike said.

'I don't care.'

'Do you know? Do you know how happy I feel if the first thing I think about in the morning is not what I'll drink? Do you know how rarely I think about my son, or my wife, before I drink in the morning?'

'Don't try and patronise me. I said I don't care.'

'Are you trying to help me?' Chibuike asked.

'No,' said Ekene.

'Because my addiction is bad. I used to be different. I told you. I had strict parents. They were disciplinarians. They never would have let me step out of line, but I found a way. I had to. I didn't know it then. I was angry. I lost my father when I was very young. I told you. I didn't know what to do.'

Ekene kept his face unmoving. Somewhere, someone was setting off fireworks. Loud, bright, lawless city. There was no occasion. No special day, for the rest of the world, but someone was always doing this. There were always these explosions that could not be seen. No reds and bright whites. Only noise, no light.

'And my addiction got worse. But I got better, Ekene. I got better. I *tried*. When he told me he was gay, I said nothing. I should have said something, but I'm not perfect, Ekene. I was on my own. My wife had died. And nobody ever told me about men and men.'

'You told me your step-father was gay.'

'That's not what I mean. I mean fatherhood. This.'

'This?'

'What I should ... What we can ... Nobody ever prepared me. I never knew what *I* ought to be. I wasn't prepared.'

'He was your son,' said Ekene. 'You should have prepared yourself.'

'I know that!' Chibuike said, and rushed forward to try to hold back Ekene's hand – he was reaching for the brandy. A leaving gift from an old colleague. Ekene shook him off and pushed him back again. This time Chibuike expected it and steadied himself on the table. But he was out of breath now, and could only watch in silence as Ekene poured the brandy down the drain.

'I *know* that,' he said, when he could. 'I'm telling you. I tried. When Achike told me he was gay ... and when you told me ... I knew I'd failed. I know that.'

'If you knew you'd failed,' said Ekene, 'you should have done something about it. He was your son, and you didn't even love him. That's on your head. Forever. Do you realise that? You can't wriggle out of this. It's you. It's on you.'

'But I did love him,' said Chibuike. Ekene scoffed. 'No, I did. In my heart, I loved him. You don't understand. You laugh. Yes, my addiction got worse, but *I* got better. When I knew I'd failed, I learned. I changed.'

Ekene made himself wait until the last of the brandy was in the sink before he turned back to Chibuike. Anger slowed his understanding. 'You *what*? I don't understand.'

All the alcohol was in the sink, now, slowly draining. The

flat was filled with the smell of it all mixed together, a sharp, almost acrid smell. The memory of something Chibuike could never have again. When Chibuike rushed to the sink and scooped out a cup of the mixture, Ekene stepped back and nearly retched.

'I think about the man I was every single day, Ekene,' Chibuike said. He was gasping for air between gulps. 'Every moment.'

'The man you *are*,' said Ekene. He hardened his heart and stood further away. He was an unforgiving deity, looking down on Chibuike's suffering.

'Ekene, you don't know,' said Chibuike. 'When Achike came to get me and move me in ... You don't know what he said to me.'

'You told me. He told you about Julian.'

'When we were in this flat and it was all done, I asked him what he'd done it all for.'

'He did it for you,' Ekene said, resentfully, blindly. He knew it wasn't true.

Chibuike took a deep swig from his glass. Why did he keep his voice so soft? 'You don't honestly believe that? You think he offered to give up his life for me? His career?'

'Shut up.'

'You think I don't know? Who was he always trying to impress? Whose opinion was he worrying about when he failed an audition, or when his films premiered? Who did he always come back to? Who was he playing music for when he returned?'

'Shut up!' Ekene had watched his father walk out on him eight times and then walk back home, and he had never said those words to him. Such things were not said to elders. 'Shut up,' he said again.

'He loved you for more than twenty years.'

'Stop.'

'The minute we got back here, I could see it in his face. He was tired of loving someone who could never love him back. And I knew I was the one who had started it. I was the one who had taught him to do it. You think you know. Why he moved me in here. You think you know.'

'Stop!'

'He did it for you! Because he hoped that if he could make *me* love him, he could do the same for you. Because he thought that if I loved him properly and so did you, for once in his life, he would find peace. Well, he's found peace now. And where are we?'

Ekene opened the cupboard doors, every one of them, looking for something else to pour away before Chibuike's eyes. But there was nothing there. While he was alive, Achike had confiscated everything he could find.

'I could see what he was doing,' said Chibuike. 'And all he needed was for me to tell him that I loved him, and that nothing else mattered. That he didn't have to be a movie star, or get married, or have nice things. All he needed was love. From me. I could see that. But I couldn't give it to him because I was ashamed. Or afraid of being ashamed. Because I didn't know how to do this and be a man. I had no words for this.'

'I don't want to do this anymore.'

But Chibuike insisted. 'So I saw him. I knew him. And I failed him. And I drank.I drank because I knew, Ekene. Because I was sorry. Very – very sorry.'

Chibuike emptied his glass, tipping his head back. But when Chibuike turned to face Ekene, he was leaning against the tall refrigerator, crying. Ekene cried almost silently, not wanting to make a sound, not deserving to be heard. What had Chibuike done to him – what had he said, to make Ekene cry this way?

Chibuike stared, too ashamed to move. Or too afraid of being ashamed. What should he do now? He was frozen in his seat. Where did a wifeless, childless, loveless old man go from here?

Could he hug Ekene? Could he encircle the grieving man in his arms, even if it would not make Ekene's guilt go away, or vanish his loneliness? Could he wrap him in warmth and hold him still?

No. There was no way through to such things, no tracks laid down for the wheels to grind. It simply wasn't what you did, or what anyone had done before. Decades had gone by, and not a single hug for the boy. He couldn't find a way. But he ached to do it. What else was he for? How long could he live like this, a father without a son to love?

He took three short steps forward. And Ekene looked to fight him off, at first, expecting some retribution for the shoving and the alcohol down the sink. And Chibuike might have given up then, and stalked off back to his room, or gone out on another long journey to find more vodka, brandy, whisky.

But, gently, he insisted. He could find no words for what he must express. Even now, when he had lost so much. The language evaded him. He could not say the words, and thought that maybe they had never been in him to begin with.

He could not say the words. But he found that he could put first one arm and then another around Ekene's now shaking frame, and draw him close, lessen his loneliness, stand with his grief, be with his guilt.

Outside, the fireworks had got brighter, or the sky had cleared, or they'd moved to a different park. The lights burst in the sky and fell on everything below in reds, and greens, and brightest white.

PART III

I know that this was Life,—the track
Whereon with equal feet we fared;
And then, as now, the day prepared
The daily burden for the back.

But this it was that made me move
As light as carrier-birds in air;
I loved the weight I had to bear,
Because it needed help of Love:

Nor could I weary, heart or limb,
When mighty Love would cleave in twain
The lading of a single pain,
And part it, giving half to him.

ALFRED, LORD TENNYSON, *In Memoriam A. H. H.*

Chapter 13

Achike is by the window while the fireworks explode. He watches the lights go on; he watches the lights go off. He watches their brightness peak, and then watches them fade away as though they have given up. He watches this several times before Ekene comes back from the kitchen with two glasses of red wine, hands one to him, and lies down on the bed with his own.

'I've never really *got* fireworks,' Achike says. 'I mean, I understand them, obviously. *Explodey go boom*. But I've never really been much for them. I don't get it.'

Ekene yawns and sips. The wine is the last in the apartment, and it will do. Oskar took the better wine with him. 'Well, you've come to the right place. Berlin's not so crazy about fireworks, either. Every year, they talk about banning them.'

'Why?'

'The noise, the air pollution. And people get hurt.'

Achike frowns his confusion. Ekene waits a moment before explaining. He watches Achike's perfect, precise face in its perfect, precise frown. Creases in his skin you could have drawn.

'Some people are a bit irresponsible,' Ekene says. 'Getting drunk. Setting off fireworks at cats and old ladies in the street.'

'Oh,' says Achike. 'Well, that does sound messy. Still. Banning fireworks doesn't sound very Berlin. I thought this was a party city. What happened to all the wild people you told me about, the ones who go to all the wild parties?'

Ekene shrugs. 'I think they're the ones firing rockets at cats. Come lie down next to me.'

He pats the bed, and Achike acquiesces, and they are lying in bed together. It's New Year's Day, a little shy of one in the morning. The last time they spoke in person was almost six months ago, when Ekene came back to London for a weekend while Oskar was there with work. Tonight, Oskar was at a party in London with some important clients; Ekene was not invited and he didn't press it.

Oskar does this. Ekene has felt him growing more and more distant for a few weeks now, and he does not try to fix it, but in ten days, when Oskar breaks up with him, he will forget that he saw it coming. He will forget how lonely he felt whenever Oskar was around, and how Oskar's presence made him lean, phototropically, away from Oskar and towards someone lighter, warmer.

Ekene invited Achike to stay and celebrate New Year's Eve together. They have talked all night, and the words drift in and out of them. They are a closed system, with nothing created and nothing destroyed. Unfinished parts of conversation are brought back later; what is not resolved is permitted to return.

Their clothes are on. Ekene is wearing the pyjamas that Oskar bought him for his birthday, when they were happier; Achike is wearing his boxer shorts and an old t-shirt. They both know sleep can't be far off, but they won't close their eyes. They watch one another faithfully.

'You've never really got Berlin, have you?' Ekene says.

'What do you mean? I like it.'

'Yeah, but it's not really your kind of place, is it? Parties, and drugs, and that. Brutalist architecture. Techno.'

'Does anyone ever stop to ask if all those things are connected?'

'You've never come to visit me here before.'

'You know that's not because of Berlin,' Achike says, quietly. Oskar has been a shadowy presence on the edge of their friendship, throwing doubt on what Achike thought he could see clearly. When Achike got to Ekene's flat the previous day, things were awkward, even though he knew Oskar would not be there. Their first day together was long and quiet. They walked around the city. Ekene showed him his favourite places to go in the long hours he had to himself. He did some freelance proofreading for an English-language publisher every now and then, worked a couple of days a week at a bookshop, but the rest of his time was his own and Oskar wanted less and less of it each week. Ekene took Achike to museums, galleries, old churches. They looked at things. They didn't touch.

Achike folds his hands over Ekene's, which are clasped around his waist. Achike's body is not his own anymore. He is getting his big acting break in his late thirties, and his metabolism is not what it was. He has forbidden himself most carbohydrates, and his phone reminds him when to eat one of his pre-prepared Tupperware boxes of chicken and broccoli. He will have to pay for the wine, somehow. He has forgotten the taste of bread. Ekene's arms are wrapped around pure muscle, hard and flat on his stomach.

'Do you ever miss your mum?' Ekene asks the question out of nowhere. He wonders if Achike's frown made him think of her coldness. Or if the closeness was too much for him and he had to say something to break it. He thinks that other people feel something he does not feel, during moments like this. He only feels afraid.

'Sometimes,' says Achike. He traces Ekene's fingers with the tips of his own. 'But she was never really much of a mum.

I don't remember her ever being happy with me. Isn't that strange? Not once.'

Ekene has heard this before, but he feels sadness and pity drop in his stomach like stones, all the same. He wonders about saying something consolatory, but thinks better of it. Best to let Achike be what he is, even if he is sad.

'Besides,' Achike says, 'it sounds kind of cold to say it, but I've kind of got used to her not being around. Anyway, my dad never talks about her, so it was hard to keep her alive. Maybe that's a good thing, in a way.'

'Do you ever hate him? Your dad, I mean.'

'No,' says Achike, firmly. 'No, I don't. He's my dad.'

Trams are still going by. One starts up and whirs away into the distance. Achike and Ekene watch one another faithfully, until Achike breaks eye contact.

'I don't know,' Achike says. 'Sometimes. Maybe. It's hard.'

'Sometimes, I miss my mum,' says Ekene. 'I know it sounds dumb or whatever.'

'It doesn't.'

'I'm too old to miss my mum, I guess. Or I should be. And I know she wasn't great. I think she saw a lot of my dad in me. It made it hard for her to look after me, and be around me. We haven't spoken in years. Maybe I should be over this now.'

'I don't think so,' Achike says, earnestly. 'Not if that's how you feel.'

'It doesn't matter. Forget it.' Ekene shrugs off the subject and avoids Achike's eyes. He is lonely, and brave, and still.

Achike flew here to talk to Ekene. He couldn't bear the silence; it has been too long. They have been in touch only in small ways: text messages here and there; a birthday card from a quirky shop in London or a museum in Berlin. Token things, dutiful things. Their relationship has never been so formulaic before. So correct. Achike has been missing his friend.

'And your dad?' he says. 'You never talk about him.'

Ekene shrugs. 'We don't have to talk about him.'

'I want to. If you want to.'

'I don't, really.'

'Okay.'

Outside, fireworks, still. Achike turns his face towards the window and his skin is lit in different colours for a while. 'I mean, I think they look nice, and everything. The fireworks. It's just that I always feel like I should *feel* something when I look at them. Other people seem to feel something. You know. Maybe there's something wrong with me.'

Ekene wraps his arms tighter around Achike and watches the lights explode over his head. Achike thinks too much. He may be incapable of happiness. There is absolutely nothing wrong with Achike.

'The premiere of *Here Again Now* is going to be amazing,' Achike says.

'Isn't the other lead dating the guy from that band?'

'Yeah. There'll be loads of famous people there. Press. Photographers.' He sighs. 'My dad says he won't come, though.'

'What? Why?'

'He thinks I'm selling out to the West.'

Ekene shakes his head, frowns. 'But that's not what the film is doing. It's about Igbo history, Igbo culture. You're bringing that to the world, Achike, don't listen to him.'

'He doesn't believe in all that stuff, Ekene. He doesn't believe in reincarnation. How many of us do, really? He thinks the whole production is selling an idea of Africanness that just doesn't exist anymore for most Africans.'

'And what kind of Africanness is that?'

'Primitive. Static. Something you put in a museum or pick up in a gift shop, not living, breathing culture that changes as people change.'

Ekene frowns and thinks. He knows the industry is a cold and difficult place. For him, Shakespeare productions in pubs with

Achike and their friends fresh from drama school never became low-budget independent films with up-and-coming directors, never became walk-on roles in big productions, never became an almost-big-budget film that his dad could decide not to see. Because there was nothing to see. He'd spent two years honing a one-man show he took to the Edinburgh Fringe Festival, and one year saving up the money to put it on. Eight people came. Achike, equally talented but with lighter skin, succeeded where Ekene did not. Ekene tries not to feel embittered.

He is about to speak when Achike says, 'I don't know. Maybe my dad isn't completely wrong.'

Ekene gets up on one elbow and leans down, speaking into Achike's hair, as though muffling unkind words will make them tender. 'Have you talked to him about it?'

Achike shakes his head, looking straight ahead.

Ekene purses his lips. He's thought about this. He has been right about this. 'Your dad is wrong. He's from a different generation, Achike. His whole life has been different. He was born in Nigeria and he grew up there. And let's be honest, nobody's ever told him he doesn't belong with his people, or that his culture doesn't belong to him. He doesn't know what it's like to be young and queer and to not have such a direct connection to the culture. He can afford to say it's all in the past because he's lived with it. We haven't. Not like he has.'

'He told me once,' says Achike, 'that his great-grandparents were the first in their village to convert to Christianity. But they died a long time before I was born, so I never got to know what it was like for them to live with both cultures. I wish I could talk to them. I still need to figure all this stuff out for myself. I'm not selling out. I'm just . . . '

'You're just thinking through it.'

'Through a movie,' Achike says, desultorily.

'Through your acting,' Ekene says. He is insistent. 'Through your craft.'

Achike nods slowly, letting Ekene's confidence settle in him. There is a version of Ekene that is persistently kind. Achike looks at him for a long moment, uncertain how long this will last.

'You know,' he says, 'I did some research for the part. The belief is that we get reincarnated into the same families over different generations. Old matriarchs become baby daughters again; great-grandfathers become sons. It's not about karma and all that. Really, it's about family. Staying close. Giving people second chances. I like that.'

As he speaks, Achike begins to feel more sure. Chibuike is wrong. Of course he is wrong. Why, Achike wonders, can he never believe in himself, the way Ekene believes in him? Being in Ekene's presence now, Achike knows: he is making art, taking risks, exploring things for himself.

'And I like that the director's thinking about the culture and how to make art in it,' Achike says. 'I like that she's brave enough to see our culture as malleable and dynamic. I want to be part of that. And Julian wants me to, as well.' He is quiet for a while.

Then Ekene says, 'I hope your dad changes his mind. Maybe he will. You never know.'

Achike hugs Ekene tighter by way of reply. Achike likes moments like these. He feels like he belongs to Ekene. He feels like his body is not his own. He wonders if this is what normal people feel when they are loved. But he also wonders if this isn't so much love, as pity. And he wonders which one he will accept from Ekene tonight. He doesn't know.

He reaches out a hand and lets it settle on Ekene's arm. It is an intimate thing he does. It is exploratory and curious, as though he has never touched Ekene's arm before, as though he is a stranger now.

'I don't think about my dad very often,' says Ekene, suddenly. Achike tries to stay very still, afraid that any movement might frighten away this unlooked-for moment of honesty, of grace. 'I try not to, at least. I was really young when he left for the first time. He just . . . left. Like it was so easy. Nothing holding him back. I just remember feeling like I was falling, like there was nothing to catch me.'

Involuntarily, Achike squeezes Ekene's arm.

'And you know, when it was just me and my mum, she used to tell me that was just what people are like. Men, especially. You know. They let you down and that. I think she was very angry, and very sad. And I was angry and sad too, so I don't blame her. But I do believe her, sometimes. I think sometimes that's just what people are like.'

'I'm so sorry, Ekene.'

Ekene continues as though he has not heard. The words are coming out of him, and he is afraid to shrug, to nod, to move a muscle in case they stop. 'I was just a kid. And mum kept saying how stressed she was, and how much she hated my dad. I was so scared she would get rid of me.'

'Get rid of you? Ekene . . . '

'I thought she'd put me up for adoption or something, or send me away somewhere. I didn't know where. I know it sounds silly now, but it was all I could think about. It's partly why I kept getting in trouble at school. That and me being gay. I was afraid of what she might really think of me, deep down. I needed to see where the line was. I needed to know what I'd have to do for her to stop loving me.'

'Ekene . . . ' Achike is helpless for a moment. He's had no practice at this. He's never heard Ekene talk about this before.

Ekene blinks slowly, and it seems as though he is far away. Then there is an explosion in the sky, and everything in the room turns green. His skin shimmers. He forces himself to breathe steadily.

Achike pleads, 'That was a long time ago, Ekene. I know it must have hurt you, but she was under so much strain, raising a kid by herself, and with your dad in and out of the house all the time. And you were in a really dark place. You weren't yourself, then. Maybe things could be different now.'

Ekene shrugs. 'You know, we talk every few weeks. She's doing better now. She's doing okay. She doesn't need my dad.'

'And you? Do you think you might ever talk over what happened?' Achike asks.

Ekene shakes his head. 'I think that would be too painful for both of us, and it wouldn't achieve anything. I know some people are really close with their parents, but I just don't think that happens for everyone. When I talk to my mum, we don't really talk. You know. Sometimes she asks if I've got enough money, if I'm well. I never ask her for things or tell her anything bad. We're not like that. But she does care about me. And I really believe she did her best, and I know I didn't make it easy for her. And I'm glad she's okay. But too much has happened. I'll never belong with her. You know.'

Achike squeezes Ekene's hand.

'Is that how you feel?' Ekene asks. 'About you and your dad?'

'I don't know,' Achike says. 'Sometimes, lately, I feel like things could change. I know he's made mistakes. And it still hurts a lot. But sometimes I wonder what it would be like if he fixed things between us. If he could be my dad again. I don't know. I talk to Jacob about it sometimes.'

A lot has happened in the time that they have been apart. Achike can afford counselling now, and he is feeling brave enough. Once a week, Jacob, a small and cheerful man, helps him probe gently into his childhood, its voids and its echoes. When Achike describes it to Ekene, he sounds far away.

'Is it as tough as it sounds?' Ekene asks. 'Talking about all that stuff, like your childhood?'

'It feels like hard work,' says Achike. 'I leave the sessions and I feel almost light-headed for a bit. I'm not used to sharing this stuff with anyone besides you.'

'I know. I know.' Ekene puts a comforting hand on Achike's.

Nobody told Achike how hard it would be to talk. He had imagined that Jacob would just listen to him for a few minutes at a time before thinking carefully and then declaring him to be right or wrong, hopeless or not, this way or that, presenting his personality to him as a *fait accompli*, presenting also the solutions he needs and a clear, bright vision of the man he will be. That was what he'd wanted: someone to deliver him to himself.

It is nothing like this. Achike is the one who does most of the talking. Much of the time, Jacob's only response is to acknowledge the pain that Achike never allowed himself to feel. 'That sounds very lonely,' Jacob says. Or, 'That must have been very hard for you.' And each time, it is Achike who has to think very carefully before he realises and says, 'Yes, it was.'

He is smiling as he tells Ekene this. 'But I feel really good about it, Ekene. I mean, I've just started, so who knows if it'll work out. I think I've got a lot of work to do, so who knows how long I'll be seeing him for. But the first few sessions have been really nice. It's just good to talk to someone objective, who asks good questions.'

He shifts his weight in the bed and turns to face Ekene.

'And I feel like, when I'm done, I'll have come through something. You know? I'll have come *through*. The way you know when a project you start is going to be really good when it's all rehearsed and everything – you know it's going to be really hard work doing it, but it's okay because you trust it. I feel like one day I'll be on the other side of something. You know? I'm not there yet, but I will be.'

'It's good to see you so optimistic, Achike.'

'I do feel optimistic. That's the right word for it. I feel hopeful about everything.'

Hope feels strange to Achike. Its arrival has been slow, and uneven, like the coming through of first teeth, but so many years late, as though each and every one of the sharp, hard things has been hidden underneath his flesh for years and is only now emerging. Not a brilliant white but a natural one; not eternal or invincible, but strong. He was built to last. There is something tough inside him.

'Do you know what I mean?' he asks Ekene.

'What?'

'I mean, are you feeling hopeful?'

'About what?'

Achike pauses for a moment to choose, as if picking a card. 'I don't know. Your life?'

'I don't know. It's hard. Sometimes.'

'Being here? In Berlin?'

Ekene hesitates. 'Sometimes, I think about my dad. I don't mean to. But I'll be alone in the flat one day and his favourite song will come on the radio. Or I'll see myself in the mirror and I'll realise I look more like him today than I used to. And I'll think of him.'

'What do you think about, when you think about him?'

'I don't really think anything. I ... feel helpless, and small. It's like being a little kid again. His kid. And then I'll remember that all that's in the past, and it's like waking up from a dream, but I never know if it's a good dream or a bad one.'

Another firework pops into life, somewhere far away. No light can be seen. Achike imagines its colours, sprinkling among trees in the Tiergarten.

'I do think about things, sometimes,' Ekene says. 'When I wake up from it, sometimes I think about things. I think, why me? Why did I get him as a dad? Why didn't my mum see anything in me, except the mistakes she'd made with him?'

Lights outside. No sound, this time.

'And I think, why do I have to be a man? Why do I have to be this hard, painful thing? Why do I have to only belong to myself? I want to be ... Why can't I be somebody's boy?'

Achike turns to him.

'And then I think about you.'

Achike watches Ekene's eyes as though a light in them will soon go out. They hug tightly, Achike's hands pressing into Ekene's back until he can feel his bones. Ekene kisses Achike's neck softly, mouths into him, *I love you. I love you, Achike. Achike, I love you.*

'I think about you too,' Achike says. 'All the time. And I know I've made it difficult. I've been difficult. But it's been difficult for me. You have to understand. I think I'm not used to – to being in control of myself.'

Ekene is surprised. Achike is the most controlled person he knows. Achike has been following scripts his entire life.

'Jacob's helped me see that it wasn't me. He was in control of me. Him. You know. I don't say his name. Him.' Achike lowers his eyes, fondles the fabric of his t-shirt. 'Even after it stopped, he was in control. For a long time. It was a long time before I could let myself be touched by anyone, or let anyone close to me. And that's because of what he did to me, and how he told me that I wasn't to tell anyone, or he'd hurt me, or nobody would believe me anyway. I . . .'

Ekene lays a consoling hand on his skin. Achike moistens his lips, takes what is offered, and continues.

'And it was more than that, Ekene. It was more than that. For such a long time, a long time after my dad found out, I felt as though this man had put something inside me, or . . . No. It was worse than that.' He takes a deep breath. Ekene lets him. 'You can't imagine what it's like. I felt as though he'd uncovered something inside me.' Ekene watches Achike retreating. He sees Achike back in his mind, thinking about his uncle's hungry, cruel hands on his skin. He sees Achike recoil, and wish he could be somewhere else, and wish he were stronger, and wish he knew why he couldn't wake up from the nightmare. Ekene watches Achike retreating and tries to catch him.

'I know that's how you feel,' Ekene says. 'I know. And I'm so sorry for you. But he didn't do that. I know what you think, but – that thing isn't inside you for him to see. It never was. You have nothing to be ashamed of, Achike.'

'Ekene—'

'No,' says Ekene. 'That isn't true. You must know that isn't true.'

'What I'm trying to say is, I always thought . . . why me?' Achike meets his eyes now, questioning, insisting. 'There were other boys. He worked with kids in a school somewhere. There must have been others who were more handsome than I was, or more . . . I don't know. There must have been others who had more of any good thing.' He breathes in again, determined to get this out. 'He must have seen something in me, something he recognised maybe.'

'Achike.'

Achike shakes his head, releases his gaze. 'That was what I thought for a long time, anyway. I try not to think that now. I felt as though there was this . . . second heart inside me, I guess. Something polluted, something beating polluted blood. And it was bigger than my heart, and stronger, and louder. I tried to hide it. I think I drove you away, maybe. I think I made things very hard for you. But you must know . . . it's been hard for me, too.'

'I know.'

'I think maybe sometimes I've taken you for granted, or I've not shown how much you mean to me.'

Ekene breathes out heavily, uncomfortable now. 'And how does your dad feel about this? The therapy, I mean?'

The subject changed, Achike looks at Ekene for a long moment before continuing. 'He's never liked talking about his feelings, or anything like that. You know, that's why my uncle was never prosecuted; things worked differently then, and they'd have needed me to testify, and Dad always thought that talking about it would make it worse. And maybe he was right about court. That would have been too much. I was only a child then. But I'm not now. I started telling him I needed it. I needed to talk to someone. Every so often, when I went to see him, I'd say I wanted therapy, to try and show him how seriously it all still affected me. He hated it when I told him that. I was trying to hurt him, I think.'

A year ago, Achike would never have admitted any such fault in himself. And yet the faults persisted, as with anyone. He could make someone nervous, make people avert their eyes, the way he was at war with himself, the way he held himself. As though he might fall and shatter at any moment. And now, does he admit a petty act? Does he smile at his own mischief?

'But one day, he just called my bluff and told me to go, if I wanted. And then I didn't have anything holding me back – I can afford it, and I just about have the time . . . So I went. I felt silly when I realised I'd been waiting for him to give me his permission. But I think I was looking for a reason not to go. It was a scary thing to do.'

'And your dad doesn't mind?'

Achike shakes his head. 'No. It's weird. He'd never go for himself, and he'd probably never have suggested I go. But now I'm going, now it's started, I think he likes it. I think he likes that something is being done, even if he isn't the one doing it. You know? I think he'd rather keep out of it really, but I think he's glad it's happening. Sometimes he asks me how it's going.'

'Your dad? Really?'

'Yep.'

'Do you think he'd ever go with you? To therapy?'

'No, never,' Achike says, roundly. 'He doesn't think of himself that way.'

'What way?'

'As someone who can be helped.'

'Oh. And what about you?' says Ekene.

'What about me?'

'Do you think of yourself as someone who . . . ' Ekene clears his throat, pauses, changes direction. 'Do you think you allow yourself to be helped now?'

Achike does not say anything for a second. They both know what Ekene means.

'I hope so.'

'This is new,' Ekene says. And it is: Achike is available to him in a way he never has been before. And it frightens him, but he wants it. Ekene calibrates the parameters of hope, plans what is sensible to dream. What he can afford.

Perhaps Achike senses this, because he continues, eagerly, 'I'm changing a lot at the moment, that's true. I feel very different from how I used to feel. And I really want you to know that, Ekene. I'm not the same as I used to be. And I'm sorry if I made things confusing for you—'

'Don't apologise,' Ekene says. He pulls Achike closer to him and looks at him earnestly. In this moment, neither Oskar nor his fear of intimacy exists. For now, this is the only thing.

'I hate myself, Ekene . . . '

'You're being silly, now.'

'Because it's too late. You and Oskar . . . I've been so stupid.'

Ekene tries to be as gentle as he can when he lifts Achike's head from his chest and stands up. He does this. He walks away.

He goes to the window and looks, directs his eyes away from the inside. Berlin is said to be like Manchester. That's what Oskar had told him, wasn't it? It would be just like Manchester. Its grittiness, its starkness. He'd been told it was dark but friendly.

'Me and Oskar are together,' says Ekene. His voice is flat, and Achike finds it unconvincing.

'I know,' says Achike. 'I'm sorry.'

What is Achike apologising for now? Ekene doesn't know how he feels about Berlin, really. He has lived in the city for

almost a year, and he still isn't sure. He watches more fireworks. Stupid, bright, beautiful city. Arriving in Berlin for
the first time had felt like stepping through the back of his
wardrobe and finding another world there: his own, but not his
own. There was something bewitching about that uncertainty,
but now the magic has worn off, and he only wants to know
where he is.

In London, on the night Ekene meets him for the first time,
Oskar is charming and affectionate in his starched white shirt,
at the wrap party of a show directed by a mutual friend. Oskar
is so engrossed in Ekene that he forgets his cocktail; Ekene sips
his champagne to keep himself steady.

Oskar is an investment banker living in Berlin, working with
one of the corporate sponsors of the show.

'Berlin?' says Ekene. 'I thought Munich was where all that
stuff happened.'

'That stuff?'

'Finance and banking and that.'

'Ah, you mean Frankfurt,' corrects Oskar, confidently. 'And
yes, you're right, mostly. But what can I say? I've never been
one for the conventional.'

'You don't consider yourself conventional?'

'Not at all.' Would it be too much to say that Oskar's eyes
twinkle? 'I'm only here for a couple of days,' he says.

'Oh?' Ekene doesn't mind how disappointed he sounds. He
wants Oskar to see he's eager.

'Yes, I'm on a little tour, I suppose. I spend so much time
working, so when I get time off work I like to get in a few
countries at once.'

Normally, Ekene hates it when people talk acquisitively
about travelling. He memorises their words and ferments little
stories to tell his friends. But there is something exceptional
about Oskar, and what had once seemed greedy and hollow

now has a second chance at sincerity.

He likes everything about Oskar, almost, but not quite, instantly. He shifts his perspective to make room for the sharper and rougher edges of Oskar's personality. He becomes forgiving with Oskar, where with others – even with Achike – he has always been critical, impatient.

Oskar is intense; 'heady' is the word Ekene will use to describe him to Achike later on. Oskar stands just a little closer than a friend might stand, his breath warm on Ekene's face. Ekene likes it. He tries to listen to what Oskar is saying, but he is too excited, and Oskar smells like bitter incense, and he is slightly taller than Ekene, looking down at him – looking, conspicuously, at his mouth – with eyes that are almost mournful with longing. They have just met.

They don't finish their drinks in the bar. They go back to Oskar's hotel room (Oskar never stays with friends – hates inconveniencing people, needs his own space) and have sex for three hours. Ekene hadn't known for certain that they would have sex at all until Oskar swept him up as soon as he closed the door, collecting the flesh of Ekene's buttocks in the palms of his hands. Ekene loves feeling himself through Oskar's touch, knowing that Oskar desires the fullness of him.

Ekene savours every moment of it. In his mind, he tries to capture mental images, afraid that it might never happen again. Maybe it is this that gives him the energy to go for as long as he does. Maybe it is the uncertainty that fuels him, pushing him a little further in case he never gets to do this again.

They fuck all over the vast, opulent hotel room, on all the furniture and in front of every mirrored surface. It is like a dream, or something only possible in a dream; Ekene will remember noticing that everything feels glassy and ideal, bright and filmic. He lets Oskar do what he wants, despite moments when Ekene himself receives no pleasure, despite moments when he does not understand the source of Oskar's pleasure, or when Oskar seems angry with him, or absent. Ekene only urges him on, as though Oskar's desires are his as well. They are his, but only partly. Ekene's true desire is only for it not to end, for Oskar not to open his eyes and realise that the man beneath him is only Ekene after all, that the mirage is only that, that the dream was always entirely his own.

When Oskar allows him to stay the night, Ekene kisses his forehead as though they have become closer than they have, and Oskar scoffs, almost breaking the spell. Oskar gets up, takes a bathrobe from a peg on the wall and throws it at Ekene. It is a half-playful gesture, but the bathrobe covers Ekene's body and he thinks for a moment that Oskar does not want to look at him. He makes himself laugh a little and says nothing. He steps into the shower. He does not want to clean himself but decides that Oskar might like some privacy. He forces himself to wash for a full five minutes, counting the seconds in his head like a child playing hide and seek. When he gets out, Oskar is waiting on the bed, his arms outstretched for a hug. Ekene doesn't think. He dives in.

The first time he flies into Berlin, Oskar is almost two hours late to meet him at the airport. The plane lands, and Ekene tries calling him but he never answers. Ekene leaves voicemail messages but gets no response. Ekene waits for him, wishing Oskar would answer his phone, then wishing he'd brought euros with him, then wishing he were braver. He imagines himself brave enough to get on a bus and figure out the route, to walk all the way to Oskar's flat if he has to, with both of his suitcases if he has to, all night if he has to.

He waits.

One flight after another comes in and lets out; the passengers collect their bags and move on, greet parents and children and friends. The security attendants watch him and grow curious, then nervous.

When Oskar arrives, he sends Ekene a text message: *here now*.

so stressed! Then he pings Ekene his location: he is in some remote part of the car park, waiting for Ekene to come to him. When Ekene arrives, Oskar hugs him briskly and tells Ekene all about how difficult his day has been, how he's had this headache, how long he's had to wait in traffic to get to the airport terminal, how all he wants to do is go to bed and go straight to sleep.

Ekene looks and looks for an opening to express his anger, his disappointment. None comes. He does not have the courage to push through and make one of his own. He had it once. But with Oskar, he is so unsure. Was Oskar's day so busy that there was no time for him to meet Ekene at the airport? Or answer his messages sooner? Is Ekene alone after all, in a strange city with a selfish man? He lets the matter rest.

Within a month Ekene has flown to Berlin three times. He loves it. Oskar pays for his flights, gives him money for taxis from the airport. Ekene speaks no German, but he does not like the silence in the car that always lasts the entire journey.

Achike and Oskar have met only once. A drink at a London bar Oskar likes and which Ekene knows Achike will hate, but hate silently. Ekene is hoping a little alcohol might make Achike more receptive to Oskar, and make Oskar, who has a tendency to become aloof when nervous, more relaxed around Achike.

Achike is on antibiotics.

'One won't hurt you,' Ekene says, but Achike will not budge. Achike simply does not do that. There is a rule to be followed. Ekene cringes at his own words, knowing that Achike will recoil from him.

Oskar arrives, certain of a warm reception in his velvet waistcoat, his cufflinks, his biggest, whitest smile. Achike recoils from him.

'What is it that you like about him?' Achike asks him, often. He asks him the same question now, to draw Ekene back from the window.

Achike is used to this; he can probably never hope to win Ekene back from this man who took him away. Instead he offers Ekene small truces, minor kindnesses, concessions to his madness. And Ekene returns small, polite, innocuous remarks. They feed themselves piecemeal this way. They try to keep their friendship alive.

'Love,' says Ekene, patiently.

'What?'

'I don't like him. I love him.' says Ekene, as though he is a little embarrassed for Achike's mistake. 'Why else would I have come here?'

'Okay,' says Achike, patiently. 'So what is it that you love about him? You've never told me. Not really.'

'He's strong. He's very strong,' Ekene says. He knows that he has to answer quickly in order to be convincing.

Achike is not convinced. He frowns, a stone deity come to life to refuse an unworthy offering. Innocently, earnestly, he asks, 'So you feel like you can rely on him? Is that it?'

'Never mind,' says Ekene. He puts on an infuriating secret smile and goes back to the bed. He lies differently this time and they are top and tail. Ekene is looking away from Achike into middle distance. His mind is on something higher.

Ekene can change like this. He can make himself cold and small. So Achike waits a few moments for Ekene to speak again, and for him to return his gaze. When Ekene does not, Achike sighs and then speaks.

'Is it my fault?'

Ekene is so surprised at the directness of this question that, for a moment, he forgets to take offence.

'It's really not like that.'

'Am I the reason you're with Oskar?'

'Stop it, Achike.' Ekene lets out a long, tired breath.

'I can't.'

'You have to.'

'This isn't you, Ekene. Ever since the airport, that day you first got here—'

'I wish I'd never told you that.'

'I'm not using it against you, Ekene. But come on, this ... this life ... This isn't you.'

'What does that mean?' says Ekene, his voice suddenly pleading. 'Do you know who I am? Do you know better than I do?' A year ago, if he had asked that question, he would have meant it sarcastically, scornfully. But now he lives with a man who is never home. He lives with a man who took four good bottles of wine with him to some party tonight, and who might not come home for a couple of days, and whom Ekene does not recognise anymore. Ekene means the questions earnestly.

Achike keeps his voice calm. 'I'm not saying Oskar's a bad man, Ekene. But there's nothing wrong with just re-evaluating where you are. I think, at some point, you have to stop and ask: is this what you want?'

'You know what I want.' Ekene looks down at his hands, clasped in his lap now. He looks weak. Frail. He feels it. But Achike can be hard to live with sometimes. Doesn't he know not to talk like this? Doesn't he know that sometimes the lie is the kind thing?

But then Achike turns himself on the bed so that his face is next to Ekene's again, and he says, 'So it *is* my fault.'

'Forget about it. I didn't mean—'

'But what if I could give it to you? What if I could give you what you want? Really, Ekene.'

'Stop.'

But Achike does not stop. He has been wrong about love. But he does not think he is wrong now. The feelings of shame and too-bright joy mixed together when his uncle let his hand fall below Achike's waist – that was not love. When the only way for him to survive was to make a new identity for himself, a carapace that was his and not his, a self who could be touched like that when he knew it wasn't right, a self that did not cry, or seek help – that was not love. How he felt when his uncle went away and it all ended, as if he had died and Achike would always be covered in his blood – that was not love. But maybe this could be.

With Jacob, he has stepped out into daylight and seen the sky turn first grey, and then black. His memories bring looming rainclouds; they speed the earth on its rotation and plunge his world into night. Jacob tells him to breathe in and out slowly, and he learns to hold his breath at the top of the intake. He has held his breath as the desires of his shameful body pluck every star from the sky and tell him they had never been shining. And he has breathed out again, and in. Impossible things arrive at his consciousness and he is there, looking them over like unexpected guests. And he has begun to wonder if his body might hold other things besides shame. Maybe real joy. Maybe love. Or the beginnings of love. He does not know.

'Ekene,' he says, his voice strong and present. His hand is on Ekene's arm. 'Ekene, this is me. You know me. And I wasn't ready before, but I'm ready now—'

'It's not like that anymore!' Ekene bursts out, tears muting his voice to a whisper. 'I'm not like that anymore. I wanted that before. But you've ruined it!'

'I'm sorry,' Achike says.

'And it's too late now.'

'Is it?'

'Achike, you don't even know what the problem is. You don't even know what you've done.'

'Every single time I told you I loved you, I was wrong. That wasn't love. I know that. But it's different now.'

'You don't know anything. So you've had a few hours of therapy. So what? Does that mean you still know me?' Another question that he means, that he needs answering. 'Do you know what it's like to have someone offer you the thing you want most in the world, but take it back at the same time?'

'But I'm not like that now. I'm not. Believe me, Ekene. Just imagine how happy we could be. Think about it. Don't you still want that? Can't you see I'm not in the same place?'

But I am, Ekene thinks.

'This is now, Ekene.' Achike is still trying. His body almost shakes with the effort of making himself known to Ekene after so much time. 'I love you *now*. I love everything that's you, every last tiny trace of you. And I'm ready for that now. Aren't you?'

'I'm with someone.' Ekene's voice is so quiet. 'I'm with someone. You know that.'

'I know. I just hoped we could find a way to—'

'We can't. Achike, we can't. Please, stop asking me.'

Achike thinks, runs his hands along Ekene's sadness for a chink, an opening. There is none he can find. 'Fine,' he says.

'Achike.'

'It's fine. I'm fine.' Achike's body moves away a little.

'I'm not saying I don't love you, Achike. I'm not saying that. I'm not saying I don't want you.'

'But?'

Ekene looks hard at Achike. He does not give in at first. His pride does not allow it. Hasn't he waited too long for this? Has he not defended himself against every thought of it?

But there is no defence from a love that slipped between his ribs like a knife, a love whose voice whispers to Ekene in the middle of the night, weakening his resolve, stiffening his flesh.

This is the reason he fled to Oskar, to Berlin. Oskar is the best hiding place Ekene knows. Oskar is beauty, and freedom, and money. Oskar is the kind of man with whom one forgets that better men exist; and Ekene did forget, and he was grateful for this for a long time. He has been living his Berlin life: he has taken long walks around the city, swum in lakes in the summer, improved his halting German, made transient friends who moved on to London, to San Francisco, to Paris. He has taken pills, gone out and found dark clubs. So what if Oskar has others? Men are like this. Ekene does, too. He has men who give him something he wants, who make him feel numb. He is used to it.

But always, the time comes when he longs for warmth again. The longing comes on like a migraine. It is only a slight ache, at first; Oskar might say something impatient to him, and then without thinking Ekene will recall the way Achike looks just before he says something disdainful, the way Achike's mouth turns down at the corners. And Ekene will think of Achike's soft lips, and his rigid sense of right and wrong.

He looks at his friend, looks at him hard. He is trying to work out how to say something difficult, the difficult thing he has to say, the thing he cannot leave unsaid.

He says it. He moves forward an inch, and an inch is all it takes. His lips touch Achike's, and he is saying the thing he has not said. What they do is language that will not translate, that conveys only itself. Ekene's eyes are open as he kisses; does he see Achike's brim with tears of joy, or is it only relief? Can Achike's mouth, his breath and lips, taste so sweet? Can he live in Achike's breath forever?

They are more than what a man has ever been. They are beyond what a man can be, alone. Achike loves the way Ekene's fingers push inside him; the way his body moves is exact and pure; it shows them both how love should be felt. Ekene can shape himself into a beautiful song they have never dared to hear.

Ekene takes too long to take off Achike's t-shirt, but Achike persists. His breathing does not slow; the slowness of Ekene's hands does not dull Achike's excitement at what Ekene's hands are doing. Achike lays his hands on Ekene's head as his t-shirt finally comes off and Ekene's breath meets the skin on his stomach. He pulls Ekene's loose pyjamas over his head. He had thought he would feel a rush of joy as he saw Ekene's soft flesh exposed, finally, the convex lay of his stomach. He feels it. The joy is almost too much.

But they do not get it right. Something eludes them. They falter, unsure whether this time, their first time as men, should be hasty and unquestioning or delicate and slow. Neither one is sure how far he may go, or who should take the lead, who should grant permission and dole out pleasure. They ask each other questions with their eyes until they cannot bear to look, until they have to avoid one another's gaze.

They need more time together than they have. Achike has imagined this moment on every night he could not sleep, but when Ekene is finally naked in front of him, his body under his hands, two hearts could not contain what they feel. Achike is too excited, and his desire begins to feel out of control. It is a little frightening. With his eyes and with his body, he feels as though he is always taking aim, and always missing, always just beyond the point at which he should arrive. He wonders why.

Until now, Ekene never knew what his love for Achike was. He never knew it was a bright, sharp blade that could cut deep into flesh and come out clean. As long as they have known each other, Achike has been the one inching towards Ekene, his best foot first, only dipping in his big toe. That was Achike.

But he is not that man this evening. He keeps his wide eyes on Ekene and keeps himself exposed. He gives pleasure to Ekene, and solace. But now, not Ekene himself but his fear rises to meet his friend. He cannot conceive of being loved by good Achike; it is too much to ask of him, he who has had so little practice, he who has never fully been loved by anyone. Until now, Ekene never knew how his horror of being loved was waiting underneath his skin, a monster waiting in the dark ocean of his body, ready to rise up and bring about the end of his little world.

When it is over, they are both uncertain. They lie side by side, their fingertips touching. What have they just done? Each of them wants the other to explain; neither one explains. Their skin touches only just enough.

The sex is done, but not gone. The fireworks have still not finished, and both of them are quietly surprised that there seems to be an endless parade of lights.

'Are you okay?' says Ekene, quietly. He wants to be kind.

'I'm okay,' says Achike. 'Are you okay?'

'I'm okay.'

'This wasn't my plan when I came here,' says Achike. 'I just wanted to see you. I wanted to talk to you. I wasn't trying to do anything.'

Ekene doesn't answer him. He finds a bathrobe and throws it on hurriedly.

Achike follows him with his eyes. 'Are you ever going to look at me again?'

'Oskar just can't know about this.'

Achike shrugs impatiently. 'Okay. Fine. Oskar.'

Ekene shakes his head, walks into the bathroom, switches on the shower. He leaves the door open and steam comes rushing out, slowly obscuring the room. He switches on a radio in the bathroom, as if he is tired of hearing Achike's voice, after what Achike's voice has done for him tonight.

'Do you regret it already?' Achike asks.

After a long moment, Ekene comes out of the bathroom. He wraps his bathrobe around himself tightly. Achike is still naked.

'No, I don't,' Ekene says. 'I don't.'

'Then why—'

'Achike. Please. I don't regret it. I just need a little time to think.'

Achike turns away from him silently.

'I do love you,' says Ekene.

'Then love me!'

'It's not that simple, Achike. I told you.'

'Because of Oskar?'

Ekene shakes his head, tears forming in his eyes.

'If I could stop loving you,' Achike says quietly, 'I would.' He is pleading now. 'I don't want to be here. If I could stop it, I would, because this hurts me, and it's difficult, and you won't help me do it. But I can't stop. Can you? Tell me: can you?'

'No.'

'So why does Oskar matter?'

Ekene is crying. He goes back into the bathroom. His footsteps are quiet, stealthy. He steps under hot water and he washes off everything they have done together. Perhaps, when he emerges, he will be cleaner, and better, and ready.

Achike turns away and cries quietly. He wishes Ekene would kiss him again. He wants his friend to take his busy head and lay it on his chest, because now the frightening kaleidoscope of lights is dancing before his eyes. It's happening again. Still naked, he wraps his arms around himself and gets under the covers, and he tells himself the lights only dance with anyone for a little while.

Chapter 14

Ekene got to the church early and sat near the back. Volunteers from the parish arranged the flowers, vacuumed around the pews. At home – home was what it was now – Chibuike was still sleeping, or perhaps awake and busy with the final few arrangements, or fretting in the kitchen. Ekene wondered if Chibuike had gone out to buy more alcohol. He seemed to be drinking a little less, but he did drink less sometimes. And sometimes he didn't.

There wasn't much more to do. Everything was chosen. They had spoken honestly about themselves, and somehow there seemed little to prevent them doing what was needed for the funeral. They'd worked quickly. They had found music, selected a coffin, picked irises over orchids. Ekene had been surprised, in the end, by how short the service would be, and how easily it had all been arranged. Only an hour. He had thought to be more troubled by the task; he wondered how his feelings for Achike would fit into the time.

Now, with everything settled, it seemed silly to have ever thought that an hour would be enough. He saw now that it was never meant to be enough; that this was not the function that funerals were meant to serve. The funeral would be made up of things Achike would have loved to see and hear, but it was not Achike. He was not here. The service, and the flowers, and the music were all for Ekene, and for Chibuike, and for the people who would come to say goodbye.

Ekene had felt a sense of accomplishment, almost peace, when everything was settled. There was a kind of quiet in his mind, where there hadn't been before. He'd written a eulogy. That was difficult work. He hadn't liked it, and he would have stopped if he could. He'd spent hours crafting something that could reflect Achike, and give some recognisable sense of the man, for people who would recognise him in what was said, and who would like to see him again one last time, if only in words. He'd studied his memories of Achike very hard, and from them he had extracted some things which he felt got to the heart of his friend. He'd done it.

But he'd studied his memories very hard – and then he'd looked away. He'd looked away at the world without Achike in it, and found that he had not really looked at it since Achike's death. He'd looked at the world, took it in with a few thoughts, in a few moments, and assessed it, coldly and fairly. It was not a good place. Things were taken unfairly. There was dishonesty and distance, and a clear line of cruelty seemed to run through everything. It was all hard, and dark, and painful. He'd thought to find something that could redeem it, any of it, but he could not. Ekene could not find in the world one single friend about whom he could be happy.

But Chibuike had brought him cups of tea, and sent him photos of Achike as a young boy, before Ekene knew him, like an extension of his time with Achike. And Chibuike had been easy and generous: he was happy for Ekene to give a eulogy, wasn't much for speaking in public anyway, didn't trust himself to be steady at the lectern. He had been gentle with Ekene, and kept his voice soft. Ekene had looked at him often, and considered him closely, and not known what he was turning into.

Today, Ekene got to the church early, to think, and be alone.
He wanted to feel clean, and to understand himself. He was
messy, and difficult. He wanted to feel free of heavy things,
to feel the new emotions leave his body, to have them shorn
like wool in spring, and to feel his flesh underneath, cool and
new again. He had never believed in God, but people came to
church to feel clean, or to feel that they could be made clean
if the right words were said. He wanted that.

Ekene and Chibuike had not requested an organist at the
funeral. Achike had never liked the sound of the instrument;
it was the piano he loved, and played. He said organs sounded
either too weedy or too forceful, always on the wrong side of
something. And for his own music, he needed the independ-
ence of the piano, the freedom to live where his instrument
lived. Organists had to go where the music was.

But an organist was rehearsing now, and Ekene was happy
to sit and listen. Sitting at the big machine, someone toiled
and advanced slowly through the music. It was practice, rather
than performance, and it came in shorter bursts and phrases. In
this time, while the people who listened were not an audience,
mistakes were things to slow down for.

What now for Ekene? There would be the funeral, of course,
but what would come next? Ekene knew that Achike had
willed the flat to Chibuike, and that Chibuike resented his
son knowing that he had nowhere to go without it, or without
the money from its sale. But Achike did not share his father's
sheepishness around money: he wanted only to give what was
needed. Achike had liked openness, and Ekene wished it could
be summer for his friend, so that the doors to the church could
be thrown open. Achike would have liked that. It was too cold
now. The year was ending soon.

No home for Ekene. Achike must have thought Ekene would
not want to live somewhere the two of them had been together,
if something happened to Achike. He had left Ekene most of

his remaining savings, which would be enough to start renting somewhere back home in Manchester, and move on, and make plans. He had options.

But options were the worst thing. What had happened to him, with Chibuike? Ekene had come to church to feel lighter, to feel free of such questions, but he could not help feeling that something was emerging from him – no creature underneath his skin, only more of himself. Ekene was still himself, still wary, still uncertain of his merits. He still liked to be alone, and trusted it more than anything else.

But something had happened to him, with Chibuike. It seemed impossible that he and Chibuike could ever be separate now. Even if they should choose to live apart after Achike was buried, something of one would always go with the other. What Ekene had wished for had come true: he was somebody's boy now, and in turn somebody was his also. He had seen the chance for Chibuike's redemption inside him, and that this chance was dear to Chibuike's heart, and that he, Ekene, would struggle if he tried to take it away. Nor did he feel ready to leave the dear old man. What were either of them, now, apart?

But also there was Ekene's desire for freedom and to be away from things. Achike had hated it, but it was as strong as the intake of breath. Ekene sometimes felt he was made for it. How could he stay? What was he, if he was someone's? Who was he, if he was Chibuike's? He could never be the man's son. Chibuike's son would not come back. So what now? Could he live with the man forever, and be his – what? Nobody else had ever done this. Surely, nobody had ever done something like this. He thought and thought, and tried to feel clean. There was no way forward. There was no language for what should happen next.

And when Ekene tried to speak it, even in his mind, he found only words that appalled him and made his senses itch. Caretaker. Martyr. Father. None of these described the whole truth. Underneath the words still moved some wild, insubordinate thing that this language could never hold. There had been rum on Chibuike's breath when he'd brought Ekene cups of tea as he worked on the eulogy. He must have gone out to get more. Did the kindness come from there? Ekene thought it might. And he worried about what would happen to Chibuike if he stopped drinking. Or if he never did.

He studied the possibility of his life with Chibuike. It was a father Chibuike needed, and the word appalled Ekene when applied to him. How could he be a father to Chibuike, listening to his dreams, keeping alcohol from him? Ekene was no such man. His entitlement was to be the child, to be looked after and protected. That was his, all the more so because it had never been his. He wanted a blanket drawn over *him* when he was cold, and a warm safe home, and a father who would come back. That was what he wanted.

But Chibuike needed care. He needed the tenderness of a father, or he would slip back into the man he was without it. Ekene didn't want that. But how could he be a father and a child?

The December wind blew in, and heads turned uncomfortably towards it as Chibuike walked in, a scarf around his neck. His arms were too feeble to push the heavy door open quickly, so he had to wait in the cold a little longer while he struggled. One of the parish committee members set down his vacuum cleaner and rushed to the door; uncertainty made Ekene sit still.

With the committee member helping, he had more time to watch Chibuike. Years of too much to drink and too little to eat had left him very thin. How many times, while planning the funeral, had Ekene had to remind him to eat, or suggest he eat a little more? Ekene would be doing this forever if he stayed. What life would he have then? He couldn't live with Chibuike forever. They couldn't both only dream of nourishment.

'Ekene,' said Chibuike, gratefully. 'You left early this morning . . .' He had ready, sure happiness at the sight of Ekene, but his words were a kind of question, a needing and reaching out that Ekene didn't like. Not for the first time, Ekene felt a kind of pins-and-needles pain, the pain of being loved and needed. He wanted to get up and walk away. Perhaps he had been wrong, and it was not what he wanted after all, to be somebody's boy. Surely, it must be too late for him to be what Chibuike wanted. Surely, the boy in him was gone. But he still wondered.

'I wanted to get out and think,' Ekene said.

'Think about what?' Chibuike asked. He came and sat beside Ekene, very close. He did it without thought or hesitation or asking, as if he had a right to it. Ekene could smell his aftershave, and he was sober. For whom had he done these things?

'Sir, after the funeral . . .' Ekene wanted to turn to face Chibuike, but he couldn't bear to look at him, or at the effort he had put into himself today. Chibuike had put on a suit and tie, and perhaps he'd not even thought of drinking this morning, because he wanted to show what Ekene had done for him, show the man he had made him want to be. Ekene couldn't be responsible for that kind of hope. It was too much.

'What?' Chibuike asked.

'Sir, after the funeral, I think we should think about what happens next.'

Even without looking, Ekene sensed Chibuike's posture adjust and stiffen. Ekene, too, sat formally, bracing himself for the conclusion of what, surely, had always been too good to be true, what had always been an impossible thing. Ekene felt Chibuike guild his disappointment, felt him guard it with whatever a man has. How high had Chibuike's hopes been, when he walked through the church doors and saw Ekene waiting there? Had he lain awake all night in readiness for something better than he'd known?

'Ahn-ahn!' Chibuike spat. 'What do you want, Ekene?' There was hardness in his voice and it shocked Ekene. Ekene saw Chibuike feel this rescission in a deep and unprotected place within. The shame in Chibuike was so strong! Surely, it must be invincible. Ekene felt the echo of it as though it had sounded in him, too, and he saw now the fragility of the man that he had never seen before. Even seeing Chibuike at his worst, even seeing him drunk and cowardly, Ekene had always thought that Chibuike must possess something that he, Ekene, did not. Childlike still, Ekene had assumed that fatherhood had gifted Chibuike a patience and strength that was not available to men who had never had a child.

How silly he had been. Ekene saw now that these things were not at Chibuike's fingertips, waiting to be reined into himself, but far beyond him and with no path towards them. Chibuike had no more of the father in him than Ekene himself. Chibuike might shatter in a million places, and it had only ever been Ekene's naivety to think otherwise.

Ekene saw that Chibuike had come as far as he could alone: father's death, wife's death, son's death. Loneliness had achieved nothing for him. He saw, too, that Chibuike had been dreaming of better things. He wanted closeness on a wide pew where two people might only sit apart. He wanted a blanket drawn over both of them. And Ekene was amazed at himself, because he had wanted those things, too, but the nearness and the asking, the abject asking made Ekene pity Chibuike, and resent him. After all that Ekene had seen and suffered, still under his skin lurked a sense that men simply did not do such things. The asking only made Ekene want to be further and further away.

The organist played their final few notes. There was nothing polished or final about it. The music stopped, and shortly afterwards there were footsteps, and a musician emerged and went home. The music would be played again, better, on another day.

'I've been thinking it might be better if I find my own place to live,' Ekene said, as calmly as he could. To Chibuike's confused expression, he said, 'I'm just not sure what we do, now, if I stay. I don't know ... I think for me to move out – I think it would be better for both of us.' And when Chibuike said nothing, he said, 'I think I might just be better on my own. Do you – do you see what I mean?' He wanted to ask for forgiveness, but could only see his way to begging understanding.

'I see what you mean,' Chibuike said, and his voice was worse than cold. He was brisk and optimistic, pretending that Ekene soured nothing between them. But the pretence was weak, and Ekene could sense the real feeling of Chibuike somewhere far off. Chibuike got up and walked away, and for a long time he pretended to contemplate a hymn book. Ekene thought he should go and talk to him again, to explain that it really was the best thing for them both; that if he stayed, he would be tarnishing the thing between them which he could not bear to spoil. He wished he had spoken in terms of this thing, and not only in terms of himself. He didn't want them to go into the funeral like this, to say goodbye to Achike while they were somehow fighting between themselves. But when he got up, Chibuike went to speak to the priest, and then he went outside, and the moment was gone.

Chapter 15

There was no funeral procession. Achike always thought they were morbid, and he didn't like the thought of his body being paraded through town. And Ekene and Chibuike were still angry and uncertain, and hadn't thought to stand at the door and greet the guests. So people walked in gingerly at first, as if unsure they had come to the right place. They looked to their left and right and took small steps, listening. Even the more forthright among them spoke softly, and only to people they knew. They smiled quick, shy smiles at people they didn't. Perhaps this was because they were unsure if such an unusual mix of guests belonged together anywhere.

There were the Okoros and their relatives, people who had not seen Achike except in photos taken by his mother when he was a baby, people among whom his beleaguered little family had been only whispered about when the children were playing outside or studying upstairs. Yet this was an extended network of aunts, uncles and cousins, that would have been a nuclear family; these were people who would have seen Chibuike's addiction, and maybe seen it put to rights, had Chibuike's pride and shame not stood sentinel, had he only let them try.

Then there was Ndidi's family, who were different. There

were far fewer of them. They were strange, cold people who looked unhappy to be there. They were impatient, and did not speak, and seemed to dislike something, perhaps the music, perhaps London. They always knew this would happen, some-how or other.

Then, at a respectful distance behind these, were the people from the film. They entered the church more slowly, just as uncertain of their surroundings as the family was of them. These were the actors, writers, producers who had seen Achike's star rise, who had been watching for his star to rise further and perhaps take them with it, perhaps renew their faith in art and what, with money, it could be allowed to do. These were people who spent months at a time filming in unfamiliar or remote locations, and who were written about in magazines and gossip blogs; they seemed to feel out of place in a small, oldish church that wasn't famous for anything.

But here among them was the art director who had seen Manhattan in Manchester. Her father was Igbo, and she had talked to Achike only a few times before the filming wrapped. She had thought he would go on and be famous. Here, too, was the music editor, who had never met Achike, but was striving to find music that could fit the love he portrayed. And here was Mercy Oruche, the director-screenwriter. The visionary, still surprised that she, barely out of film school, could have suffered the bereavement of someone not even old enough to be her father. She smoothed down her black linen shift dress and took a seat in a pew at the back.

And here was Chibuike, walking into the church with his arm through the arm of someone he did not recognise and whose name he could not remember. Chibuike had heard it only a few moments ago, but he forgot names so easily, always had. He was not drunk yet, although he pined for it.

And things moved. Chibuike swayed, and needed the man's arm. He leaned heavily on it. Perhaps the man was about

Chibuike's age, or a little younger, but he was white. The man seemed terribly sad, sad enough to be a relative of Achike's, but he wasn't. Chibuike was sure of it.

After his conversation with Ekene in the pew, Chibuike had been finishing a drink behind the church when the white man had approached in a black suit and put out a cigarette briskly. He'd offered to walk Chibuike inside, and Chibuike accepted only because the white man had kept his face so gentle, and because Chibuike felt so weak. They walked up the aisle of the church together, slowly, taking their time so as to keep steady. The white man was almost walking for him, but slowed down for family members to greet Chibuike, to offer their commiserations, to let their voices crack for him, to try to hold him up with the firmness of their hands in his. Chibuike let them try.

The white man found a seat for him at the front of the church and then melted away. All around Chibuike was family: his sisters and their families, their cousins and elderly uncles and aunts. Ekene was somewhere. Chibuike could not see him. He could not meet anyone's eye.

To his right, in stained glass, was an image of Christ with His mother. He was walking towards Calvary and towards His crucifixion. This image had always transfixed Chibuike, and it held him again now. He remembered it from years ago, before he had stopped going to church; from the years before his father died, he remembered it. There was much suffering ahead; there would be hours of death. In the image, Christ could only bow under the weight of his own cross. His mother could only cry.

He had seen this image before in many iterations, and he knew it well. He could have rendered it again blind. Mary was at her utmost, here. She bowed her head in grief, because to bow her head and weep was the most she could do. To bow her head, and not try to hold it up. To let herself be vulnerable.

She could cry. Behind him, women cried openly, as they

might. But Chibuike did not; he felt himself only teeter on the edge of tears, as at the farthest reach of land before the drop of cliffs and the wide sea, before flight for creatures who could. He stood on the brink, and felt clean air on his skin, and he thought: were tears only a woman's? Mary could do nothing more than weep, but weeping was *hers*. She could love through her bowed head, outstretched hand, wet face. She was remembered for it. Women, denied so much, were given this when they needed it. But a man, a father, could not do such things. Why? He did not know – he could not see what purpose it served but he kept himself back, or someone might look at him askance, or afraid. But where did his love go now, if not through him and out?

It could be his fault. He had made so many mistakes, and it did not seem possible that he could have survived his addiction with everything intact. Drinking men lost other things, why not the ability to cry? Something had been settled in his body for some time now. He should not be surprised. Stupid man. Weak man. Failure of a father.

Or maybe it was the way he had always been. He had not cried at his father's funeral, either. Or his mother's. And he knew what people said about him for it, and he could not say if they were wrong.

As more people took their seats, the pianist played a hymn. This was Achike's favourite. He always preferred the older hymns, even more than his parents had. There was something about the darkness of those melodies that he had liked. It was Christmas carols he had loved most of all; more than Christmas itself, with its miracles he couldn't believe, more than candles, or prayers. He had tried to keep a smooth wall between himself and God.

And yet the music had entered him. Chibuike and Ndidi had spent long Christmas Eves listening to him sing carols whose tunes seemed rather to dread the approach of Christ than to celebrate it. Music that crawled through broken glass towards salvation. Chibuike preferred things in a major key, but to Achike, God was to be found in the darkest night. God was a stern figure, bent and frowning over a serious and struggling world. To Achike, God was what you saw if you screwed your eyes shut in fear; when you opened your eyes, he was gone. Chibuike took the blame for that, too.

On the other side of the aisle, at the front: Ekene. He had wanted to sit with Chibuike, but Chibuike's relatives had come and sat next to him before he'd had the chance. There was no room, now, and Chibuike was still angry with Ekene. Besides, he would not leave his sisters; he and Ekene were not family, and things must be done correctly. There was a rule to be followed.

They'd had no visitors in the house. Only now, seeing all the guests arriving, did Ekene realise how odd this was. There should have been families within families, ready to help. Ekene was sure they had wanted to. Not one person had come to the flat when they'd heard about Achike's death. Chibuike had asked people not to, of course. He knew he would not be in the right frame of mind to receive guests until after the funeral. He needed to prepare himself. He needed solitude, and Ekene.

But this was not so for Ekene. He had not realised until it came to arranging the funeral – sending out invitations, choosing a location – that he had no friends to call, no family he wanted to see. The whole world was happy to go about its business.

'I like this music,' said the man to Ekene's left. His voice was familiar, and he spoke confidentially. It was the man who had helped Chibuike into his seat. 'I think Achike would have liked it.'

'It was one of his favourite songs,' said Ekene. He only spoke to be polite, and meant to say nothing more, but the man continued.

'Did you know him well?'

'I did,' said Ekene, smiling faintly. He turned away again and asked no questions, and in so doing he tried to end the conversation. He wanted to be alone. He wanted to feel clean. But the man only waited a couple of moments before speaking again.

'I'm sorry,' said the man, 'I don't think we've met. Julian Trent.'

'Oh! Julian!' Ekene turned towards him involuntarily. He had never even seen a photo of Julian online, although he'd looked, the night after they spoke on the phone. Looking at him now, he tried to hide his disappointment. He had expected someone who looked more tired, perhaps. Someone who looked busy and important. He had thought to see a greyer head emerging from this starched white shirt and black suit. But Julian could have been anyone, almost; he looked about fifty, a few years younger than he was. His hair was only greying slowly, or maybe he dyed his hair well. He spoke as he had done on the phone, precisely and with his consonants clipped, but measured. He had the trimmings of a good man.

Why was he sitting next to Ekene, at the front of the church? What was his business here?

'I'm sorry,' said Julian, shaking Ekene's hand. He did this in a very proper way, as he did everything else, as if he'd been taught to do it by someone, as if someone was still watching, and nodding. 'I didn't catch your name?'

'My name is Ekene,' he said. This was how he spoke to non-Igbos. Not 'Ekene,' or 'I'm Ekene.' People got confused.

'Ah, I thought it might be you.' Ekene wondered why. 'It's so good to put a face to a name. Ekene.' Justin said his name again, slowly this time. He seemed to be deep in thought for a moment, and then added, 'I wanted to pass on my condolences in person.'

'Thank you.' Ekene searched for the next right thing to say. 'Achike spoke very highly of you.'

'And of you,' Julian said. 'I know the two of you knew each other for a long time.'

'Since we were teenagers, really.'

'Yes, yes. Goodness. You must have been through a lot together.'

'Yes,' said Ekene, simply.

'It must have been very hard for you,' said Julian. 'Both of you.'

'What do you mean?'

'Oh no – oh no, I didn't mean that.' Julian's eyes widened and he shuffled uncomfortably. His hands had rested on his knees but he lifted them up now, palms outwards, as though he had angered Ekene and must pacify him. Ekene sat quietly and observed these hands, pale and old, advancing. 'Nothing bad! I just know how hard it must have been for you both, being gay in the black community. That's all.'

Ekene's heart sank. He gave a very slight nod and kept his lips tight.

Julian studied Ekene's face very hard and decided to continue. 'I tried to support him as well as I could. And I think he did well in the film. I haven't seen it in full yet, of course. But I gather he did very well.' He babbled now. He was conscious of having been clumsy, and spoke while he searched for the next right thing to say.

Ekene tried to give what kindness he could. He tried to reply calmly, and let this calm Julian. 'That's very good of you to say. I was really proud of him.'

'Not kind at all,' said Julian. 'It's true. He'll be sorely missed. And to have come out of the home he came from. He told me a lot about his father. Do you know? I mean, you were his best friend, you must know. He worked so hard. To escape. And he did.'

Ekene nodded and tried to seem grateful for whatever good thing Julian thought he'd given. But all the same, his heart sank. Was this it? Was this the man who had loved Achike? Ekene was galled. The man had touched perfection itself, had approached a man who demanded admiration, but he could speak only of pity. Ekene's heart ached for Achike, and the nights he must have spent in this man's arms. He wondered how it had started. He wondered if, one fresh morning in his offices, Julian had ever spoken softly, shyly, and expressed pity for the young actor, and if Achike had ever acquiesced, happy to give in to the gentle, clumsy man, even if Julian could only ever see a fraction of the spectrum of his worth.

And could Ekene begrudge Achike this? Could he deny him kind words, softly spoken?

He wanted to. Achike had been wrong about love, clearly. And Ekene had been wrong about Achike. Ekene did not realise until now that he had maintained parallel images of Achike in his mind: one was of Achike as he saw him in the day-to-day, kind, beautiful, but in terrible pain. And yet there was another image of him as flawless, that did not properly correspond to what Ekene knew about him.

Achike's affair with Julian tore down this second image. Achike had only ever been some of the things Ekene had thought he was. Ekene felt foolish when he realised. He had thought he'd known Achike entirely, that he'd kept a faithful watch over his friend. But he saw now that he had drunk a kind of poison, and slept.

He felt lost. He had thought to mourn a saint; he saw now that he was utterly unprepared to mourn a man. From where Ekene was, there was no heaven he could see for the lonely and the lost. What kingdom belonged to such as these? And to what paradise could he release his friend today, if the only release was a bitter one, and hurting?

Ekene noticed his eyebrows had grown tense while Julian

talked, and he relaxed them. Achike had been wrong about love, but so had everyone else. Julian was no worse than Ekene was. Having brought the best of himself to bear on Achike, having brought the best love he could extend, Julian was no worse than him. Julian was not the man Achike deserved, or the monster Ekene had feared, but somewhere in between. Clumsy, blind, eager.

For some time before his death, Achike had lived in transit, measuring out his life in journeys. Aeroplanes to locations, trains home, chauffeured journeys with drivers who were themselves alone and away from somewhere. He had fled from one location and one role to another, making friends briefly, the idea of home dissolving further with every trip. He was never home, never where he most wanted to be.

But perhaps he had found a home in Julian. In Julian, perhaps, he had found an older, gentle man who wanted to look after him, and who could give something like tenderness freely. Julian was the man who'd walked Chibuike up the church and seated him. Ekene tried to forgive, and put his shoulder to the act. He was confused, immature, afraid. Even now, he might be years away from being able to offer a steady hand.

The work of self-forgiveness lay ahead of him for the rest of his life. He must live with his failings for a while, and live with his guilt. That was for him. But that must not tarnish what he could give to his friend on this day. Achike had died not knowing, never really knowing what Ekene really felt for him; with Julian, perhaps, he had lived.

He thanked Julian for his kind words and turned away, back towards the altar, where the coffin waited. He hadn't thought it would look so small.

The priest began, and made her way through the service gently, knowingly. She must have done this before, countless times. Chibuike had wanted this surety. Achike hadn't been to church since he was a child, but in his will he'd allowed for a church service because he knew that would please his father, or his father's spirit.

Chibuike never went to church either; he'd stopped going a long time ago. But he wanted God now. He wanted the funeral to feel bigger than itself, and beyond itself. The idea of burying his son was intolerable without this notion of someone directing Achike's soul – and the day – towards something holy and important. He wanted the priest's old, steady hand, knowing he could not give it himself. He needed to pray, and to be heard.

The woman read on, and ordered things. There were readings and hymns, and silence, and lit candles. This was it. It was ritual he'd wanted, the going where others had been. You could put God in rituals, in the smell of candle smoke. You could smell the smoke and know that you were in His presence, and let Him work on you. You needn't fuss. That was what people thought.

One needn't fuss, and yet there was energy in the priest. She led the service watchfully. She was in everything she did; her keen heart was in everything. She half sung each prayer, thinking through the words and putting feeling in them, not letting them go unblessed by her earnestness but insisting that the words take on part of herself before she released them to the mourners before her. It was a good thing she did. Chibuike wanted her surety, and he wanted this, too.

They stood up and sat down and kneeled, for readings and hymns, silence and lit candles. For nave and flowers and coffin they stood and sat and kneeled together, all against the cold day outside that they must face when it was over. It was what was done, and Chibuike liked to be following that. This was a language all its own.

And then came time for the eulogy. Only Ekene stood up,

because it had been agreed between the two of them. He would speak. What did Chibuike know about his son, enough to speak for minutes at a time? All he knew was how his son had survived him, and not survived him. That was not for a eulogy; he would have the rest of his life to think those words to himself. There would be years for it.

And still there was shame in him about Ekene, and about whatever was between them. They were two men, after all. And there were people among the pews who knew what Ekene was. If he were to stand up with Ekene and speak, or to introduce Ekene's words – if he were to publicly acknowledge whatever was between them – it would be unthinkable. He had a fear that he would be undone, or that whatever was between him and Ekene would be undone. And there would be daylight showing between the threads, and something else there, too. Something gaudy and ridiculous. That would be the end of something, if people saw. What were they, after all? His love for Ekene was real in his heart, but largely without form, and he felt it could only exist safely while it was shapeless and took no space. He had loved Ekene as his own son and he had shown that love, but only for a short time, and only within the flat, where Achike's spirit still seemed to breathe, and to smile on them and their kindnesses. Everything they had done and said was secret. To acknowledge Ekene publicly would be to acknowledge the shape and form and size of his love for the man, to put it into the hands of others and feel their skin contract around it, test its substance. He shivered. No. That would be the end of something.

And who knew what this uncovering would initiate, or what he could be, then? Bad enough that Ekene had scorned him as he had, before the service began. Chibuike had felt shame enough. It was as though his eyes had been closed before Ekene turned him away, and he had only then seen his own true and naked form, his ugly, frail body. Stupid man. Weak man. Who was he, to offer love to another man? Men did not do such things. Men did not presume on other men, or hunger after anything another man could give. Men must take only what was certain. Who was he, to think he could be loved? Who was he, to think he could offer anything into the heart of another man, and be enfolded in?

Across the aisle, Ekene stood and walked slowly up to the lectern, a golden eagle at the front of the church, its wings spread wide to hold a heavy text. His legs were cumbersome to move, and he felt suddenly very afraid.

He tried to cope. He kept his eyes away from the eyes of the people in the pews. He had a fear that if they saw him, and he acknowledged what they saw, he would turn to stone, or be something weaker, and disintegrate. He had written his eulogy carefully, knowing that he knew Achike better than anyone else in the world, and he had felt glad to have a good weight on his shoulders then, but now he felt he could not sustain it. He began to feel that he would be crushed. Even to reach the lectern was too much, and he felt his body start to slowly fall, almost through the floor. To fold like paper, as though along old lines of failure. He heard a ringing in his ears like high bells far away, and his hands began to sweat. He looked up to the ceiling, but no angel intervened. He felt a very sudden shock, a profound feeling that there was no heaven Achike or anyone else would ever see; no God, and yet he felt greatly chastised, as though he had upset some great and terrible power. His stomach churned. There again, too, was the pins-and-needles pain, in his legs now, and his arms and wrists. He felt as though he was dying. He wanted to die. He should have known this would happen to him. Stupid man. Weak man.

Chibuike watched Ekene falter. He panicked in his heart as Ekene stopped on his way to the lectern and seemed to struggle to move, to breathe. Ekene clutched his chest, and looked like crying. Chibuike panicked. Men did not do such things.

And yet Ekene persisted, or his upset persisted. Slow moments unrolled themselves in which Ekene struggled, and struggled. Chibuike looked to the priest, whose surety he'd wanted, but she hung back as if unsure where her purview began. She was moved, but unsure, and she looked out to the people gathered. Her place was not with the family; she was of God, and did not want to be where some kind relative should be, who might want to offer support from a vantage point she could not occupy. She looked out at the people. But the people only looked back, not knowing Ekene, or not wanting to. Nobody moved.

Chibuike panicked in his heart, but sat still. He searched for the next right thing, but knew that he was failing Ekene while he searched. He was not such a stranger to fatherhood that he did not know when he was failing. Ekene tried to stand upright and breathe, and Chibuike sat, watching him.

Chibuike hated himself again. Stupid man. Weak man. But something had been erected between him and Ekene, and would not let him pass. It was a high wall between the two of them. It was shame, and fear. It was the foreignness of what must be done, of the kind and tender thing between two men.

He looked around. There were eyes on him, from Ndidi's family and his own, watching to see if he knew this man, and what his place was in Ekene's life. What would he do? Only that morning, Ekene had not wanted him there. It was distance Ekene had wanted, maybe even to move away. And could he begrudge Ekene that? That was the expected thing. There must only be distance and sex between men, and distance was ordained and respected, and sex was foul, it was death. There was nothing else.

The people looked at him to see what he would do. The priest, relinquishing her reservedness, began to step forward.

*

Ekene's breath was pushed out of him as he folded down on himself. He felt profoundly lost. And he was partly glad to be lost. He only wanted to be left alone, irredeemable, struggling. The service could go on without him, or it wouldn't. The cold day outside would carry on without him, and then it wouldn't. He only wanted to be able to breathe, or not to breathe at all. To try, and then to fail, was too much.

Then Chibuike's arms around him recalled him to himself. Ekene was still far away from his body, and it felt at first as if someone else was being comforted. It was not his own faults that were being smoothed over, and he could still hear a ringing. It was not his own damp palms that were worthy to be touched, even held tightly. Not his face that was worthy to be examined, and softly called to under light that came through stained glass. He flinched at first, and felt more conscious of the eyes of the people on him, each one of them also unsure what this meant. He could not understand what was being said to him. Chibuike's words – and more so his actions – felt like a language Ekene could not read. There was something behind Chibuike's presence that was inscrutable. But Ekene began to return to himself, as though he had been given something that was enough, or as though something had been appeased.

And he saw with surprise that Chibuike did not try to push him forward, or hold him up. Chibuike's presence was entirely pure of force, wanting only to help him breathe slowly in and out, wanting only to offer some good thing forward to his heart, and to encircle him with the best love he could extend. It was only to bring the best of himself to bear on Ekene. And so they sat together on the floor, Ekene still heavy under the weight of himself. He breathed.

The music stopped. The priest spoke, said some things to which Chibuike should have listened, but could not bring himself to hear. She did good things, again, and thoughtful things. The service was almost over without the eulogy, so she ushered the people out of the church, to say their prayers by the grave while the two men recovered themselves. People filed out quietly, leaving the men to themselves and to what was between them, but many people passed by and said prayers for them. Many of them touched one or the other's arm in compassion, before walking out to the graveside. The people had only been afraid to be the first one stepping forward, and now that someone else had done so – Chibuike, who had until now never stepped forward before it was too late – they were kind, and a little ashamed.

The priest was the last to leave, and she said kind things to them quickly and quietly, and she walked out of the church, leaving the door a little ajar. She told the pianist to carry on playing a little longer, to carry on playing something light, and merciful.

When Ekene could breathe easily again, he stood up and covered his eyes. He did not want to think that Chibuike had offered him shelter of any kind, or embraced him like a good father in front of people. He avoided Chibuike's eyes, that were quick and concerned. He told Chibuike that he was fine. He didn't want any more of what he had been given. He kept to himself.

It was time to bury Achike now, and everyone else was ready. Ekene walked a few steps towards the church door, but his legs began to give way and Chibuike held him gently, with a hand under his elbow, and Ekene accepted that. They walked together, slowly around the building, towards the graveyard. The piano could only be heard faintly, and the pianist was coming to the end of the piece.

Everyone else was ready. They were standing, for prayer and saying goodbye, and for dust on the coffin. Everyone else had already accepted that it was time. This was what was done.

Chibuike held Ekene up, and tried to be ready himself. They would stand. They would try. They would put Achike into the ground, and there would be no more music.

Chapter 16

'I'll do it.' In the flat, Chibuike pre-empted Ekene and took plates from the table for him, ordering them and stacking them for washing. He was swift and capable.

'I don't mind, sir,' said Ekene.

'It's fine. You rest.'

The wake was over. Not all the people had come, but enough to make the flat feel fuller than it had for a long time. Before Achike died, Ekene had lived there alone, waiting for Achike to come home. It could take weeks. And then, for days, he and Chibuike had been isolated together in the flat, holed up, brewing.

Enough people had come to pay their respects, with their cards of condolence, and their food, and their questioning eyes. Chibuike and Ekene had greeted them, ignored their questions, stayed within sight of each other as they spoke to relatives. Many people wanted explanations, too, of Achike's death. That was difficult – the iniquity of it was still very fresh – but they made people understand, as much as they themselves had understood.

Now, everyone was gone, and all the plates were collected in, standing unwashed in stacks by the sink and on the worktops.

Parts of the flat were tidy but needed cleaning, parts were clean but needed tidying.

Between Ekene and Chibuike, there was daylight now, and something else. Love had taken form, and had been seen. Their eyes were opened, too. They must speak, but they spoke hesitantly, knowing that their words had more in them.

They sat down at the table together and rested for a moment. Ekene still felt winded. He wondered if he should have called an ambulance, but he couldn't bear the thought of one, and Chibuike had looked up some things online anyway. Ekene would call a doctor in the morning.

There was no more tidying that couldn't wait. They knew they would do the dishes together, one washing, one drying. They would put the radio on and find music they both liked. They knew that. That could wait.

Ekene took Chibuike's hand. Had it always been so thin? The skin on it was like leather. It was not, he thought, like skin, but more like something you would wear or not wear.

'Thank you, sir,' Ekene said. 'Thank you for what you did.' It was so hard to say the words, but he insisted. He wanted to push his gratitude out whole, and recognisable. Things must be right, this time around.

'You're welcome,' said Chibuike, simply. He laid a hand on top of Ekene's hand on top of his. He said nothing else, not wishing to make Ekene feel as though anything really extraordinary had been done for him. Chibuike did not want gratitude, or struggle. He wanted to shrug off those things and continue to be kind, and be a father again. He wanted this to be a pattern they followed. He could look after Ekene, Ekene could look after him. It felt as though they were without form, more ideas than men. How strange, and how wonderful, that love was possible.

And how long it had been possible – their whole lives, they'd been lights that danced around each other. Chibuike, in his long life, had danced around love many times. He'd stepped, ducked, slid through the thicket of life, fleeing joy, fleeing the unfamiliar thing. How strange, now, to want only to be the fled-to, to be the haven, the happy end. How strange it was to know that where one went, the other would go; that where one lived, a part of the other would live with him.

But what form would that take? It must take some form or other. What shape would things take tomorrow, or the next week? They did not know if the going and living together would only be in spirit. Maybe that would be enough. They had done the good thing for Achike: he was buried, honoured, always remembered. All other things were for the two of them alone, now.

'Have you decided what you want to do?' Chibuike asked.

'About what?'

'Whether you want to live here or not.'

'I've thought about it a lot,' said Ekene, quietly.

'I'll always keep a room for you.' Chibuike waited for Ekene to say something that might break his heart.

Ekene took a deep breath in. 'I can't stay here,' he said. 'Not day after day. I can't do that, I'm sorry. My life can't be here. I could stay for a while, but one day . . .'

Chibuike shook his head, crying, and hating himself for crying. The indignity. And worse, he could not bear Ekene seeing his shame. But Ekene wouldn't take his eyes off his face.

'I can't stay here day after day,' Ekene said again. 'But I can't leave you, either. Not completely. I can't be your child, sir. I'm not a little boy anymore, and I can't bring myself back like that. I can't do it. After everything, we both need to live life, and I think that living together would be . . . I think that would be something other than life.'

'It's fine,' Chibuike said, but he got up and turned away from Ekene. He walked over to the sink and looked outside.

Everything was wet, and greyer than it had been, but there was still some light. It was deep enough in winter now, but there was the sun. It was what English people called good weather: cold, bright. Not the golden warmth of English summer, or what Lagos had, the warmth that surrounded and accompanied everything, even when rain came. This light was silver; it was second best.

Chibuike reminded himself that second best was still good. Why, then, did he feel as though the day only told him how bleak his life would be, if Ekene would not live with him, if Ekene left him and that was the end? When his heart spoke he could listen, finally: it was father and son he wanted. It was family. Staying close. Second chances.

But Ekene had spoken too. Chibuike must accept it. If Ekene did not live with him, that needn't be the end of something, he told himself. And he had thought this might happen. It had occurred to him that he might be left alone with whatever was left of his life, and that he must try not to waste the remaining time.

And there were other things. After the funeral, in the intimate space that they had made with their embrace, he had promised Ekene to give up alcohol, to go to meetings, to look after himself, and Ekene had accepted warmly, like his child. Chibuike told himself now that he could live on this, and it would accompany him.

But the winter light answered, and his old skin answered, and his frail bones answered that nothing would ever be enough for him, without Ekene in his home. How else could he be whole? How else could he be a father, a good father? What else could life offer him, this late in the day? The light outside seemed not silver, but grey.

Ekene watched the old man's form attempt stability. He watched, and thought to feel disdain. For a long time he had felt contempt for anything resembling what he saw now: the weakness, and the loneliness of others, just as in himself. He had been so wrong about the heart, and he'd learned to be cold when he was very young. Since he was a boy, loneliness and even anguish were things to be ignored while they were endured, not things to be remedied. He'd kept a smooth wall between himself and others.

But he was more than what a man was, now, and he could not go back. He'd thought to feel contempt, but none came. Instead he remembered Chibuike's arms around him, so feeble in themselves but communicating something infinite and strong.

Ekene knew he must not stay forever. He knew there was a kind of blinding euphoria in him because of what they had done that day; he was liable to bleed himself out in service of the kind old man. If he lived with Chibuike as Achike had hoped to do, he could lose himself forever in service. That was not love, to him.

But if he stayed for some time, he knew they could be more than what men had been. And what would that be?

'Sir, I can't be your child. I don't have that to give to you. I don't.'

Chibuike nodded gravely.

'But,' said Ekene, 'I could still be a kind of son to you. If you want.'

'What?' Chibuike's shoulders froze in the middle of a breath. He dared not turn around.

Ekene thought for a moment before speaking again. The right thing felt just within his reach. 'I can't be everything you need. Not at once. I can't. You'll need to go to meetings, and you'll need to give up drinking – all the things you promised. And maybe I need to look after myself better, too. But I don't have to move out right now. And when I do, maybe I don't have to be very far away.'

'Are you sure?'

'I've thought about this a lot,' Ekene said.

'I'm glad you have, but so have I,' said Chibuike, sighing heavily. 'And I think we'll probably have to sell the house.'

'What? Right away?'

'Soon. I can't afford the kind of mortgage Achike would have got, not on a place this expensive. Even if you contributed, it would be too much. But with the money from the sale, and if you get another teaching job somewhere . . .'

'We could afford somewhere else. A fresh start. Somewhere new.'

'It's better than living with strangers,' said Chibuike.

Bright, new city.

'And I was thinking something else,' said Ekene. 'I wondered if you still felt the same way about the premiere.'

'Of Achike's film?'

'Yes. He told me once that you didn't want to see it.'

Chibuike shook his head, and he was terse when he spoke. 'That was a different time. I was angry with him. I'd see it now. Of course I would see it.'

'I was hoping you would say that,' Ekene said, eager to show Chibuike that he was not trying to accuse him. 'I was hoping you'd see it with me. You know. I thought maybe it would be easier on us both if we saw it together.'

Chibuike looked outside but his eyes were in his mind. His eyes were on the thought of his son again, his son walking across a screen, or speaking some last words.

'What made you change your mind?' he said.

'I never did,' said Ekene. In the silver light of this day, everything looked like a gift. 'This was always what I'd thought to do. Please understand. I know you need me. And I don't need you any less, sir.'

Chibuike nodded, still crying, and they moved to hug each other, but hesitated before this first mutual thing, each approaching the other. Neither one moved in brave and lonely service of the other, but now together and whole. Their form was still unprecise, and might only ever be second best to what they'd lost. But wasn't that still good? Even if it was too late for Achike, even if he would never see it – hadn't they both come so far?

Yes, it was an impossible thing they might do now.

They did it.

I wage not any feud with Death
For changes wrought on form and face;
No lower life that earth's embrace
May breed with him, can fright my faith.

Eternal process moving on,
From state to state the spirit walks;
And these are but the shatter'd stalks,
Or ruin'd chrysalis of one.

Nor blame I Death, because he bare
The use of virtue out of earth:
I know transplanted human worth
Will bloom to profit, otherwhere.

For this alone on Death I wreak
The wrath that garners in my heart;
He put our lives so far apart
We cannot hear each other speak.

ALFRED, LORD TENNYSON, *In Memoriam A. H. H.*

Slowly, Achike lets his eyes open. There is still some noise, still no light. Or ... what lights can he see now? Not daylight, surely? Surely, the bright day is done?

He cannot tell; his dreams might still be following him. He cannot have been asleep for very long, but he has slept deeply enough to almost be away somewhere, and he feels it. But he is still in Berlin, in the flat with Ekene. He remembers. He feels heavy with rest, even though he does not know how much he has had.

His skin feels tired. Maybe it's the migraine: he is in the quiet moment between the aura and the pain. He thinks to steal some time from the pain, while he can.

Maybe he's just getting older. Before he became a film actor, he was barely conscious of his age, only dimly aware that he was over thirty. Now he must confront the fact of his mortality every day. He is tired. His work tires him, and his rest tires him. Is it worth it?

What time is it? Ekene must have finished showering by now, but he is still in the bathroom. He doesn't sing this time, like he normally does in the shower. Sometimes, at home, Achike will sing back to him when he comes out of the bath-room, while Ekene's face is wet and vague.

Achike walks to the window and strains to see over the buildings across the street, as if he need only stand on tiptoes to see the lights in the sky. Didn't Ekene say people often misused fireworks, in Berlin? Achike looks down at the street below. There is nobody around. If anyone is getting hurt, he can't see them.

Ekene is right: Achike doesn't *get* Berlin. Ekene calls it a party city, and Achike has tried his best. But it's not a city to him, only a loud party with the doors closed, all noise and no lights, and no candles to blow out. Somewhere, someone is having a much better time than him, always. He doesn't want to stay and see the party.

But to be in Ekene's presence, to watch Ekene watch the fun, is close to happiness. Achike thinks to himself: he could do this. If it weren't for his work, he could stay here and do this, or be in any other city. Where can they not go, black and gay and safe if they're together? Maybe one day they could even move back home to Manchester. If it weren't for his work.

Is it worth it? He's been asking himself this for a little while. He has been thinking about another life. He could be a father, maybe. It's not impossible. He could be a husband. Even a son. He wants family. People around him, people who don't have to leave in the end. He wants to walk into another life as he might walk in, out of the rain. He is tired.

Another firework, and the headache starts. He knew it would. He has stolen all the time he will have. He lies down on the bed again, puts on the sleeping mask from the plane and tries to think of something happy and permanent. Migraines have changed the way he thinks about darkness.

The bathroom door clicks and releases, and he hears footsteps. Somewhere in the big room, Ekene is standing.

'Migraine?' Ekene says.

Achike nods. He knows Ekene is smiling softly, somewhere on the other side of his mask. But it's important for Achike to conserve his energy. A migraine is a fight he must fight and must lose. He must keep quiet. Words cost too much. They have already cost too much.

'Do you have your medicine?' Ekene asks.

In his darkness, Achike opens his eyes, surprised. 'I forgot to take it,' he says. 'I completely forgot.'

Ekene does not pause. 'But you have it?'

Achike nods again.

'Is it . . . ?' Ekene asks, but he is already looking. He knows Achike's packing: shoulder bag, side compartment for easy access. He takes out the little box of pills and pads over to the sink to get water. 'Here you go.'

He holds a cup of water to Achike's mouth as if it's nothing, and slides the pill between Achike's lips. Achike moves to take the mask off.

'Don't,' Ekene says.

Achike doesn't. The pain is starting and it makes him soft, docile. He only wants someone who won't have to go. He wants to be the kind of man who gathers people around him, makes them want to stay.

Ekene lies down on the bed with him, but not face to face. He moves to the other end and arranges himself, places his head on Achike's feet. He is quiet for a while.

'I'm sorry I hurt you,' he says.

Achike breathes deeply and stills himself. He wants to move as little as possible, to change nothing. The pain is building. It will get worse. 'I know,' he says.

'I know you think we'd be good together,' Ekene says. 'I know that. Sometimes I think so, too.'

Achike is entirely still.

'But I'm not there yet.'

'But you could be, Ekene. If you only—'

Ekene lays a hand on his thigh to quiet him. 'I know that. I'm not hopeless. But I'm not there yet. We've both been through stuff when we were kids, and maybe that's why we work as friends. But we've been through stuff, Achike. I'm not there yet.'

'You'll get there.'

Ekene shakes his head gently, then lets it fall on Achike's body again. What can he say, against this? *I'm getting there*, he thinks. *And sometimes I wish you'd just let me. Like this, sometimes. I wish we could just be like this. Do you have to be so far ahead all the time? Will you always be far away from me?*

'I'll get there,' he says.

Achike breathes a long breath out, satisfied. They listen to the fireworks for a while. Somewhere, someone may be getting hurt. Someone may be looking at the lights, their eyes in the sky.

Ekene looks over to Achike, ready to say the thing that he has thought, but his friend is already completely still, breathing softly in his darkness. Is he asleep? Ekene cannot tell. He will not ask.

Ekene may still become brave and true, when Achike wakes up. He looks at Achike again, at his face, his perfect form. Confronted with such beauty, what else can Ekene do, but sing to him, softly, and wait for him? He knows Achike cannot hear him in his sleep.

Achike might sleep all night. Perhaps, in a new day, Achike will be different. Perhaps he will wake up closer to Ekene, and then both of them will be different, and emerge from their darkness together, and be close.

Ekene thinks, and breathes, and he hopes for this bright new day. It could be light, when Achike wakes up. It could be warm and safe. There is no knowing what might happen. It could be golden. So what else can Ekene do, but whisper all night, in readiness?

I love you. I love you. I love you.

Acknowledgements

Somewhere in my emails, there is a draft message from me to my agent, telling her I couldn't write this book after all; that it was too difficult, too far beyond what I could do; that I would have to abandon this novel and write something easier. Without the people who have supported me in a thousand ways, that draft might have been sent, and my draft of a novel might never have become a book. The list of your names could fill another chapter, but for now there are a few people I'd particularly like to thank.

Sharmaine Lovegrove, Maisie Lawrence and the Dialogue Books team, for your hard work, for your creativity, for your passion. My agent, Cara Lee Simpson, for encouraging me and advising me so well and so consistently. Alice Malin, Andrew McMillan and Seán Hewitt, early readers and dear friends. I'm not sure which job is harder.

In addition to the research I did myself, there are some very kind, very knowledgeable people who helped educate me about the themes and settings of this book, and I'd like to thank them. Andy Smith, for your knowledge and advice. Dr Fiona Hansell, for your invaluable advice on the details of brain haemorrhages, alcoholism and other crucial medical information. You were so generous with your time, and so patient with my endless questions. Maddy Kelly and Euan Sutherland, for explaining how hospitals work. John Young, for explaining how paramedics work. Tian Glasgow and James Northcote for explaining how actors work. Bernard Travers, for explaining how engineers work. Ed Crowley, Rosalia Delfino and Mike Cullen, for explaining some of the details about London and city life.

Last, and most, Aunty Chinelo, Uncle David, my brother Udobi Nzelu and my partner James Stables, for your love, faith and encouragement.

Bringing a book from manuscript to what you are reading is a team effort.

Dialogue Books would like to thank everyone who helped to publish *Here Again Now* in the UK.

Editorial
Sharmaine Lovegrove
Amy Baxter

Contracts
Anniina Vuori

Sales
Caitriona Row
Dominic Smith
Frances Doyle
Hannah Methuen
Lucy Hine
Toluwalope Ayo-Ajala

Publicity
Millie Seaward

Marketing
Emily Moran

Design
Charlotte Stroomer

Production
Narges Nojoumi

Copy Editor
Rachel Malig

Proof Reader
Amber Burlinson

Operations
Kellie Barnfield
Millie Gibson
Sanjeev Braich